ANGELS
& Whiskey

A Saddles & Racks Novel, #1

USA Today bestselling author

Kimberly Knight

COPYRIGHT

DEDICATION

For every Autumn.
Say No More.
Your life matters!

PROLOGUE
Gabe

March 9th

I NEVER THOUGHT I'D SEE A DAY WHERE MY WORLD WAS MORE consumed by one person than by serving my country.

My life was set to follow in my grandfather's footsteps. It was my destiny. I'd forgotten he'd met my grandmother while serving in Vietnam, so I should have known I would meet my future wife while serving in Afghanistan.

"You gotta girl back home we don't know about, Cap?"

I glanced from the computer screen to First Lieutenant Paul Jackson as he spoke and then to Cochran, who was sitting across the room. The moment I'd laid eyes on Cochran when she joined my crew, I had no idea she'd become my first love.

For a few seconds, I watched as Cochran laughed with Stone, her fellow medic. "Something like that," I murmured, turning back to the website on the computer that was allowing me to *secretly* design an engagement ring for her. I was Specialist Cochran's Captain, and because of military regulations, no one could know we had been dating for nine months and that I wanted to make her my wife.

My life's plan had always been to work my way through the ranks until I was no longer breathing. But now I wanted to be with Cochran and spend the rest of my life making her happy. It was hard not being able to kiss her whenever I wanted—to touch her as she

1

walked by or hold her hand. I felt like a stalker; always secretly watching her.

"Why are you designing an engagement ring?" he asked, interrupting my thoughts.

I looked over my right shoulder at him. "Are you a moron, LT?" I chuckled.

"I just didn't know you gotta girl is all." He shrugged, still peering over my shoulder and looking at the computer screen.

"Well, I do." I glanced to Cochran again and then back to the computer before Jackson noticed. "Get out of my hair and go check your gear before Major Dick rips you a new asshole."

"You don't have any." He laughed, looking at my bald head.

"I like it that way, Lieutenant. Now fuck off." I ran my hand over my bald head. I'd been losing my hair for a few years, so I finally said fuck it and shaved it all off. Cochran thought it looked sexy on me. I was his Captain, but we were like brothers and even had that brotherly banter. Honestly, he was the closest friend I had on base, so it was no wonder he was questioning me about my love life.

"You know I'm going to get you to show me naked pictures of her."

"In your dreams, P.J. Now really, fuck off."

"All right," he huffed. "By the way, the gear's good, Cap. But I feel ya. I'll leave you to your girly shit." He laughed again then slapped me on the back and left to join the rest of the crew. They were binge watching *Lost* while we waited for any MEDEVAC (medical evacuation) calls.

I was tired of the war. I never thought I'd say that. For as long as I could remember, I'd wanted to be an American hero. Not anymore.

I'd already completed two tours and as soon as my third was done, so was I. I didn't want to be in the sand anymore. I didn't want to hear gunfire in the distance twenty-four-seven. I didn't want to have that sinking feeling in the pit of my stomach on a MEDEVAC call as we potentially stepped into the line of fire.

I wanted Alyssa Cochran—on a beach in Hawaii.

I wanted to wake up next to her and see her blue eyes sparkle while the sun rose.

I wanted to see her blonde hair fanned across my pillow.

I wanted to be with her openly.

I wanted her as my wife.

Cochran rose from her seat on the couch and I minimized the computer screen. I glanced at her a few times as she made her way across the room, trying not to be obvious that I was watching her. She brushed her finger along the bridge of her nose. *Our sign.* I tried to hide my smile as I saved my design in my online account on the computer, then erased my browser history and closed the window. I couldn't wait to have her in my arms.

I made my way down the hall, pretending to need the latrine. I looked over my shoulder and when I saw no eyes on me, made my way through the door across the hall where Cochran was waiting.

"Have I ever told you that I love a man in uniform?" she whispered, grabbing my arm and pulling me into a vacant room.

I closed the door behind me. "I'll make sure to keep my uniform after this tour." I wrapped her in my arms, holding her as if it were our last day together. I hated the whole situation: the sneaking around, not being able to kiss her whenever I wanted, not being able to cuddle on the couch and watch a movie.

"Good." She smiled as I leaned down and kissed her soft lips enjoying the faint taste of cherry Chapstick.

Taking her hand, I led her to one of the cots and sat in the center, pulling her down to sit on my lap. Her arms wrapped around my neck and she leaned into me. "What were you and Stone laughing about earlier?" I asked, then took a breath of her scent. She always smelled like vanilla ... warm vanilla sugar.

She leaned her head back and gave me a wicked smirk. "I can't tell you. You're my Captain."

"Alys—"

"We were playing Fuck, Marry, Kill," she blurted.

My jaw clenched. I didn't want to hear who she wanted to fuck, but curiosity won. "Who'd you pick?"

After a few beats, she finally spoke. "You can't get mad, Gabe. It was just for shits and giggles."

"All right, I won't. Tell me." I brushed a piece of her hair behind her ear that had fallen from her bun.

"Well, of course, I'd marry you—I love you. And Stone and I both want to kill Major Dick even though he's not bad on the eyes." She paused and took a deep breath before continuing. "Now this is the part you can't get mad at—"

"Just tell me, babe." I knew I couldn't get mad over a silly game, but it was just like when you had a dream and someone pissed you off in it; you'd wake up mad at them for no reason. And that's how I was feeling. I wanted to know who my *competition* was.

"I'd ... I'd fuck Jackson."

My back straightened and my arms wrapped tighter around her. Yeah, I wanted to throttle him even if he was my best friend.

"It's just a game C.H." I smiled. CH stood for Captain Hottie. I knew she used my nickname to lighten the mood. "I only want to fuck you—and *do* only fuck you."

"I know, babe. But my best friend?"

"Just a game, C.H. Just a game."

"I need to come up with my own list." I grinned at her. Two could play this game.

She slapped my arm playfully. "Don't you dare!"

"All right, I won't. But I hope these next six months go by fast. I want Jackson to know you're mine." I brushed my hand under the hem of her army green T-shirt, feeling her smooth belly and needing to feel her soft, warm skin.

She gave a tight smile. "Me too."

"Maybe ..." I paused for a moment before continuing to make sure I wanted to suggest this. "Maybe we *should* tell Jackson and Stone? I trust them and they can be our lookout people."

"You want to risk them telling?"

My hands had worked Alyssa's T-shirt from her pants without me knowing. I wanted her and at that moment, I didn't care if my whole crew knew. If someone ran and told Major Dick, I'd deal with it. I'd risk getting kicked out of the army just to be with her and a chance to kick Major Dick's ass. Major Dick wasn't his real name, but he sure as shit earned it, and I'd leave with the respect of everyone in the army because no one liked *Dick*.

"I'd risk anything for you."

"Okay, let's tell them. I trust them. Stone's my best friend too."

"Good." I agreed and began to lift her shirt over her head until there was a knock on the door. We both stilled, me holding my breath.

"Cap, we gotta Dustoff," Jackson called out behind the closed door. While I wanted to spend the rest of the day with Cochran on my lap, we had a MEDIVAC call we had to go to.

"Shit, he already knows," Alyssa whispered, her eyes wide with concern then scurried off my lap.

I watched her, not saying anything while she tucked her shirt into her pants. Jackson knocked on the women's door. He knew I was in there with her.

"How many?" I asked while Alyssa righted herself.

"Two."

"How bad?"

"Urgent. No enemies in the area."

I rushed to the door, swung it open with Alyssa on my heels. "You know nothing." I pointed a finger in his face in warning.

He smiled. "I found you in the shitter. I don't know what you're talking about."

"Good. We'll be right behind you." I grabbed Alyssa's hand and halted her as Jackson continued walking down the hall. "One down and one to go." I smiled and kissed her cherry lips.

"Stone won't be a problem. Tonight I'll show you how happy I am to finally tell people."

5

"I like the sound of that. But real quick ... Since you want to marry me, what shape of diamonds do you like?"

"What?" she asked, scrunching her eyebrows.

"In your game of Fuck, Marry, Kill, what ring would you hope I'd give you?"

She laughed. "You're silly."

"Just tell me. We don't have time for you to question me."

"I don't know. I'd never really given it much thought. I'd like any ring you'd give me."

"All right. Good to know. Let's go so we can get back and tell Jackson and Stone. Then I can take my time tasting you and not have to worry about anyone catching us." I kissed her again before we joined the rest of the crew.

The crew chatted about what was happening in the current episode of *Lost* as we made our way to our coordinates. My thoughts were only of Alyssa. I couldn't wait for tonight so I could take my time making love to her somewhere other than a supply closet.

I stared at her as she laughed with Stone, the desert sand behind her, and I envisioned her in a bikini laying on the beach in Hawaii. I hated Afghanistan. I wanted to be back on American soil with the Pacific Ocean in the distance.

When we finally touched down, the helicopter caused the sand to blow around us. Every day I found sand in places on my body it didn't belong. It felt as if I could never be one hundred percent clean no matter how hard I scrubbed.

The popping of gunfire could be heard in the distance as we made our way from the bird. Heads down, gear in hand, we made it to the soldiers that were covered in crimson blood. After Cochran and Stone had patched up the bullet holes on each soldier with enough gauze so we could transport them back to base, the crew and I strapped them on the gurneys. I faintly heard the gunfire getting closer as we stood.

Pop. Pop. Pop.

"I thought you said dispatch radioed there were no enemy troops in the area?" I asked Jackson.

"That's what the 9-Line said."

Usually dispatch was correct when they'd called in a 9-Line MEDEVAC request for us. They'd tell us where the location was, how many patients, if we needed special equipment ... Nine items to prepare us. Obviously they were wrong this time.

"We need to move. They're getting closer."

The wind kicked up, blowing the rough sand in the air and making it hard to see our own hands in front of our eyes. I fucking hated Afghanistan.

The gunfire got louder.

Pop. Pop. Pop.

"Let's move!"

Jackson radioed base. "Charlie Tango, this is Delta Sky. We have enemy fire and we're being ambushed. Send backup, stat."

My crew and I picked up the two gurneys and began running toward the helicopter. The gunfire was close as we slid one gurney in.

Pop. Pop. Pop.

"Cap!" Jackson yelled.

I looked back seeing enemy troops in the distance, the wind dying down enough to see them crouch and take aim.

7

Before we could pull our weapons, they fired.

"Get this gurney in!" I snapped, drawing my gun and covering my crew.

Instinct took over as I aimed, firing my gun and praying we didn't get hit with bullets as we stood in the open desert with nothing to hide behind. As we fired back, Cochran and Stone tended to our downed soldiers.

"Heads down, keep firing!" I barked.

Pop. Pop. Pop.

"Watch Cochran's and Stone's six, Woodring!"

Pop.

"Move, move, move!"

Pop. Pop.

We continued to fire. I didn't know how many enemy troops there were. I couldn't see with all the sand in the air, but we kept firing until the wind wasn't blowing and we saw all of the enemies down.

"Everyone good?" I asked. I turned around to see one of my medics down. I couldn't tell who, but my heart stopped.

"Jackson!" I hollered as I ran to the downed medic.

When I reached her, I fell to my knees, flipping her over —Cochran.

"No!" I yelled, my heart pounding so hard that I thought it would beat out of my chest. Alyssa wasn't moving and blood started to seep and stain her uniform.

"Fuck!" Jackson shouted, kneeling beside me.

"No!" I yelled again. This couldn't be happening. This was Alyssa, the love of my life. She was part of my crew. The crew I was trained to protect and the one person I wanted to protect the most was down, her chest covered in dark red blood and not moving.

"Cap, we gotta get her in the bird. More enemies could be coming," Jackson affirmed.

I was numb, unable to move. Alyssa was in my arms still not moving and barely breathing. I held her asking her to open her eyes ...

But she didn't.

"Open your eyes, Cochran." I could feel the tightness in my throat as I fought off the tears that were building. Everything around me didn't matter anymore. I only cared for Alyssa and she was shot— shot on my watch.

"Cap, we gotta move," Jackson persisted.

"Put her in the bird so I can stop the bleeding," Stone begged.

I hesitated for a minute, still looking at Alyssa. The severity of the situation hadn't hit yet.

"Cap—"

"All right!" I picked her body off the ground, placing her inside the helicopter. We piled in and I removed her helmet. Her beautiful blue eyes didn't stare back at me. Her smile wasn't spread across her face like it had been thirty minutes prior.

Tears rolled down my cheeks. No one had seen me cry before. I was a soldier. I was an American hero. I was a fucking captain—I didn't cry. But as my worst fear came crashing down around me, I lost it.

Tears trickled down my cheeks and onto Alyssa as she lay in my arms, her breathing diminishing every second. I didn't care anymore. This was real and she was the love of my life. I wanted to go back to thirty minutes ago and prepare everyone for the ambush. I wanted to be the one in front of the bullet—not Alyssa. I wanted to save her.

We started to fly back to base, the tears still rolling down my face. No one said anything. Stone and Jackson worked on Alyssa while my other crew members tended to the original soldiers the best they could since they weren't medics.

Alyssa started to cough up blood and then before I knew it, she stopped.

"Stay with me, babe," I pleaded, brushing my fingers down her cheek.

I looked up to see Stone's eyes fill with tears as she listened through a stethoscope, then she shook her head at Jackson, advising my gaze.

"No!" This couldn't be happening. Alyssa wasn't dead. We were going to get married. She was going to take my last name. I was going to wake up next to her every morning—I was counting on forever.

But we weren't.

Alyssa died in my arms on the way back to base and worst of all ...

I didn't get to tell her how much I loved her.

ONE
Autumn

Two years later …

VALENTINE'S DAY.

The most romantic day of the year.

Like most girls, I'd fantasized about receiving candy and roses on this day and being treated to a nice dinner with the one I loved for as long as I could remember. For the twenty-six years of my life, that had never happened—until today.

Rich and I had been dating for six months and he was the most romantic guy I'd ever been with. He took care of me. He made sure my car had enough gas to make it to work, he'd slip a note in my lunch bag when I wasn't looking that always made me smile when I found it, and he always told me he loved me.

He was perfect.

I smiled as I read Rich's morning text telling me that he loved me and couldn't wait to see me for dinner. I wasn't sure how I was going to make it through the day. It was like Christmas and the anticipation was killing me. This was my first official Valentine's date and it wasn't with a bottle of Pinot and a box of chocolates I bought myself. I was on cloud nine, to say the least. I'd even woken up before my alarm, wanting to hurry and get the day started.

I changed out of my pajamas and into black slacks and a red blouse to celebrate Valentine's Day for work. After all, red was the color of love. After making sure my makeup was just right and my long, chocolate-brown hair was straightened with a flat iron, I hung my little black dress on the shower rod. I didn't want there to be any wrinkles in it for tonight.

Rich and I met one afternoon in August. He'd walked into the bank I worked at to open a new checking account, and the moment I saw him walk in the door in his army uniform, I was love struck. What woman didn't love a man in a uniform? Especially a military uniform.

Sigh.

I couldn't tell he was nine years older than me at the time. He didn't look it. He was gorgeous. The way he smiled a sly smirk as he stepped up to my desk when our eyes met, the way his piercing blue eyes checking me out, and the way his voice made me turn to butter … It made me forget how to speak.

"I need to open a new account … Autumn." He smiled, his gaze lowering to my nametag—or my boobs. I wasn't one-hundred percent sure which, but I didn't care.

I stammered as I tried to find my voice, and his smile widened. "Y-Yes … Please, um, sit. I can help you with that—"

"Richard. Richard Jones." He stuck out his hand. Mine instantly became sweaty at the thought of touching him.

I reached out, taking his hand in mine, silently praying to God that he wouldn't notice my clammy palm. His hand was rough like a man's should be, and I swallowed hard before speaking. "Nice to meet you. Have you had an account with us before?" I felt my smile widen a little too much as infatuation overtook my emotions. The way he was still smiling at me in return clearly told me that he could see the lust radiating from my body.

I wanted to run my hands through his finger-length light brown hair while staring into his piercing blue eyes. He had just enough stubble on his face to frame his features that showcased his strong jaw.

Down, girl!

"No." He smiled again, and my fixed stare took in his perfect teeth

as he sat in the chair in front of my desk. "I haven't been in town for seventeen years."

"Right." *I gestured to his uniform.* "Thank you for your service."

"Anything to protect beautiful women like you."

I sucked in a breath. Holy shit. Men flirted with me sometimes, but not usually men I wanted to see naked. I cleared my throat. "Thank you. Let's ... uh ... get started."

I opened the checking account for Rich and before he left, he took my business card, telling me he'd be in touch. The rest of the week I thought about him—sometimes with the help of my battery operated friend. But the longer I waited for his call, the more I thought he was just flirting with me to be nice. I was starting to give up hope until the following Friday when he called me on my direct line and asked me to dinner. We'd been together ever since.

His parents had been killed in a hit and run accident while he was deployed during his first tour, so he spent Thanksgiving and Christmas with my family. My parents took him in like a son and instantly fell in love with him, especially my dad.

"We should go shooting sometime." *Dad beamed then took a sip of his beer as we waited for the turkey.*

"Do you go to the range often?" *Rich asked.*

"A few times. I'm not a marksmen like you, but I'd love to see what you could show me, Major."

"Sir," *Rich smiled his perfect smile,* "please just call me Richard or Rich like my close friends."

Dad smiled in return as if he'd won the lottery. "Rich, you can call me Dan."

Dad never liked any of my boyfriends. No one was ever good enough for his baby girl, but an American hero was perfect and I couldn't agree more. Of course my mother agreed.

"He's so handsome," *Mom praised while staring at Rich.*

"I know." *I sighed, leaning on the kitchen counter, my chin resting in the palm of my hand as I also stared at Rich from the open kitchen into the living room where he and Dad watched football.*

13

"Better hang onto that one. A man who takes care of you like he does is worth keeping."

Still staring at Rich, I responded, "I plan on it."

As I drove to work, I remembered the last six months. I couldn't believe how happy I was. I never thought I'd find the perfect guy. Most of the guys I dated only wanted me because I had a pretty face. They'd stop at nothing until they got me into bed. Most of the time they'd fail because I wasn't that type of girl, so they'd move on, looking for the next piece of ass.

No one saw me for who I was on the inside until Rich. He made me feel like a lady. On our fifth date, he told me he was in love with me and had continued to tell me every day since.

"Someone's a lucky girl," my co-worker and best friend, Brandi greeted as I walked through the lobby toward my desk.

"What's that supposed to mean?"

She gestured to my desk that held a vase with two dozen red roses. I smiled instantly.

"Why couldn't I have been the one working that day instead of you?" she pouted.

"You're married, silly."

"I know, but *damn* ..."

"Hey, it's not my fault your hubby doesn't wine and dine you anymore," I joked, picking up the card that sat between two rose buds.

"Like he ever did that. Once he got me in bed on our third date, he stopped all the romance."

"And you still married the guy."

"True. What does the card say?"

She stepped closer, trying to read the card. I held it to my chest and grinned. "Why are you so nosey?"

"I'm living vicariously through you. Let me pretend the major is my lover."

"Let's not and say we did." I shook my head, laughing as I pulled the tiny two by two card from the envelope.

Princess,

I hope you're ready to never spend Valentine's Day alone again. I love you.

-Rich

XOXO

I smiled again as I read his words and held the card to my chest, looking at Brandi with love in my eyes.

"Well?" she prompted.

"It just says that he loves me and we'll always be together."

"I hate you." She snickered and walked off.

I sat at my desk staring at the roses. Ten hours and counting until my first Valentine's Day date.

My little black dress was paired with my black Louboutins with the red sole. I saved up for a year to buy them. They were my go-to heels and perfect for Valentine's Day.

When I got off work at five thirty, I rushed home to get ready for my hot date. It was by no means my first date with Rich, but the butterflies in my stomach thought it was. I was nervous and I had no idea why.

I put a fresh coat of makeup on my face, gave my hair a few curls to highlight my face and slathered my whole body with vanilla lotion. At seven o'clock sharp, Rich knocked on my apartment door. I opened it with a smile.

"Hey, princess." He smiled back and pulled another two dozen roses from behind his back.

"More?"

"I wanted to buy you the whole flower shop, but I thought that'd be overkill."

I took them, smelling the sweet fragrance. "Just a little, but my apartment would smell especially good."

"Not as good as you." He stepped forward, wrapped his arms around my waist and kissed me. His tongue parted my lips, the faint taste of mint lingered in his mouth. I moaned as his hands slid down my back, resting on the curves of my butt. After a few seconds, he pulled back. "Let's go or we'll miss our dinner reservation."

I grabbed my purse and overnight bag and he led me to his sleek black Mercedes. After he'd opened the passenger door for me, I slid in and he took my bag, placing it in the trunk before getting into the driver's seat.

"I missed you today," he confessed, starting the engine.

"I missed you, too. And you made Brandi jealous."

He grinned. "Oh yeah?"

"Yeah. Her husband didn't send her flowers."

"That's a shame. I need to show my woman how much I love her."

"You do. Every day. You don't need to show me with flowers though."

"You didn't like them?" He took his eyes off the road as he looked over at me.

I smiled, reaching over and placing my hand on his muscular leg. "Of course I did. I'm just saying that every day I know you love me and not just because you gave me roses."

"I do." He lifted my hand and kissed it before linking our fingers together.

I looked out the windshield, the sun setting behind the surrounding mountains and the sky painted with a gradient mixture of red, pink, orange, and blue. "Where are we going for dinner?"

"Paris."

"Paris?" I asked, quickly snapping my head toward him.

He laughed. "Well, not Paris, France."

"Oh ... right." I chuckled.

We arrived at the Paris Hotel and Casino and gave our key and car to the valet before walking through the smoky casino floor to the elevators that led up to the restaurant in the Eiffel Tower. "I've never eaten here," I commented, watching the numbers count down, indicating the elevator was descending. I'd always wanted to eat at the lavish restaurant, especially at night as the fountains at the Bellagio shot water into the air, and danced to the music, but I could never afford it.

"The chef's a personal friend. You'll love it."

Rich placed his hand on the small of my back as he led me into the glass elevator with the other diners who were also going to spend their romantic evening eleven stories above the strip.

We were escorted through the kitchen, then led to the dining room where the panoramic view of the strip spread across the large windows around the entire room. The sun had fully set by the time we sat at our table and the glittery lights lit the view in the most breathtaking way.

"I haven't seen the fountain show in years. I rarely come down here," I mentioned, not taking my eyes away from the view of the Bellagio fountains.

"Really? I'm down here all the time for work."

Since moving back to Vegas, Rich had opened a loan office, trying his hand at being an entrepreneur. He had several clients who he'd loan money to for business startups or gambling debts.

His family was well off and when they died, he was left with their money, plus the money from his service in the army. I wasn't used to having money. My parents were middle class. They owned their own photography studio and while it paid the bills, we didn't have thousands of dollars saved up. We made it through even if it was paycheck to paycheck.

I've worked since leaving home eight years ago at the age of eighteen. I didn't attend college because I was ready to start making my own money and live my life. I also wanted to help my parents out by not needing to take care of me anymore, so I got a job at a bank as a teller and moved my way up to the new accounts department. If it weren't for that job, I wouldn't have met Rich and having my first Valentine's date. Everything happens for a reason they say.

"Yeah, there's too many people," I scoffed, still staring out the window as I answered Rich's question.

"That's true."

A waiter walked over and explained the prix fixe menu to us. As we waited for the meal, we made small talk and watched the fountains continue to do their show every fifteen minutes. Everything was perfect and I was no longer nervous as we held light conversation and ate the best meal of my life.

"Are you ready for dessert?" Rich asked.

I was stuffed, but since it was a set menu, I'd been eyeing the crème brûlée that some of the other guests were already eating.

"You bet."

"Good." Rich grabbed my hand as we waited for the waiter to bring our dessert. Another waiter poured us more champagne and I took in the view once more, knowing the night was coming to an end.

The waiter finally brought our desserts and Rich let go of my hand so we could eat. I was mid-sip of my champagne when I felt something hit my lip. Pulling the glass away, I examined it, noticing something metal inside the bubbly liquid. The realization hit as I saw Rich slide from his seat and kneel at my side.

"Rich ..."

He reached into the glass, pulling out the biggest diamond I'd ever seen that sat on what I assumed was a platinum band with two smaller diamonds beside it. The three princess cut diamonds sparkled in the candlelight as the brut champagne dripped down his fingers.

"Autumn Summers, since I first laid eyes on you, I knew you were meant to be my princess. I've wanted to ask you a question since I told you that I loved you on our fifth date. I know we've only been together for six months, but when you live your life in war, you tend to not take anything for granted. I know I want to spend the rest of my life with you and I'm done waiting. Will you marry me?"

I felt a tear roll down my right cheek as my hand covered my mouth in surprise. "Yes!"

Everyone clapped in the restaurant while Rich held me in his arms and kissed me until I could no longer breathe.

For twenty-six years, I'd envisioned how my first Valentine's Day date would go and none of them played out like my day had.

It was perfect.

TWO
Gabe

Three years later ...
Present day

WE CONTINUED TO FIRE. I DIDN'T KNOW HOW MANY ENEMY *troops there were. I couldn't see with all the sand in the air, but we kept firing until the wind wasn't blowing and we saw all of the enemies down.*

"Everyone good?" I asked. I turned around to see one of my medics down. I couldn't tell who, but my heart stopped.

"Jackson!" I hollered as I ran to the down medic.

When I reached her, I fell to my knees, flipping her over —Cochran.

"No!"

I woke up screaming, clenching the sweat covered sheets, panting and trying to catch my breath. It was always the same. If I didn't consume enough whiskey to make me not dream, I dreamt of the day Alyssa died. It was like a movie on repeat. It played over and over and over and always ended the same.

Glancing at my alarm clock, I figured I'd gotten enough sleep with the six hours I'd received and got out of bed. With my current job, I usually stayed out late, going to lavish parties, going on dates, whatever they wanted as long as I played my role.

After my final tour with the army, it took six months to take the required post-deployment health assessments and post-deployment resilient training exams. Somehow I'd passed even though I had nightmares nightly about Cochran. I thought about moving back to my hometown of Chicago, but a part of me knew that I'd miss the sand. Plus my best friend, Paul Jackson, moved back to Malibu at the same time and promised he could get me a job.

Sure as shit he was able to get me one all right.

When he first told me what he was going to be doing, I laughed. I laughed for hours. When I stopped laughing, I would laugh some more. I laughed so hard I cried.

"I wouldn't be laughing, Captain. You have no idea how much money you can make."

"You don't need to call me captain anymore. That's behind us."

"Habit." He shrugged. "Look, haven't you heard the expression 'don't knock it till you try it'?"

I laughed harder, tears starting to prick my eyes. "Oh, I bet you'll be knocking something."

"Hey, man, it's a beautiful woman on my arm. What more can I ask for?"

"What if they're ugly?"

He shrugged again. "I'll cross that bridge when I get to it. I'll fake it. Plus, Bobby said we're escorts, not gigolos."

"What's the difference?" I chuckled.

"We don't have to sleep with the ladies unless we want to. We're not paid for sex. We're paid to be a companion for a few hours. Saddles & Racks is a legitimate company."

I laughed again, tears rolling down my cheek. "Saddles & Racks?"

"Come on ..."

"I don't know—"

"Just think about it, Cap. It might be good for you to—"

I stopped laughing. "To what? To move on from Cochran?" The silence that filled the air could be cut with a knife as I waited for him to speak.

"No ... For you to be happy again," he pleaded.

"You think fucking a lot of women is going to make me forget her?"

"God no." He paused, thinking of what to say next as I felt my blood boiling. He didn't know what it was like to lose the love of his life. "Look. We're young. You're what? Thirty like me? We have a long life ahead of us and you can't use your hand forever."

"Thirty-one."

"What?"

"Thirty-one. I just turned thirty-one before we came back." I sighed.

"How did I not know about your birthday?"

"No one knew when my birthday was but Cochran."

We stared at each other. "All right. Well, just give it a chance."

I'd thought about Jackson's proposition for a few hours while he begged me to go with him to meet Bobby. I was still laughing at the name of the company while I contemplated Jackson's employment venture. Finally, I gave in. What could be the harm in getting paid to go on dates? After talking it over with Bobby, I finally became a "stud" at Saddles & Racks Escort Company. I was a fucking male escort!

How does a United States Army Captain become a male escort? Well, it's simple really. Losing the love of my life in my arms changed me. The amount of whiskey I consumed should have gotten me kicked out of the army before my tour ended. I was lost, broken, and had a hole the size of Texas in my heart ...

Texas was where Alyssa was from.

In the twenty-six years before I met and fell in love with her, I was a horny motherfucker. I'd fucked a lot of women before I'd signed up for the army, and then I'd fucked a hell of a lot of women in supply closets. But Alyssa had changed me. I never wanted to be with anyone else but her, and it took me over a year to finally be able to have sex with someone else. And I did it while getting paid. But I couldn't just go in there with my dick out. I was nervous as fuck on my first date.

"What do I wear?"

"You sound like a girl." Jackson laughed.

"You realize I haven't been on a date in ... well, since high school."
I shrugged.

Even though I had dated Alyssa, we'd never officially went out on
a date. Sure, we'd hang out together on our days off, but we were never
alone unless we were sneaking off to be together. I could never take her
to dinner, hold her hand in public, or kiss her in front of people.

"It's Valentine's Day, so wear jeans and a nice shirt. Something
simple, but dressy. It's not rocket science, Cap."

I exhaled. "I know, man. I'm just nervous to pull the trigger."

"You only pull the trigger if you feel a connection. She's not paying
for sex."

"Right." I nodded. I didn't know why Jackson was acting as if the
date wouldn't end in sex. All his dates ended that way. When you
think of an escort, you think of sex.

I pulled a pair of dark denim blue jeans, a long-sleeved solid black
T-shirt and a bluish-grey and white striped scarf out of my closet.

"Don't you have something red?"

I stared at Jackson as if he'd lost his mind. "I should wear red
because it's Valentine's Day?"

He grinned. "Yeah."

"No, I don't have anything red." I walked into the bathroom to
change since Jackson was obviously not leaving my bedroom. Red
reminded me of blood—Alyssa's blood.

After I'd changed, I stared at myself in the mirror. "You can do
this. Cochran would want you to be happy." People had been telling
me that since she died. "Cochran would want you to be happy." But
how did they know? Sure she'd want me to be happy, but did that
mean she'd want me to date someone else?

"Cap, you gotta go before you're late. You don't want to be late on
your first day and have Bobby pissed at you," Jackson called from the
other side of the door.

I took a deep breath. "You can do this."

I was nervous. Bobby said that Christine, my date for the evening, wanted the whole boyfriend experience. I was to pick her up with flowers, open doors for her, pay for the meal (even though I really wasn't paying), drive her home and then kiss her goodnight.

Simple.

After knocking, I fidgeted with the scarf that was draped around my neck with one hand as I held the roses in the other. If I didn't know any better, I'd think I was on my very first date—ever. "Get it together, man," I whispered to myself as the door opened.

"Hi," I greeted Christine with a smile, holding out the red roses. "Happy Valentine's Day ... sweetheart." I threw in sweetheart for the whole boyfriend experience.

She reached out, taking them from me and smelled them before speaking. "Thank you, handsome."

I smiled again, trying to calm my nerves. "Ready?"

"Just let me put these in water first."

I followed her inside and finally noticed that she was wearing a bright red dress that matched the roses and her lipstick. My eyes continued down the curves of her ass—she had a nice ass—and to her legs. Damn, they looked good too. It had been a long time since I'd seen a woman in heels, and these made her legs seem as if they went on for days. I had a flash of them draped over my shoulders as my face was buried between her thighs. A year without sex was wearing on me for sure.

I shook my head, trying to clear the image as I looked around her living room while I waited. I was looking at her pictures on the fireplace mantel when she came out of the kitchen. "Okay, now I'm ready."

"Great." I smiled, gesturing for her to walk in front of me. I placed my hand on the small of her back, trying the best I could to fake that I was her boyfriend. Her long, chestnut-brown hair brushed across the back of my hand and I had to fight the urge not to remove it.

After she'd locked her front door, I led her to my white GMC Yukon. Opening the door for her, she climbed in and I went around to the driver's side. I already knew where we were going. I wasn't supposed to ask. She'd planned the entire date and told Bobby. I was just supposed to act as if it was my idea.

"I hope you like Thai." I started my SUV.

She grinned. "I love it."

I wanted to tell her that I was nervous. That this was my first time, but she didn't seem nervous and I didn't want to make her.

"Thank you for picking me up. I've gone on a couple of these and I was always extremely nervous that I met them at the restaurant."

I breathed a sigh of relief. It was natural for me to feel nervous, but I still wasn't going to tell her that this was my first time. "Of course. It's Valentine's Day and I wouldn't feel right having you meet me at the restaurant."

"That's sweet of you. I've never dated an army captain before."

I started to ask how she knew I used to be a captain in the army, but then remembered that Bobby had added it to my online profile. He'd said that the women would be enticed by a military man. He even asked if I had my uniform in case some wanted to role-play. Of course, I did, but it brought back too many bad memories.

"You haven't?" I asked, not having anything else to say.

"Nope. When did you get out?" she asked, looking over at me as I drove toward the restaurant.

"It's been about a month ... ten months since I left Afghanistan."

"Wow. I bet Malibu is so different from Afghanistan."

I laughed sarcastically. Of course it was. "You have no idea."

"Tell me about it."

I looked over at her. I knew she was just trying to make small talk and get to know me. After all, we were on a date, but I had too many wounds and talking about it brought them all back.

I heard the voices in my head, "Cochran would want you to be happy."

I took a deep breath before I spoke, "To be honest, it fucking sucked." I laughed, trying to act as if everything was okay. I wasn't going to tell her about Alyssa. "Sand, wind, the fucking sun was hot as hell. And you know," I shrugged, "gunfire."

"I can't imagine risking my life like that. It's very brave of you. Thank you for your service." She patted my knee and I looked down at it as if it were burning my skin through my jeans.

She's just a woman. An attractive one at that. You can do this. Have fun. Who knows, sex might be good for you.

"You're welcome." I took her hand in mine, brushing the back side with my lips before linking our fingers—boyfriend shit.

I saw her smile out of the corner of my eye, not removing her hand from mine. I had to admit, it felt nice to hold a soft hand again.

After dinner, we walked along the beach. The air was cold as the wind blew through my light long-sleeved T-shirt, but since I wanted to give Christine a good experience, I acted as if it didn't bother me at all.

Over dinner, I'd loosened up. It really was as if we were on a date. I'm sure it helped that she'd gone on a few dates with other escorts before me. She told me that it was easier to date an escort because she was too busy trying to run a million dollar PR firm. She didn't really have the time, but she still needed a hard body once in a while. Who was I to judge what she did with her free time?

We walked hand in hand along the cool sand, the moonlight casting a path for us. "I've had a very nice time," she beamed.

I smiled. "Me, too."

"Would you ..." She paused, kicking the sand with her bare foot. "Would you like to come in for coffee when you drop me off?"

Coffee after a date was the universal code for sex. I heard the voices again. "Cochran would want you to be happy." I knew Christine was just a client, but it had been too long since I'd had sex. This was a stepping-stone into moving on. I'd never forget Alyssa. I never wanted to love another, but I had needs and Jackson was right; I couldn't use my hand forever.

"Yeah, let's go. I bet you're cold in your dress."

As I sat at my dining room table, drinking my morning coffee, I realized I'd come a long way since my first date three years ago. Christine was a regular for me, but I still hadn't been able to fulfill any requests to put my uniform on. Every time I saw it folded in my bottom drawer in my dresser, flashes of Alyssa ran through my head. I just couldn't do it yet—maybe not ever.

Taking a sip of my coffee, my phone dinged with a text from Bobby.

Bobby: *I need you to come have a chat with me when you pick up your paycheck.*

His text threw me. He never wanted to talk to me unless it was about a date, and that was done through our online profile on the computer. If it were a date for the same day, he'd text to make sure I checked the back-office on the computer—not face to face like he was now.

I decided to get it over with. The women never seemed to complain, especially the ones I fucked, so I couldn't imagine what he wanted to talk to me about.

"Hey, Kylee, how's your day going?" I asked the receptionist when I arrived at Saddles & Racks.

"Hey, Gabe, it's going well. How about yours?"

"Well, I've never been called into the principal's office before." I laughed.

"He's in a good mood. I don't think it's anything bad."

"Good to hear. Can you let him know I'm here?"

"He said to send you back when you stopped by."

"Awesome. Thank you." I started to walk away, but then stopped. "By the way, are you still upset the Giants kicked the Royals ass?" I tried not to laugh as I waited for her answer.

"Low blow, Gabe. Low blow."

"I couldn't help it." I roared with laughter. "It's not every day I get to see your smiling face."

"Bye, Gabe!" Kylee huffed, crossing her arms over her chest.

I waved goodbye, still laughing as I made my way down the long hall toward Bobby's office. The door was closed, so I knocked.

"Come in," he called out, so I opened the door.

"Hey," I greeted. "You rang."

"Yeah, come sit down, Gabe." Bobby gestured to a chair in front of his desk.

I stared at him for a beat. This wasn't going to be good. "Am I in trouble?" I smiled, trying to lighten the mood as I sat in a chair in front of his desk.

"Should you be?" he asked, smiling back.

I raised an eyebrow. "No, don't think so."

"Relax." He leaned back in his black leather office chair, his hands folded in his lap. "I have a proposition for you."

"You know I only do threesomes with chicks, right?" I grinned.

He laughed. "It's nothing sexual."

"All right. Well, let's get to it then," I teased, crossing my arms over my chest as I sat back in the chair.

"How do you feel about Vegas?"

"Like for a vacation destination?"

"No, like to live."

"What?" I scrunched my eyebrows in confusion and leaned forward.

"Hear me out." He put his hands up as if to calm me. "Our Vegas office needs two guys. While I don't want to lose you, I think you and Paul would fit in perfectly."

"You want me and Jackson to move to Vegas?"

"Yeah. The clientele is in high demand there and I think you two would work out well in the desert."

I stared at him for a beat. Vegas wasn't like Afghanistan, but hearing the word "desert" didn't sit right. "Have you asked him?"

"Not yet. You came in first."

At that moment, there was a knock on the door. Bobby said for the person to come in and it was Jackson.

"Speak of the devil. Sit next to Gabe," Bobby instructed.

Jackson gave me a "what the fuck?" look. I just smiled. I didn't know my answer for Bobby, but if Jackson were on board, I'd do it. He was my best friend. My lieutenant. My brother. I wouldn't survive the *desert* without him.

"As I was saying to Gabe," Bobby started to say as Jackson sat down next to me, "our Vegas location is in high demand and we want you two to join that office."

Jackson gave me a shocked look, probably the same one I had on my face when Bobby told me the same thing. "You want us to move to Vegas?" he asked.

"Yes. It can be—"

"Hell yes!" Jackson shouted, jumping out of his chair and giving the air a fist bump. "Vegas, dude." He turned to me, grinning from ear to ear.

I chuckled. *Guess we're moving to Vegas.*

THREE
Autumn

I STARED AT MY REFLECTION IN THE MIRROR, SEEING THE bruises that marked both of my biceps. You'd think that after two and a half years of being told what to do, I'd learn when I needed to shut-up.

"Did I ask for your opinion?" he snarled, shaking me as if I were a rag doll.

"I just—"

"You what? Thought you'd know what I liked?" His hands clamped down harder against my skin. I swallowed hard, trying not to show that it hurt.

I stared at him for a minute. I thought I had good taste. I had picked out several outfits for him before. "I just like the blue one. It matches your eyes."

He let go of my arms. They burned and throbbed where he'd grabbed me as the blood started to flow again.

"I don't need you to tell me how to dress," he hissed and walked back to his closet.

I wasn't going to tell him how to dress. I just wanted him to know I liked the blue tie—my mistake. Before he could see the tears that wanted to spill over my bottom lids, I turned and left the room. If he saw me cry, the wrath would be ten times worse.

We had been married for almost three years. I heard about men that changed as soon as they got married, but I never thought Rich was going to be that way. When we were dating and engaged, he never so much as raised his voice. I should have known he was too good to be true. Now I'm married to a controlling asshole and I can't leave him because I have no money, let alone the fact that he'd send his thugs after me.

Yep, Rich has thugs on his payroll.

After he'd proposed, he convinced me to quit working. *"Princess, I have plenty of money. You don't need to work anymore. I want you to stay home and get ready to have my babies."*

It took me a few months before I finally caved and quit my job at the bank. Rich was persistent, promising he'd always take care of me, and while he had, he's also controlled my every move since we'd been married.

We dated for six months, got engaged and married three months later. My parents loved him. My friends loved him. My family loved him—I loved him. Everything was perfect ...

Or so I thought.

I never thought I was a weak person, but I was. I didn't have the courage to leave him. I felt stuck, alone, used—worthless. He's never hit me, not really, but he's grabbed me, pushed me ... screamed at me. I felt as if I were an adolescent child trying to learn how the world worked, not someone turning thirty.

After he would yell at me and grab me, he'd be the sweetest person ... like the man I fell in love with.

"Is this the blue tie you were talking about?" he asked, coming into the kitchen where I stood.

I couldn't hesitate before answering him because he'd get mad again. I'd done that too many times and I was slowly learning. "Yes," I whispered.

"Good. Are you going to the coffee shop to meet Brandi?"

"Yes." I swallowed hard. I was scared the storm hadn't fully passed and the slightest raise of my voice might set him off again.

"Good. I'll see you after work and then we can see about getting you pregnant." He leaned down and kissed me on the lips before walking toward the bedroom.

I watched as he turned the corner, my heart continuing its heavy beat.

As I stood in front of the bathroom mirror, getting ready for my coffee date with Brandi, I realized the bruises on my arms were already starting to show. Rich knew I bruised easily, so he'd never lay a hand on me where someone could see. He was too smart for that. No one knew what went on behind closed doors; he scared me enough not to tell.

Or run.

It was as if Rich planned his attacks—as if he waited for me to make one wrong move so he could show me who was boss. Maybe he saw me as weak. I knew I felt as if I were at times, but things needed to change. I was tired of lying to everyone and pretending he was the perfect man. Things needed to change starting today. I was strong before Rich. I was independent before Rich. And I'd be damned if I were going to let him continue to control my life. This wasn't love. This wasn't how a marriage should be. I had too much going for me to let a man run my life.

Sure I'd let him control me for three years, but that was about to change—starting with today.

The weather in early March was still cool enough to wear long sleeves or even a jacket despite living in the desert of Las Vegas. I drove my black Mercedes to Starbucks where Brandi and I had our usual coffee date. After Rich had proposed, he took my old Honda Civic and surprised me with the Mercedes. When he gave me the car, I was ecstatic. I'd never had a nice car before. I should have realized it was part of his master plan to control me. *"I need my princess safe. Can't have her driving around in a car that might break down at any moment,"* he'd insisted.

Safe from everyone but him.

I parked my car then walked into the shop. The smell of fresh coffee hit me as soon as I entered. I saw Brandi sitting at one of the tables, and I waved before I stood in line to order my vanilla latte.

After ordering, I walked over to her table. "Hey," I beamed, excited to see my friend.

"Are you pregnant yet?"

She knew that Rich and I had been trying for two years. What no one knew, especially Rich, was that I was still taking birth control pills. While some people think that children might save a marriage, there was no way I was going to bring a child into the world for Rich to potential abuse.

"No. I need to tell you—"

The barista called my name, announcing my latte was ready. "Hold that thought." I grabbed my coffee and sat back at the table across from Brandi.

"Tell me what?" she asked, taking a sip of her coffee, her brown peering over the lid as she tilted the paper cup back.

"I'm still taking my birth control pills," I whispered.

"What? Why?" she asked, raising her voice in surprise.

"Shh. I have my reasons."

"I don't understand. Don't you want kids? Haven't you been trying?"

I took a sip of my warm, vanilla goodness before replying. "There's more to it than that."

"I don't understand."

"I know." I sighed. I looked over at the menu that hung behind the cashier, not really seeing it as I thought of what to say next. I wanted to tell her about Rich—who he really was, but I was scared. I'd been living my life in denial for too long.

"Explain yourself," she teased.

I looked back at her. This was my best friend. Best friends help each other out and if she knew, she could help me figure out a plan to finally leave him. "Remember that J. Lo movie, *Enough*?"

She raised her brows in confusion. "Um ... yes?"

"Do you remember why she had enough?"

"Her husband beat her."

"Right ..."

"What? Rich *beats* you?" she asked in a whispered yell.

I hushed her again. "Shh. Not exactly."

"Jesus Christ, A. Spit it out."

"Never mind. Forget it." I shouldn't have brought it up.

"If Rich hits you, you need to tell me."

I could feel the lump in my throat start to form. I was tired of being yelled at. I was tired of having bruises on my body that I had to hide. I was tired of living on eggshells. I pulled my sleeve down from my shoulder, exposing one of the bruises.

Her eyes widened. "He *does* hit you," she whispered.

"He grabs me," I corrected—as if that were any better.

"How long?"

"I can't go into details here. People are around."

"Fuck the people, Autumn. You're my best friend. How long?" Her voice had escalated to just below a yell.

"Almost since we've been married."

"What?" she shouted, the people around us turning their heads to look at us.

"Please. Not here." I looked down at my coffee cup, tears pricking my eyes as I avoided her judging scrutiny.

"Fine. Let's go to my place."

I exhaled. "I can't."

"Why not?"

"Today I'm only allowed to meet you for coffee."

"Are you listening to yourself right now?"

"Just ... Please." I fidgeted with the brown coffee sleeve that was wrapped around the paper cup. I couldn't look up at her. She had no idea what I'd been through—no one did.

"You need to leave him," she urged, lowering her voice.

"I can't."

"Why—"

I finally lifted my eyes to hers. "He has people. It's not good, B."

"Go to the cops."

I took a sip of my cooling coffee. "Yeah ... he has people there, too."

"Of course he does," she muttered.

"I promise I'll let you help me, but we need to come up with a smart plan. That's why I decided to tell you. I'm ready—I've had *enough*." I felt a tear roll down my cheek.

"Dammit, Autumn." She stood and reached for my hand, pulling me out of the chair and wrapping her arms around me. "You know it's going to kill me letting you go back there."

I wiped my tears from my cheeks. "I know. I'll be okay. I promise."

We sat back down and I glanced at my phone. "Shit. I gotta go or I'll be late. Rich always calls me on the house phone while he eats his lunch at two."

"To make sure you're home?"

Rich went into work around ten and was home by eight unless there was a *problem* he needed to handle. Every day I was allowed to go to the gym and get coffee on my way home, but I had to make sure to be home by two for the call from him. I'm sure he checked our security cameras too to make sure I had no visitors that he didn't know about and to see what I did throughout the day.

"It will be okay. I've dealt with this for almost three years. What's a few more months?"

"Months?" she shrieked, raising her voice again.

"Maybe sooner. The plan really needs to be solid and I need to somehow put money away. I don't use cash and I'm not sure my name is on our bank accounts."

"I hate this," she muttered, leaning back in her chair with her arms crossed over her chest.

I gave a weak smile. "Me, too. We'll talk about this next week. We'll have coffee in your car."

We stood, throwing our empty cups in the trash. I opened the door and walked right into a hard body, face first. "Oh my God. I'm so ..."

I couldn't finish my sentence.

The most intoxicating green eyes looked down at me as he held my elbows to steady me.

"It's okay. My mistake." He smiled, still holding me up. "Are you okay?"

"I'm ... fine. Thank you." I stepped passed him, Brandi right behind me.

He smiled again and walked inside, but not before turning around again so our eyes could lock.

"Who the fuck is that?" Brandi asked as if I knew, looking at where the mystery man stood staring at me.

"I have no idea," I said finally breaking our gaze.

Brandi walked me to my car. "If you need anything, call me. No matter what time. Call me. I'll be there in a heartbeat and ready to cut the major's balls off."

"Okay. Thank you."

We hugged goodbye and then I drove home, speeding down the streets so I'd make it home in time for Rich's call.

By the time Rich arrived home after work, I'd thought about how

I was going to leave him a hundred different ways. I couldn't just leave because he'd find me. I had no doubt. I couldn't come up with a good plan and needed more time to think, but as I stirred the pasta sauce for dinner, Rich walked in.

"Hey, princess," Rich greeted, opening the garage door that led into the house when he saw me standing at the stove. I tried not to shudder at my nickname. I hated it. At one time, I'd loved thinking I was his princess, but no anymore. Now I felt as if it were all an act and he said it simply to make me feel at ease.

"Hey, honey. How was work?" I plastered a smile on my face, pretending as if nothing was wrong.

He shrugged walking toward me. "You know—loaned some money and made sure others paid me back."

I never wanted to know how he *made* sure people paid him back. "Good." I smiled, tilting my head back so he could kiss me like he did every night when he came home.

"I have good news." He stepped around me, walking toward the bar for his nightly drink.

Our kitchen was massive. My old apartment could have easily fit in it. A black and brown marble granite breakfast bar sat in the middle and beyond that was the family room. The cherry wood bar with a matching granite top sat along the wall to the left that led to the family room that housed our giant flat screen TV.

"Oh yeah?" I returned to stirring the pasta sauce.

"I've decided to run for mayor."

I turned around, the wood spoon still in my hand. Rich was smiling as he poured himself a finger of amber liqueur. "The mayor of Las Vegas?"

He smiled the smile I fell in love with. "Yeah."

"Wow ... Honey, that's—"

"I know. It's going to be good for *us*."

I had no idea what he meant by that. I wasn't a political person. I had no idea what would be involved in running a campaign to manage a city—especially a large city like Las Vegas.

I set the spoon in the spoon rest and walked over to him, a fake smile on my face. "I'm proud of you, honey bunny."

"We're gonna run this town."

I wrapped my arms around his neck. "I like the sound of that, Mr. Mayor."

"I like that name; Mr. Mayor—Mayor Jones—Mr. Richard Jones, Mayor of Las Vegas." He nodded his head as he tried the names on for size.

"Me, too." I kissed him again then went back to the stove.

"Hurry up with dinner so we can celebrate and try to get you pregnant. It would be perfect timing. A baby would win me some votes."

I had no idea, but I agreed to keep him in a good mood. I wasn't sure how it would look for a mayoral candidate to have his wife leave him without a trace.

And I didn't care ...

"I want you naked and ready for me when I get back," Rich barked, pointing a finger at me as I stood at the end of the bed. "Don't disappoint me."

Sex with Rich used to be something I craved. He'd take his time, making sure I'd gotten off multiple times before he did. Sometimes he'd please me and not expect anything back. But like everything else, that changed when we got married. At first I just thought he was role-playing, but I finally realized that he craved control—not me.

I hurried and stripped off my jeans and purple sweater, tossing them in the laundry basket followed by my bra and panties. I'd made the mistake a few times of not being "ready" for him. He wanted me wet. *As if my pussy instantly became drenched because he said so.*

I used to be wet for him all the time. Just the thought of his touch would turn me on. Not anymore. I didn't enjoy it like I used to. I'd still get off, but it lacked the passion. He was basically a stick it and *not* lick it person now. Damn, I missed a good tongue lashing down south.

Crawling under the plush white covers, I slid down, my back coming into contact with the cold sheet. It felt nice against my hot skin as stress coursed through my body. I couldn't disappoint him. The bruises on my arms already hurt when touched and I didn't want anymore.

Spreading my legs, I slid my hands down my chest, caressing my breast with my palms and making my nipples pucker slightly. I teased them for a few seconds, trying to send signals to my brain that I was horny—but I wasn't.

Fuck!

One hand slid down further, not stopping until I felt the slit of my pussy. I heard Rich in the bathroom. I didn't know what he was doing, but if he caught me playing with myself, he'd be pissed. Continuing my path, my hand slipped lower, the other still trying to get my nipples to harden. I could hear the sound of water running from the bathroom sink, and I knew I only had a few more seconds— maybe a minute tops. My middle finger slipped down, running through my folds and straight to my clit. The moment I felt the nub, green flashed behind my closed eyes—green intoxicating eyes.

I smiled, thinking of the stranger as my finger pressed harder, creating circles on my clit. I moaned slightly as I pictured *his* hand in place of mine. My finger started to glide effortlessly as my arousal finally coated my finger. Pressing two fingers to my clit, I circled faster, trying to come before Rich stepped out. I knew I shouldn't, but the eyes and smile of the stranger played in my head ...

Damn.

I faintly heard the water turn off in the bathroom and I stilled. *Fuck!*

Kicking the covers off, I scurried to lay on the top comforter, waiting for my husband. He stepped out of the bathroom, naked. He really did have a nice body. He was cut in all the right places, especially the V that led to his cock.

You've licked that. Nothing changes. Use him to get off while you think about Mr. Green Eyes with the bald head.

"You ready for my dick?"

I nodded, biting my lower lip.

Rich walked over to the side of the bed and reached, grabbing a fistful of my brown hair. My head tilted back as he yanked—not hard, but enough to move me. He pressed his lips to mine, licking the seam. I opened, allowing his tongue to enter.

He kissed me for a few seconds then released my hair. "On your knees," he ordered.

I didn't hesitate. I knew better.

Raising on all fours, I turned my ass to him as he stepped closer, running his finger down my butt crack and through my folds.

"Damn, princess. You *are* ready for me. You're fucking dripping."

I smiled, my head turned so he couldn't see me. I wasn't wet for him that's for damn sure.

Not waiting to agree with him, I moaned my response as his finger entered me, making my back arch like a cat. He thrust a few times before withdrawing, leaving me empty. I turned my head slightly, looking over my right shoulder as he stuck his finger in his mouth, licking my arousal.

"Sweet as pie, princess. Sweet as fucking pie."

I smiled in response. *Use him to get off while you think about Mr. Green Eyes.* I turned my head back, closing my eyes. As Rich entered me, I thought about how Mr. Green Eyes would feel. I moaned, feeling *his* hard cock stretching me from behind. I didn't know who he was. I'd probably never see him again, but things happen for a reason. I needed to bump into him today. Without knowing it, he helped me please my husband so I didn't piss him off again.

Rich grabbed my hips, urging his cock in as I fantasized about the stranger. I wondered what *his* hands would feel like as he pounded into me ... the smell of his skin ... the way his tongue would lick the sweat from my back as he made his way down ... not stopping until he was sucking my clit into his mouth from behind ...

"Fuck, princess," Rich hissed, breaking my thoughts. He grabbed my hair again, pulling my head back, my back arching. I knew he did it this way to control me. I couldn't move as he rammed into me over and over and over. "You better be fucking close."

I'd be closer if you'd shut the fuck up!

I moaned again, playing my role as his balls slapped between my thighs. He groaned, pulling my head back farther. I kept my eyes closed as I pictured my stranger again. Pictured his bald head, his eyes, his smile, his rock hard body as *it* pounded into me.

"I'm coming and you better too," Rich groaned.

Rich pumped a few more times as I thought about Mr. Green Eyes stretching me with his cock and then I cried out, my body convulsing as my orgasm shook me.

"That's a good princess," Rich praised, his hot seed running down the back of my thigh.

Just in the nick of time. Thank you, Mr. Green Eyes.

FOUR
Gabe

WE LEFT MALIBU AT 0600 SHARP. THE SIX AND A HALF HOUR drive to Vegas was torture. It should have only taken five hours, but driving a U-Haul truck had set us back an hour and a half.

I drove the giant truck while towing my Yukon—five miles an hour under the speed limit. Jackson was lucky. He drove his Jeep and listened to satellite radio while I had to scan the stations looking for anything enjoyable. The moment I'd find something I liked, I'd drive out of range, leaving me bored to death on the open stretch of road that was nothing but dirt.

Once we hit the city limits, I followed Jackson as he drove through the streets of Las Vegas to our new house. Saddles & Racks had paid our moving expenses and our first month's rent on a two-story, tan colored, stucco house that we'd be sharing. We didn't mind sharing a house; we'd been in worse situations when we were in Afghanistan and it would be nice to live with Jackson in a new city.

I parked the truck on the curb while Jackson parked his Jeep in the driveway. I needed a beer. "P.J., get back in the Jeep and let's go buy a twenty-four pack."

"You don't want to see the inside?" he called back.

"I just drove almost six hours straight. I need a beer."

"Well, I need to piss," he countered, walking toward the front door.

"Fine, I'll go. Throw me the keys."

He did. "Get lunch too."

I stared at him. Was I his fucking bitch? "Is this how it's going to be living with you?" I joked.

"Fuck you. I gotta go piss or I'll give our neighbors a show when I pull my dick out here on the front lawn," he said, walking backward to the front door. "Just get me a burger or something." He turned and ran for the door.

I laughed at him as I climbed into his Jeep. I didn't know where I was going, but I figured a grocery store must be nearby or at least a liquor store. Shit, it was Vegas. I could stick a dollar in a slot at any casino and wait for a cocktail waitress to bring me a beer if I needed to.

I drove a few blocks, then pulled into a parking lot of a Starbucks after realizing how tired I was from the drive. Alcohol would just make me exhausted, and we still had to unload the truck. Stepping out of the Jeep, my phone dinged with an incoming text.

Jackson: *Bobby gave me the number for a few of the guys at S&R and they're coming over to help us move our shit. Get a few cases and more food.*

I groaned. I wanted to meet the guys, but I was fucking exhausted. I didn't want to be social. I just wanted to move my bed and pass out.

My head was down as I reached out and opened the glass door for Starbucks ...

And smack into a body smaller than my own.

"Oh my God. I'm so ..."

"It's okay. My mistake." I smiled, taking in the blush on her face that led to the biggest, most beautiful hazel eyes I'd ever seen. I held her up by her elbows so she wouldn't fall. "Are you okay?"

"I'm ... fine. Thank you." She stepped to the side, the wind blowing in the right direction as I took a deep breath, smelling a scent I'd never forget.

"Who the fuck is that?" the woman she was with asked.

"I have no idea," she admitted, turning around and walking away.

I went inside, trying to shake the scent, but at the same time remembering Alyssa's smile. There wasn't a day that passed that I didn't think of her. As I stood in line, the smell of coffee in the air, I realized I wasn't sad about smelling the vanilla scent but more intrigued by the stranger wearing it.

After leaving Starbucks, I found a grocery store nearby and bought enough beer for ten guys. Even though I knew there weren't going to be that many hands on deck, I figured there was no harm in having beer be the first thing to christen our fridge. I also bought a bottle of Jack Daniels for me and some toilet paper—the necessities. I knew without a doubt that smelling the familiar scent would cause me to have a nightmare and I needed the whiskey to prevent that from happening. I had them most nights, but I couldn't relive Alyssa dying again.

I stopped at a fast food drive-through for five burgers and fries before arriving back home. A silver *Ford* pickup truck sat on the curb, and the U-Haul was backed into the driveway with the garage door open. I still needed to pound a beer or two before I was able to move anything. Moving fucking sucked.

"It's about damn time!" Jackson bellowed, coming out of the garage.

"I don't know my way around."

"I'm just fuckin' with ya. The guys just got here." Three men walked out of the garage behind Jackson. "Cap—I mean, Gabe. This is Brad, Nick, and Vinny."

"What up?" Nick gave me a nod and stuck his hand out. Black ink lined his arms and up part of his neck.

I took his hand. "Hey."

The bald guy gave a big goofy grin as he stepped forward with his hand out. "Vinny."

I shook his hand too and then turned to Brad. "Paul says your ex-army. I'm ex-marine." He said with a southern drawl and a strong grip.

"Awesome. Three military men and two bald guys."

We all laughed.

"And one wanna be rapper." Vinny nudged his thumb toward Nick. "Plus a Cali boy." He looked over at Jackson.

"Vegas better watch out," Jackson boasted.

"Let's drink some beer and move shit," I offered, holding up one of the twelve packs.

It took three hours for the five of us to move all our shit. Afterward, we finished a few more beers before the guys called it a night. We made plans to get a round of drinks later in the week so they could tell us how the Vegas scene worked in our line of work.

When I stepped out of the shower, Jackson was in the kitchen. He held up the brown sack with my bottle in it. "What triggered it this time?"

"Life."

"I thought you didn't have nightmares anymore?"

I sighed. "That's just what I told you."

"Now that we live together, we're gonna fix this."

I scrubbed my hands down my face. "Can't fix dreams, P.J."

"*Working* doesn't help?"

I knew Jackson really meant fucking. I walked up to him, snatched the bag out of his hand, "For the most part. I had a bad day."

"Bad day? I've been with you all day. What was bad about it?"

"Fine! I had a fucking trigger. I bumped into a woman at Starbucks and she smelled exactly like Cochran and now I can't get her out of my head."

Her ... the stranger ... not Alyssa ... *Why was I thinking of the stranger?*

"Gabe," he groaned. "I really think it's time you talk to someone. It's been three years, man."

"I don't need to talk to anyone," I disagreed, turning on my heel and walking to my bedroom, bottle in hand.

"Shh, stop giggling. You're gonna get us caught." I grabbed Alyssa by the hand and tugged her through the dirt parking lot.

"They're all in the bar drinking." She giggled again.

"Where'd you park?"

"In the back like always."

I tugged Alyssa faster, not wanting to waste another second. "Keys, babe."

She pulled her keys from her front jean pocket, pressing the unlock button on the fob. I reached out, opening the backseat and let Alyssa get in before me. After closing the door behind me, I turned facing my blonde angel.

I leaned slightly toward her, grabbing the sides of her face with both hands and bringing her lips to mine. She moaned when my tongue thrust inside her mouth, tasting her cherry Chapstick coating my lips in return.

"I've missed this," I groaned against her mouth.

She smiled, not breaking the contact. "Me, too."

"Let's take off your shirt so I can taste your titties now."

"Titties?" She laughed, her head tilting back, exposing her neck.

I smirked. "Titties, boobies, tits—whatever."

I helped her lift her black tank top then threw it into the front seat. "You have perfect titties."

"Shut up and taste them already." She chuckled, reaching for my shirt to bring me down to her as she lay back on the bench seat.

"Yes, ma'am."

I didn't hesitate as I started at her lips again, working my way down her neck, her chest valley and to her right breast. Pulling the cup of her bra down, I licked her puckered nipple. Her back arched and a moan escaped her mouth.

"You like that, babe?"

"Yes," she panted.

I pulled the other cup down, doing the same to her left breast as I did to her right. Her legs wrapped around my waist, bringing me closer as I rubbed my jean covered crotch against her heat.

I traced my tongue down her flat stomach, inching down to unbutton her jeans. I popped the button and—

There was a knock on the door.

Stilling, I looked up at Alyssa, her eyes huge as she looked over my shoulder. "It's Major Dick."

My neck instantly tightened and I took a deep breath to calm down. I pulled away from her, throwing the car door open.

"What the fuck do you want?" I snapped.

"I can't wait to bring you up on UCMJ charges, Captain. I'll love watching your ass be thrown into jail for fraternization." He grinned like the fucking Cheshire Cat from Alice in Wonderland.

"You think they'll believe you?" I crossed my arms over my chest, my legs spread wide as I stood there glaring at him.

"You think they won't?"

"You have no proof."

"It's crazy how technology has changed over the years." He held up his cell phone still smiling like the asshole he was. "Takes video now."

I lunged at him, reaching for the phone to break it into a million pieces. He turned, sending me stumbling.

"Now, Captain, that's no way to talk to your commanding officer." The evil smile never left his face as he taunted me. "Maybe I should *get in on this action." He looked down at Alyssa as she sat in the back-seat, averting her eyes.*

"You fucking lay a hand on her and I'll kill you!" I barked.

He clucked his tongue, tsking me. "Come on, Captain, you know I can't touch what's dead."

"Dead?" I looked at Alyssa. She was no longer in her jeans and black bra. She was now wearing her army uniform, blood covering the right front side of her chest.

"What did you do?" I shouted, stepping forward to rush to her, but he held me back. "Let me go. I need to save her!"

"She's already dead."

"No!"

I woke up screaming, clenching the sheets around me. Fucking Major Dick. My dream wasn't even real. Alyssa and I had never been caught.

"Gabe?" Jackson knocked on my closed bedroom door. "You okay?"

"Yeah," I murmured.

"Nightmare?"

"Yeah."

"Wanna talk about it?"

"No ... Just leave me alone." I fell back against my pillow.

"Okay. I'll be in the living room. We need some fucking food."

"I know."

"And coffee. Fuck I need coffee," he groaned.

"There's a Starbucks a few blocks over," I called back.

"Perfect. Let's hit that shit up before breakfast, then the store. We can't spend all day though, I got a date. Fuck, and we need to find a gym."

"You have a date already? We just got to town."

"Yeah, man. Might wanna check your back-office, too."

I groaned, grabbing my cell phone. Sure as shit, I had a date too.

When Alyssa first died, I drank like a fish. Jackson had covered for me numerous times while we were still in Afghanistan. Once we were home, I still drank enough to pass out. Over the years, it got better. Sure, some days were worse and I had to drink to shut my mind off; especially March ninth each year. It usually took me a few weeks to get my heart to calm down enough so I could sleep after the anniversary of Alyssa's death—which was only a few days before we left for Vegas. Smelling Alyssa's scent made it worse, but when I saw the face of who I was smelling, made it better. It was a weird feeling and when I lay in bed the night before, I thought of the stranger and not Alyssa.

After changing into jeans and a light sweater, I drove us to the Starbucks I'd discovered the previous day.

"Thank God there's a Starbucks on almost every corner," Jackson joked.

We stepped inside, waiting in line to order, and that's when I saw *her*.

FIVE

Autumn

I woke up to Rich yelling in the master bathroom. Thankfully, it wasn't at me.

"No, he can't fucking have until the end of the week! He either pays by the end of business today or he'll meet Remo—yeah, fucking deal with it." There was a loud crash and I rolled over, pretending to still be asleep. The less I knew about his business, the better.

"Princess, it's time to wake up." Rich brushed the hair from my face to stir me.

I groaned, rolling over as if I was still sleeping. "Morning, honey."

"Get up. Time to go to the gym."

I smiled. I didn't want to go to the gym, but if I put on weight, he'd get pissed. "Okay, and this afternoon I have a nail appointment, remember?" I had to make sure everything was done perfectly: my hair, my nails, and my clothes. And I *always* had to let Rich know.

"Right. So you're going back to Club 24 or staying there the whole time?"

"I don't like the coffee at Club 24, so I'll go back after I have my coffee and lunch. Can you call me on my cell when you have your lunch?" Honestly, Club 24 was perfect and the food was spectacular, but I needed that extra stop so I didn't feel trapped. I felt as if my wings needed to be spread, not clamped down by Rich's claws.

"Yeah, but you better answer before three rings." He stood and walked back to the bathroom.

"I will, honey bunny. I promise."

He came out of the bathroom, straightening the cuffs of his long-sleeved button down white dress shirt. "Also, I'm going to have Lea stop by. I want to throw a party to announce that I'll be running for mayor. You'll need to help her."

I smiled tightly, trying not to show how pissed off I was. "Of course. I'm excited. I should buy a new dress."

"Not today. Gym, coffee, nails, home and wait for Lea." He counted each stop on his hand as if to remind me there were only five things I needed to do today.

"You got it, Major." I sat up on my knees, waving Rich over so I could kiss him goodbye and he could leave me the fuck alone.

"I'm serious, Autumn. Don't disappointment me."

I swallowed hard at his threat before I smiled brightly. "Honey, I won't. Gym, coffee, nails and home. Lea and I will plan a kick ass party for you."

"Good. I gotta go. There's a problem with a client I need to take care of." He gave me a quick kiss on the lips and left the bedroom.

"Love you," I called out—for good measure.

"I love you too, princess."

I cringed. There was the nickname that made me feel like an adolescent child.

I walked into Starbucks in my black yoga pants and black razor-back tank top, sweaty from my vigorous workout. I'd started to lift more weights; if I was going to leave Rich, I needed to become stronger—inside and out.

"The usual?" Alexis asked, grabbing a paper cup.

"Yes, please." You know you go to Starbucks too much when they know your name and order by heart.

I sat in my usual maroon wing-backed chair by the window as I took sips of my latte and ate my salad. I still didn't have a plan. I had no money to leave town, and my parents couldn't afford to help me. My head was a mess.

As I ate my salad, my phone dinged with a text.

Brandi: *Are you at Starbucks?*

Me: *Yeah.*

I waited for her to text back, but she didn't.

The coffeehouse music played in the background as I continued staring out the window. I couldn't search anything on my phone in fear that Rich would see. I couldn't look on the computer at home and he made sure I made no extra stops in my day, so I had no idea how to plan my escape. You didn't grow up and study ways to leave your abusive husband in school, and Rich had too many people in his life; I was certain he'd find me no matter what.

As I looked around for a newspaper to check prices of used car in the classifieds, my gaze landed on a familiar face.

"We don't have time to drink our coffee here."

"Yeah ... we do."

My heart stopped when I heard his voice and our fixed stares locked.

"No ... we don't."

Mr. Green Eyes walked over and sat at the wood table across from me, my gaze watching his every move. "Yeah ...we do," he said, not taking his ogling eyes off of me. Mine lowered to my salad as I instantly became nervous.

If you only knew what I thought about last night, Mr. Green Eyes.

"Oh ..." his friend sang, "we *do* have time."

I looked over at his friend. His short brown hair and brown eyes were the complete opposite of Mr. Green Eyes and his bald head.

"Excuse me," the friend said. "We're new in town and I see that you might have just worked out at a gym. Do you know the best one around here?"

"Um ..."

"You did just come from a gym?" The friend motioned to my attire.

Finally finding my voice, I answered with a smile. "Yes, sorry, I go to Club 24. It's just down the street." I pointed in the general direction.

"Perfect," the friend clapped once, nodding his head at Mr. Green Eyes.

My gaze fell back on Mr. Green Eyes as he sipped his coffee and stared at me. I had no idea what was going on, but it was awkward—especially after I'd thought about him while Rich fucked me the night before.

"So ..." The friend whispered, leaning in closer to his friend (but I could still hear him), "This the trigger?"

Mr. Green Eyes looked at his friend then back at me. "Yeah."

I tried to look away before he saw me staring, but I couldn't help it. I was too confused to form rational thoughts. I wanted to know what he was thinking. Why he came over and didn't even say hello when clearly he sat near me for a reason.

"I see ..." The friend nodded, then turned his head back to me. "I'm Paul and this is Gabe. We might be seeing you at Club 24. Gotta stay in shape for the ladies and all." I giggled and Gabe kicked his friend. "Ow!"

"It's a really nice facility. They have everything," I affirmed.

"Like what?" Paul turned his body around in his chair to face me fully.

"Well, all the basic equipment you'd find at a gym, but they also have a spa, salon, barber shop, café, juice bar, a volleyball court, basketball, racquetball—"

"Damn, they do have everything," Paul exclaimed.

I looked back to Gabe, waiting for him to speak, but again he stayed quiet as he sipped his coffee. "Yeah, they just opened a few months ago too. I bet you can get a good deal for signing up."

"Do they have a referral bonus? Maybe you can go with us and get an incentive?"

I knew I couldn't go with them. I, without a doubt, knew that Rich had eyes on me all the time. Before I could respond, Brandi walked in and over to where we sat.

"Oh my God, what are you doing here? Why aren't you at work?" I asked, looking up at her as she stood next to me.

"I wanted to check on you." When she stopped talking, she looked at Gabe and Paul. "Am I interrupting something?"

I smiled. "No, just having coffee and lunch." I motioned to my latte and salad.

Paul stood, sticking his hand out to Brandi. "I'm Paul. This is Gabe. We were just asking your friend where a good gym was."

"Oh ..." She looked back at me then to Paul. "Club 24."

"So we hear." Paul smiled. "We good to go?" he asked Gabe.

"Yeah," Gabe finally spoke.

"Ladies, it's been a pleasure. Hope to see you both around," Paul smirked. Gabe just gave me a tight smile before he turned his back to walk away.

Brandi turned back to me. "Was that ..."

"Yeah ..."

"The guy ..."

"Yep."

"Damn. What'd I miss?" she asked, sitting in the chair that Paul vacated.

"Nothing. It was weird. Gabe didn't even say anything."

"Hmm," she grunted. "Weird."

"Yeah. Anyway, why are you here?"

"I just wanted to check on you and didn't want to text or call in case Rich is monitoring your phone."

"Oh ... I'm sure he is."

"I've been thinking ..."

I perked up. "Yeah?"

"What if Todd and I took out a second mortgage on our house and gave it to you?"

"What? Why?"

"So you can leave town. You can pay me back once you get settled somewhere."

"B, it's not gonna be that easy. Rich will find me."

"Then we need to kill him. I can't take this," she huffed, crossing her arms over her chest.

I laughed. "We can't kill him."

"I know. Figure of speech." She waved her hand in the air to brush off the comment.

"I gotta go get my nails done and be home in time for Rich's event planner. Oh, that reminds me. He's running for mayor."

Brandi's eyes became huge. "Shut the fuck up!"

"I know, right? I'm so fucking screwed."

"No, you're not. No one deserves to live in hell like you. Verbal or physical is still abuse. I still think you need to go to the cops," she whispered, leaning toward me.

I knew she was right. But I couldn't. I was too scared.

I walked into Club 24 and my gaze immediately fell on Gabe and Paul at the front desk. My steps faltered.

The receptionist looked up, noticing me. "Welcome back, Mrs. Jones."

I tore my eyes from Gabe's back. "Thanks, Cassie. I have an appointment at the salon."

"Perfect." She nodded.

I could feel green and brown eyes on me as I started to walk to the salon. "Ms. Jones," Paul reached out to stop me. "We forgot to get your name at Starbucks, so it's good you came by. They do have an incentive program here."

I smiled. "Awesome, but really, it's not needed."

"Nonsense. You get one hundred dollar gift certificates for each of us." Paul gestured between him and Gabe.

I perked up. Somehow I needed to turn the certificates into cash to save for my escape.

"It's true," Cassie affirmed. "As long as they sign a year contract."

"We are." My eyes shot to Gabe as he finally spoke. "Ms. ..."

"Autumn. My name's Autumn."

"Autumn referred us," Gabe spoke.

"I'm sorry, but I really need to get to my appointment. Can you do everything without me to get them signed up?" I asked.

"Of course," Cassie confirmed.

"Start with Paul. I'm going to walk Autumn to her appointment," Gabe insisted, stepping toward me.

I pulled my head back in shock. "You are?"

"Yes, ma'am. After you." He motioned for me to start walking, but I hesitated before taking my first step.

"You don't need to walk with me," I protested.

"I need to ask you something."

I held my breath. I had no idea what he wanted to ask me. I didn't know the guy and I was wearing my wedding ring, so I'm sure he knew I was married. "Okay."

"Please forgive me if this is overstepping, but I noticed the bruises on your arms and I just wanted to make sure you're okay. I overheard your friend asking if you were okay, and you looked sad at Starbucks."

I closed my eyes, taking a deep breath. "Yeah, I just ran into a wall when I was drinking." I shrugged, trying to play off the lie.

He eyed me. "Both arms?"

I looked to my other arm. "What can I say? I'm a wobbly drunk."

I laughed. No one had ever seen the bruises before—or commented about them. I was always good about covering them up, but I'd completely forgotten about them as I'd dragged my sweaty body to Starbucks.

"Ma'am—"

"Autumn. Please."

He smiled his intoxicating smile and I fought to suck in a breath. "Autumn. I know you don't know me, but would you like to have coffee with me sometime?"

I would. I really fucking would.

I was tired of being pushed around by Rich—literally.

I was tired of being screamed at.

I was tired of fearing that one slip of my tongue would cause more bruises.

I was tired—period.

But at the end of the day, I was still married to Rich. And even though I was insanely attracted to Mr. Green Eyes, I couldn't do anything about it.

I held up my left hand, showing Gabe my ring. "I'm sorry, I'm married." We stopped at the doors that led into the salon.

"All right. Maybe I'll see you around."

"Yeah, maybe," I agreed with a smile.

"Thank you for telling us about this place." He waved his hand in the air, motioning to the gym. "Have a nice day, Autumn."

My cell phone started to ring in my purse. "Thanks, you too."

He gave a tight smile as he turned and walked away.

I answered Rich's call after two rings.

SIX
Gabe

SHE SAT NEAR THE WINDOW, THE SUN GLOWING BEHIND HER AND casting a halo as if she were an angel. I did a double take, making sure what I saw was real—or who for that matter. But as I stared, I knew she was the same woman who smelled like Alyssa.

Today *her* brown hair was pulled into a ponytail and she had on workout clothes. When I'd first bumped into her, she was wearing jeans and a sweater, her hair long; it had brushed against my hands as I steadied her.

There was something about her that I was drawn to. It wasn't because she brought back memories of Alyssa—this was different. I couldn't look away from her as I felt my heart start to beat faster and nervousness coursed through my body.

"What are you getting?" Jackson asked, bringing me out of my daze.

"What? Oh ..." I stepped forward and ordered my vanilla latte, then stepped aside, letting Jackson pay for it.

"I'm buying you coffee?" he questioned, raising an eyebrow at me.

I shrugged. "You owe me."

"Fine. All right," he huffed with a chuckle.

As we waited for our coffee, I stared at the brunette angel. I wanted to go over and talk to her. Ask her for her name—*smell her*—but something was off. She didn't have the same smile on her face that I'd seen the day before, but more of a solemn vibe and for some odd reason, it bothered me.

I stepped closer, pretending to play on my phone as we waited for the barista to make the coffee. I was hoping *she* would look up at me. I wanted to see her smile again. I wanted to be the cause of her smile.

The closer I got, the more obvious I felt I was being. In my line of work, I could talk to anyone. I had to. I had to make women feel comfortable. So I didn't know why I was nervous.

"We're drinking here," I said, reaching for my coffee that the barista set on the bar after calling our names.

"We don't have time to drink our coffee here," Jackson whined.

"Yeah, we do." The brunette angel looked up, our fixed stares locking, but she didn't smile.

"No, we don't."

I sat at a table near *her*, hoping that I could at least get her name. "Yeah—We do," I gritted through my teeth.

The brunette angel broke our stare and looked down at her salad. I looked her over, loving what I was seeing in her tight outfit. But that's when I saw her arms. My stomach dropped. She had bruises on each as if they were from fingers wrapped around her biceps.

"Oh ..." Jackson said, finally understanding what the fuck was going on. "We do have time."

Jackson started to talk to her as I stared, sipping my coffee. I caught bits and pieces as my mind wandered, trying to figure out how I was going to find out about her bruises. I was a stranger—she was a stranger, but I wanted to ask her as my protective side came out. I wanted to know who would hurt someone as beautiful as her. No man is to ever hit a woman, no matter how much they nagged, bitched or moaned. And if I ever saw a man hit a woman with my own two eyes, I'd kill him.

"So," Jackson whispered, leaning into me and bringing my gaze to him, "this the trigger?"

I looked back at her. "Yeah."

I watched as they talked about Club 24. I wanted to interject, but

I let Jackson take over, finding out all the details while I thought about how I was going to find out about her bruises. Maybe it wouldn't be today. Maybe it wouldn't be tomorrow. But if I saw more, I'd make sure she knew who I was and the same with the fucking asshole that was doing it to her.

"Oh my God, what are you doing here? Why aren't you at work?" she asked. The girl who was with her the day before appeared at her side.

"I wanted to check on you." The friend looked over at us. "Am I interrupting something?"

The brunette angel smiled. "No. Just having coffee and lunch."

We said goodbye ... well, Jackson said goodbye. I was still too pissed at the sight of her bruises to speak.

"Why didn't you talk to her, you fucking creepy motherfucker?" he asked, buckling his seatbelt into the passenger seat.

I cranked the engine. "Did you notice the bruises?"

"What bruises?"

"The ones on her arms."

Jackson thought for a moment. "I wasn't looking at her arms."

"Well, she had them on both arms. Looks like someone grabbed her really hard."

"Damn," he exhaled.

"Look up directions on your phone for Club 24," I said, putting my Yukon in reverse.

"We're doing that now? I don't think—"

"Yeah, we're doing it now. *She* goes there and I want to see her again."

He smiled a big toothy smile. "You got it, Captain."

We found our way to Club 24, Jackson bitching the entire way that he was hungry. I was hungry too, but the coffee could tide me over until after we signed up for the gym. It wasn't as if we were going to actually workout today. We had a long list of shit to do and work tonight.

"Jesus Christ, it's like a compound," Jackson said as he looked around the massive space we'd just entered. "I guess they really do have everything."

"Hi, can I help you?" a woman behind the front desk asked.

"We're here to see about a membership. We were referred by ..." I turned to Jackson. "We didn't get her name."

"Shit," he groaned.

I turned back to the staffer. "Do you have an incentive program, Cassie?" I asked because if they did, I'd find the brunette angel and get her name. It was another reason to talk to her.

"We do," she confirmed. "If you sign up for a year, the person who referred you will get a hundred dollar gift certificate to use at our facility."

"Well, we gotta wait," I advised Jackson as I turned to him. "It's another reason—"

"Welcome back, Mrs. Jones."

I watched as the brunette angel put on a fake smile as she spoke. I motioned for Jackson to get her name, figuring it would be more awkward for me to ask her since I didn't speak to her at Starbucks. Fuck—I was creepy.

"Ms. Jones," Jackson said, reaching out with his hand to wave her down. "We forgot to get your name at Starbucks. It's good you came by because they do have an incentive program here."

She smiled as she spoke. Still not the one I wanted to see again. "Awesome, but really, it's not needed."

"Nonsense. You'll get one-hundred dollar gift certificates for each of us."

"It's true," Cassie confirmed. "As long as they sign a year contract."

"We are." I blurted. "Miss?"

"Autumn. My name's Autumn."

"Autumn referred us." I turned back to Cassie.

"I'm sorry, but I really need to get to my appointment. Can you do everything without me to get them signed up?" Autumn asked.

"Of course," Cassie confirmed.

"Start with Paul. I'm going to walk Autumn to her appointment." I stepped away from the desk and toward Autumn.

"You are?" she asked, her beautiful, big eyes widening. I stared at them, trying to figure out the color. They weren't brown. They weren't blue. They weren't green. They were a mixture of all three. *They were beautiful.*

"Yes, ma'am, after you." I motioned for her to start walking, but she hesitated.

I asked her about her bruises. She lied. Most abused women did. I wasn't going to push her. If her husband wasn't helping her, then he was the culprit and I had every intention of finding out. I didn't know why, but I was drawn to her. I wanted to know everything about her. She didn't smell like warm vanilla sugar today, and that was okay. I wasn't attracted to her because I thought she could mask my pain. I was attracted to her because she was the first woman to make me feel since Alyssa.

I felt nervous.

I felt happy.

I felt *for* her.

We signed up for a year with Club 24, had lunch at a hole in the wall Mexican restaurant and found a grocery store where we bought enough food to feed an army.

By the time we put everything away and unpacked a few boxes at our new home, it was time to get ready for our dates.

My date tonight was Michele. Luckily the date info in my back office only said that she wanted to meet up for drinks. I didn't have it in me to role-play; pretend I was her boyfriend, her husband, her boss ... her whatever the fuck she wanted. She only wanted a drinking buddy and, of course, whiskey was calling my name.

I drove to the bar that she wanted to meet at. The job info stated that she'd be wearing a black dress, drinking a Cosmopolitan, and she had long, straight brown hair. As I walked to the bar, scanning it for her, I didn't feel nervous. The nervous energy left after the very first date three years ago.

I had to admit, the moment I saw Michele, I was attracted to her. But she didn't make my pulse race. If she suggested we go back to her place or fuck in her car, I'd be down with it.

"Michele?" I asked, placing my hand on her shoulder.

"Gabe?" she asked, turning around on the barstool.

I gestured toward her drink. "Starting without me?"

She smiled warmly. "It's my first one."

I slid onto the stool next to her, flagging down the bartender and ordered a Jack and Coke.

"Whiskey man?" Michele grinned.

"It's my poison of choice, yes." I laughed.

"I don't know how you can drink that stuff." She shuddered. "It's gross."

"It's not that bad when you're used to it."

"I guess that's true."

"Do you come here often?" I chuckled at my cliché line.

"Sometimes for happy hour with my friends."

We made more small talk. I told her how I'd just moved from the Los Angeles area while she told me that she moved to Vegas ten years ago to try and make it in show business. We ordered another round of drinks and I inched closer to her, trying to give her the best experience possible. Women paid decent money for a companion for a few hours and we did everything we could to make them think they were the only woman we were thinking of.

"Would you like another drink?" I asked, pointing to her empty martini glass.

"Actually ..." she bit her lip as if to entice me, "we have an hour left. Would you like to come back to my place for *coffee?* I live right down the street."

Oh, the good old coffee line.

If you hire an escort, just fucking say, "Would you like to go back to my place and fuck?" I mean, seriously. Escorts are at your beck and call. It may not be plastered on the walls of our company because it's illegal to pay for sex, but if you're feelin' it, just come out and ask.

I smiled, looking at her lips as she spoke. "Sure. I love *coffee.*"

I followed Michele to her house. An hour wasn't a lot of time, but with my job, we didn't have to stick around and cuddle after—unless we still had time and they wanted to.

"How do you like your coffee?" she asked, walking toward her kitchen as I closed the door behind me.

"Michele." I chuckled. "You and I both know I didn't come here for coffee."

She smiled back with a nervous smile, averting her eyes as she asked, "So do we just start?"

"Is that what you do with other guys?" I walked closer to her.

"I don't have much sex. Hence why I hired you." She waved her hand, gesturing toward me.

"No, you hired me for drinks. This is just a bonus." Reaching up, I brushed her bangs out of her eyes so I could look into the blue irises.

"This is—"

I cut her off, bending down and sealing my lips over hers to calm her. She moaned in response, my hands cupping each side of her face as my tongue entered her mouth.

"How do you want it?" I asked.

She pulled her head back. "What?" She blushed.

"Aw, it's no time to get bashful. We're gonna fuck now. How do you want it? Hard or slow?"

"I ... I don't know."

"It's all about your pleasure, sweetheart. So what is it? Tell me your fantasy."

What I'd learned from the three years as an escort was we were the boyfriend in public and the escort behind closed doors. Some only wanted the boyfriend experience. Some wanted to role-play. And some wanted to be fucked harder than they'd ever been fucked before.

"I've always wanted to be fucked hard on the kitchen table," she choked out.

I smirked, reaching down and hoisting her up by her ass. Her legs wrapped around my waist, her arms around my neck as I walked to the kitchen in search of the table. "Lean back," I instructed, setting her down on the table once I reached it.

She did as I asked and I reached under her black dress, pulling her thong down and tossing it onto the floor. I could already smell how aroused she was. Running my hands up each of her calves to her thighs, she arched her back, moaning. I pushed her dress up, exposing her bare pussy, and licked my lips. Her eyes were closed as I reached out and ran two fingers down her folds and through her glistening juice.

"Damn, sweetheart. Getting fucked on your kitchen table turns you on that much?"

She nodded her head, biting her lip again while I slipped a finger in her then two, spreading her arousal around her lips. I pumped them a few times, bringing her close to the edge, then stopped.

I felt her ogling eyes looking at me as I shrugged out of my long-sleeved, button-down blue shirt and unbuttoned my jeans to push them and my boxers down my legs. Glancing up, I caught her stare and paused. For a split second, I saw hazel eyes looking back at me and not the blue ones. Shaking my head to clear my thoughts, I stepped closer and she reached out and grabbed my dick, stroking it a few times.

"Ready?" I asked.

She nodded.

I reached into my jeans pocket and pulled a condom out. After sheathing myself, I stepped closer, spreading her legs wide and teasing her clit with the tip of my dick. Her eyes closed as I inched in. I didn't care. This was her fantasy and she could do whatever she wanted. I didn't need to look into her eyes as she came. I didn't need her watching me. I just needed to fuck her the way she wanted and call it a day.

Sliding all the way in, her hands kneaded her tits through her dress. She pulled the top of her dress down, exposing her nice boobs, and started to play with her nipples. I let her play with them a little while I pumped a few times. They were a nice view.

"Lift your arms above your head and hold on, sweetheart."

Her eyes opened, but she didn't say anything. My thrusts continued to be slow, building her up, and then I picked up speed, pumping my hips. Michele held the table as I rammed over and over. Her eyes closed again and I closed mine too, focusing on the feel of her warm pussy wrapped around my dick. My thoughts drifted to Autumn again.

Fuck!

My eyes opened, looking down at Michele as she moaned with

pleasure, my hips still pumping. Sweat was rolling down my chest and my back as I brought her closer with each thrust. Letting go of one of her legs, I placed my hand on her stomach and held her while I continued to vigorously thrust into her.

"Oh my God. Don't press on my stomach, I'm gonna pee."

"It's impossible, sweetheart. Trust me."

Our eyes locked as she started to wiggle.

"Gabe, I'm gonna pee."

"Trust me. Relax." She closed her eyes again, her pussy tightening as my firm hand pressed down on her stomach. "That's it," I coaxed.

"Oh my God," she moaned as her back arched and her lips parted. "Oh God!" she shouted as she started to come. I pulled out, her pussy spraying and hitting my chiseled stomach. "Holy shit. Did I just squirt?" she panted.

"Yeah, I told you to trust me." I smiled as I ran two fingers through her cum and stuck them in her mouth so she could taste herself.

"Oh ... wow. That was ..."

After she had come down from her high, I stepped toward her, spreading her legs wide as I slid back in. "Hold the table again, sweetheart."

I started to thrust, needing to get off. She held onto the table and I closed my eyes, pumping hard as thoughts of Autumn popped into my head. I let them in this time. I wanted them. I pictured her tight pussy wrapped around my dick as my hands roamed all over her beautiful body. The bruises would be gone and her real smile would be looking back at me. She'd shatter under me as I sent her over the edge into bliss.

I groaned my release, opening my eyes to bring me back to reality. Michele moaned as she tipped over the edge again. After pulling out, I disposed of the condom and cleaned my chest off using the kitchen sink.

"Thank you." She sat up, straightening her dress.

I smirked. "You're welcome."

"I may need to hire you again. That was amazing."

"You know where to find me."

After a hug and a quick kiss on the lips, I climbed into my car and drove home, dreaming of the brunette angel's smile.

SEVEN
Autumn

Lea and I worked for two hours straight as we started to plan Rich's party. I knew better than she that everything needed to be perfect. If one thing went wrong, the wrath of Rich would reappear.

We decided to have the party at my house. It was large enough to hold at least two-hundred people if we used both the inside and outside, and it sat beautifully on a golf course that would be the perfect backdrop. White lights would be strung across the yard allowing enough light for people to mingle while sipping drinks. Both a caterer and bartender was hired.

I didn't know anything about throwing a party for someone who wanted to run a city, but I knew enough to make it a stunning engagement. With Lea's help and expertise, everything was perfect. All that needed to be done now was to go over the guest list with Rich.

Lea left shortly before six that evening. Her petite frame hoisted up in her SUV and her dark brown hair shined in the sun when she rolled down the window to tell me goodbye. It was a beautiful day. The sun had been out for most of it and it wasn't too hot or too cold. I wanted to lie out in the sun and work on my tan to match Lea's, but instead, I knew I had to get dinner ready.

After searing off a few pork chops, I threw them in the oven while I made an arugula salad with balsamic vinaigrette. Lean proteins and low carbs equaled a leaner self. From working out hard at the gym, my body was already craving the extra protein so I made myself a protein shake and drank it while the chops cooked and I checked my email.

I received an email from one of the CEOs of Club 24, Brandon Montgomery, thanking me for referring two people. A smile spread across my face as I thought about Gabe and how I wanted to see him again. I was surprised when he noticed my bruises—I should know better, but the way he was concerned made me want to run to him and have him help me plan my escape.

I didn't know anything about him other than he was sexy for a bald guy. He had strong arms, and thighs so thick and powerful that I wanted to—

I shook my head, shaking off the daydream.

Checking the clock, I noticed that it was almost time for Rich to arrive home. I scurried to my bathroom and freshened up for him. I'd already taken a shower before Lea arrived, but I had to make sure my hair wasn't flat and my makeup looked natural and perfect.

I heard his car enter the garage and I ran to the kitchen so he could see me cooking for him. If he were anymore old fashioned, I'd have to greet him at the door with a cocktail and a kiss. Luckily, he preferred to pour his own drinks at night, depending on what kind of day he had. It was also my clue as to how to approach him.

Vodka martini meant that he had a bad day at work. Someone either didn't pay or something didn't go his way.

Whiskey sour meant that he had a decent day at work. I was still on edge because it could change at any time.

Shot of something meant he was pissed off at someone and was going to make me pay, usually with sex.

Beer meant that he was relaxed and in a good mood, so nothing I did pissed him off. *Usually.*

Wine meant that he was horny and wanted to fuck me—no questions asked.

Nothing meant I was to let him yell at me until he cooled off enough to have a shot followed by a vodka martini.

I stood near the stove, my usual vodka cranberry on the counter behind me as I held my breath. The door flung open as Rich strode in, slamming the door behind him as he walked toward me. I swallowed hard.

Today was a nothing day.

"Who the fuck were you with today, Autumn?" he yelled, walking toward me. *Fast.*

I blinked. "Lea."

"Before Lea. Who the fuck were you with at Starbucks and Club 24?" His face was red, forehead scrunched and a few inches from my face, yelling. Luckily, not touching me—yet.

"Brandi texted me and asked if I was at Starbucks. She showed up during her lunch—"

He grabbed my throat, pushing me against the refrigerator. "Not Brandi. Who the fuck were the two guys?"

I blinked again, trying to speak, but it only came out as a whisper as his hand pressed firmly on my trachea. "I don't know."

His grip tightened and I stared into his stormy blue eyes. "What have you learned about lying to me?" he hissed.

"I'm not—" I choked out.

"You're not what? Not lying to me? Don't you know I have eyes all over this town? Tell me who the two men were."

His gripped loosened enough so I could answer. "They were just asking what gym I went to. They were new in town and needed to know the best place."

"Are you lying to me?"

I shook my head and he searched my face for a few seconds before he finally let go of my throat. Grabbing my glass, I chugged the remaining magenta liquid. I needed something stronger, but Rich was at the bar and I didn't want to go near him.

He poured a shot of vodka, downed it, then proceeded to make himself a vodka martini. I had to turn my back, fearing he'd see my watery eyes. I opened the oven, checking on the pork chops.

"What's for dinner?" he asked. *No, I'm sorry. No, I'm an asshole. Nothing.*

"Pork chops and salad," I replied.

He walked over, martini in hand, and pressed a soft kiss to my lips. "I'm going to go change."

And just like that, Dr. Jekyll was back.

While we ate dinner, I told Rich of Lea and my plans for his party. We went over the guest list. He wanted to invite as many people as we could fit in the house, and the invitations were to say that it would be a black tie affair.

As we lay in bed, both reading, Rich glanced over at me and asked, "You're still ovulating, right?"

I looked over at him. "Yes." I was ovulating, but given that I was still taking the pill, I knew it didn't matter.

"Good." He set his ereader down on his nightstand then rolled over, facing me. "I want to make love to my wife," he stated, running a finger down my arm and staring at my dark purple bruises.

Of course, I had no say in the matter. He would take what he wanted no matter what I wanted. But "make love" Rich was only around once in a blue moon and my emotions were all over the place. I didn't want to miss the opportunity to be with the man I fell in love with and not the one who I feared.

I smiled at him, goose bumps pricking my arm where he stroked. "Mr. Jones, are you trying to seduce me into having your baby?"

"Is it working?" He smiled.

No. "Maybe," I smirked, playing my naïve role.

His hand brushed over my flat belly and under my T-shirt, inching upward toward my breasts. "I'm gonna taste your pussy. Get you so relaxed that your eggs will be distracted and my little guys will find their way past the wall. You're gonna have my baby, Autumn. One way or another, we're gonna be one big *happy* family."

His words did something to me at that moment. Usually, I'd be turned on by his sweetness, but I caught a glimpse of one of the bruises on my right arm as I peered down at him, and the pain in my heart resurfaced. Rich was anything but sweet. He was a snake and a liar. He didn't want to please me to satisfy me. He wanted to please me in hopes that he'd create a child. Maybe he read online that it was worth trying to get me relaxed and opened up. Maybe someone told him.

If the asshole only knew.

I knew the pill wasn't one-hundred percent effective, but if God wanted me to have this man's baby, then it was meant to be. I wasn't a very religious person, but I knew that God knew what he was doing. He wouldn't want to put a child in harm's way—would he?

Rich massaged my breast, caressing it in his palm, and I moaned, faking my response. I tried to tell myself that this was the man who got me wet. Not the one from last night, but the one who cared for my body. I needed to fake my body out. I knew I couldn't fake my mind, but my body only knew touch and was easily swayed.

His finger traced my nipple, making it pucker. My deceiving pussy started to moisten at the anticipation and I knew I needed to give in and enjoy myself. Last night's pleasure was because of Gabe …

My mind trailed off as I thought about Gabe. I was trying to remind myself that I got off the night before because of Gabe and not because I enjoyed my husband's touch. I couldn't enjoy a touch that could be gentle one minute and the next capable of hurting me.

"You know I don't want to hurt you," he confessed.

I looked down to his face that was eye level with my stomach. Confused wouldn't even be the correct word to describe how I was feeling at his words. He'd never addressed the bruises before, and he'd certainly never apologized.

"I really do love you, princess. I'm sorry I get angry, but work is stressful. And when someone I trust tells me that he's seen you with someone I don't know or someone that I didn't know you're with, I get pissed. I know you fear me. I can see it in your eyes."

I swallowed hard. I never tried to hide that I feared him. I just tried to hide my tears. "Don't you trust me?" I choked out.

He took a deep breath, his hand leaving my breast. "It's hard for me to trust anyone. That's why I'm this way."

"I'm your wife. I've never done anything to make you not trust me."

He rolled onto his back. "It's not you—it's me."

"If I ask you a question, will you get mad and hurt me?"

He looked over at me. "No, that's what I'm saying. I do it when I'm caught off guard."

"Okay ..." I took a deep breath. He opened the can of worms and I wanted to know the answer. "How were you okay before we got married? You never hurt me then."

He thought for a long time. Maybe searching for the right words to say to make me believe him. Maybe to figure out how to tell me the truth. "It's because of work. When we met, I'd just started my business. Over the years, it's been challenging. I want to provide for you. I want everything perfect for you, but I can't do that when people don't pay and I lose my money. I give a lot of money away, princess. A lot."

"But I don't need money—"

"But I do," he countered. "I don't want to talk about this anymore. I hate seeing the bruises on your arms that I create and I know you fear me. Maybe that's why you can't get pregnant. I don't know, but I want to fix this. I need to fix this because once I'm mayor, I can't have my wife looking as if I beat her."

But you hurt me.

After dinner, I went to the bathroom to look at my neck. There were red marks on each side of my throat, but nothing like my arms. I silently hoped the marks would be gone by the morning so Gabe didn't see—or anyone for that matter.

I nodded in agreement. I didn't want to talk about it either. "Will you make me come now?" I asked, biting my lower lip.

He smiled, the tension leaving his face. "Yes, princess, I will. I'll even do it with my head between your legs. It's been a long time."

"It has." I agreed.

He pulled the sheets down my body, bunching them at the foot of the bed as he lay between my bent, parted knees. His warm breath tickled my lips right before his tongue licked up to my clit.

"I really have missed this. You have the best tasting cunt I've ever fucking had. One of the reasons why I married you." He smiled up at me.

"Less talking, more licking."

He licked. He rubbed. He pumped his fingers—sometimes all together until I was crying out and shattering in ecstasy.

Then he made love to me, nice and slow until we were both covered in sweat and panting. The next morning, I looked at my throat as I got ready for the day. There were no visible bruises. I thought there would be. Maybe he was learning how to punish me without leaving a mark ... since he wanted to become the mayor.

EIGHT

Gabe

SHE WAS STUNNING. HER LEGS GLISTENING WITH SWEAT AS SHE ran on the treadmill. I wanted to see her sweat while she was under me, screaming my name.

As I stepped forward to say hi to the brunette angel, she turned and smiled at me.

"It's about time you showed up," she said, her breathing not skipping a beat as she ran flawlessly.

"I wasn't sure you wanted to see me again."

"Why wouldn't I?"

"Because you're married." I stepped onto the treadmill next to her.

"What he doesn't know, won't hurt him."

"But he hurts you."

"I deserve it."

"Bullshit, Autumn!" I growled. I was thankful I hadn't turned on the treadmill because I was sure I'd fall at her stupid words.

"Look Gabe. I've been thinking about you nonstop. I don't want to talk about my husband. I want to follow you into the men's locker room and blow you in one of the private showers."

She pressed the stop button on the treadmill as I stared at her in shock. "Okay."

"Good." She reached for my hand. "I even brought a friend so she can go down on me while I go down on you."

"You brought a friend?"

"Yep."

We walked into the men's locker room. Usually there was a handful of men in there, but today it was empty.

"She's waiting in the shower for us."

I walked to the wall with the showers, opening the one that I could see the silhouette behind the glass door. The stall was already steamy and when the air from the outside pushed in, the steam blew away and left her friend standing there. She turned with a huge smile on her face.

"I've missed you, babe."

"Alyssa?"

I woke up hard and panting. It wasn't my typical nightmare, but it might as well have been. My heart didn't know they were dreams because it still ached every time I dreamt about Alyssa. I was hard and crushed—not a good combination. I'd kill to have a threesome with Autumn, but I'd die if Alyssa appeared out of the blue. The sun was seeping through the blinds as I replayed the dream in my head. My mind wanted Autumn, but my heart wanted Alyssa back.

I wanted to stop hurting.

I'd never forget Alyssa. I still loved her, but I needed to stop waking with sweat dripping over my body—my heart can't take it anymore.

Finally getting out of bed, I tugged on a pair of sweats and made my way to the kitchen for coffee. The closer I got, the more I could smell breakfast.

"P.J., if you cook for me every morning, I may just have to marry you."

He turned. "Who said I'm cooking for you too?"

"Well, if you're not, then you should. I know you secretly want to marry me." I grinned.

"You're outta your mind, Cap. I'm into *pussy*."

"I know," I smirked. "But seriously, you're making some for me right?"

He paused for a beat. "Of course."

I grinned. "That's why you're my best friend. Tell me about your date." I poured a cup of coffee while he spoke.

"Cap, man ... this chick was into some freaky shit."

"Do tell." I sat at our kitchen table, the smile never leaving my face as I sipped my coffee and listened.

"Whips, chains, floggers, butt plugs ... You name it."

I laughed. "How is that freaky?"

"That part isn't. It was that she wanted her husband to watch me use them on her."

I choked a little on my coffee. "No shit?"

"You have no idea how scared I was. I almost didn't get it up to fuck her properly. I thought her husband was going to want my asshole, dude!"

"Oh my God." I laughed hard, so hard I was doubled over with tears.

"It's not funny. I made sure my ass was clenched so tight that he couldn't stick anything in there while I made his wife come."

"Seriously, I thought my date was weird, but it doesn't compare to this *at all*."

He gestured for me to grab a plate to put food on. "What happened on yours?"

"The chick was cool. She wasn't the problem. The problem was that when I was fucking her, I thought of Autumn."

"I think that's good. It's about time—"

"Nah, dude. Autumn turned me down. She's married."

"I take it that she doesn't have a husband who wants to watch his wife get spanked by another dude?"

I shook my head. "Not getting that vibe." My smiled faded quickly. "Actually, I think her husband's the one who hurts her."

We were both silent eating the sausage and eggs that Jackson made. Finally, he spoke. "All right, here's the deal. We don't know Autumn from a glory hole." I glared at him for using that reference to compare our relationship with her. "But if you want, I'll help you stalk her to see if this fucker keeps hurting her—"

"Stalking?"

"Let me finish." He took a bite of eggs. "We'll hang out at Club

24 for an entire day … hell, for a week. That place has everything and it won't be suspicious. We'll learn what days she comes and what hours. We'll chat her up, get to know her and if we see more bruises, maybe she'll tell us about them."

"I don't need you to do that."

"You were a creepy motherfucker yesterday. No wonder she brushed you off."

"Fuck you!"

"I get it." He held his hands up in front of him. "I know you don't want to replace Alyssa. But, Cap—"

"I know," I hissed. "Maybe Vegas will be good for me."

"That makes me happy." He smiled.

"Whatever," I mumbled. "Let's finish eating and go to Club 24."

We split up when we arrived at the gym, trying to cover the mass space to search for Autumn. We both came up short.

"Maybe she's already left," I groaned.

"Then we'll come earlier tomorrow. Let's go shoot some hoops or something."

We started to walk toward the basketball court. "You know what? Your plan is stupid. Why don't we just ask Cassie at the desk?"

"Ask her what?"

"What time Autumn comes in."

"You think she'll tell us?"

"She knows Autumn referred us. It's worth a try." I shrugged.

"Let me talk to her. I'm not sure how you're even an escort," he teased.

Cassie gave us the information we were seeking. Autumn comes in around nine, Monday through Saturday. Looking at the time on my phone, we'd just missed her by an hour.

"Let's go check Starbucks," I suggested.

"We just got here and haven't worked out," he whined. "I need to keep my stamina up for work."

"Fine, I'll go. Uber a ride home."

"You're just going to leave me here?"

I shrugged. "Yeah, I'll call you when I'm done and come get you if you're still here. If she isn't at Starbucks, I'll come right back."

"Don't be creepy."

"I won't," I groaned.

I couldn't believe that I was trying to stalk a stranger. I *was* creepy—definitely creepy. But I needed to see Autumn again. From the moment I ran into her, I couldn't get her out of my head and I had to figure out why. It wasn't like me. I hadn't thought of any women other than Alyssa since she died. I'd been on dates for work with plenty of hot women, but I'd never thought of them outside of work before, so there was definitely a reason I thought of Autumn. I was attracted to her for sure. Maybe it was because I was sent to protect her somehow. I was certain I hadn't bumped into her by accident, especially since I saw her the next day and at Club 24. Vegas wasn't a small town by any means.

Walking into Starbucks, my gaze fell on the chair she was sitting in the day before, and my heart skipped a beat. She was sitting there, staring out the window. She looked beautiful even in her oversized grey sweatshirt; it was seventy-five degrees out and I was certain she was hiding her bruises. Only women who are abused hide them like that, especially drop dead gorgeous women like Autumn.

After ordering my coffee, I walked to the table where Jackson and I sat the day before. "Hey," I greeted her.

"Oh ... Hey." She smiled a tight smile, her face blushing.

"I thought you didn't want to have coffee with me?" I joked, trying to keep her smiling.

Her smile didn't falter as she looked down at her paper cup, twirling it between her palms. "I never said I didn't—"

"But you want to?"

"Gabe—" Her gaze met mine as she tilted her head slightly.

"Having a good day?" I asked, cutting her off. I didn't want to hear her excuse that she was married. If she were happy in her marriage, I'd let it go. But she didn't look happy.

"Pretty good. I was just leaving." She stood to leave.

"Wait!" I reached out and grabbed her wrist. "Don't go."

"I have to." She kept her stare focused on the door, not looking at me or my hand on her.

"Just five minutes," I pleaded.

She took a deep breath. "We can't keep meeting like this."

"Why? Because you're married?" I let go of her wrist, hoping she wouldn't leave.

"Exactly."

"I understand. I'm new in town and just trying to make friends," I explained.

She turned her head finally and looked at me. "I bet you're a really nice guy, but I just ... can't."

"Because *he'll* get mad and hit you again?"

"Please," she begged, still not making a move to leave.

I stood, my chest rubbing on her arm as I stepped closer to her. I could smell the slight scent of warm vanilla sugar and I swallowed before speaking. "I can't get you out of my head, Autumn. You have no idea what that means to me. And the fact that your husband hits you ... I want to save you," I whispered in her ear.

I meant to say help instead of save, but my tongue slipped. I wasn't sure why I said save. Maybe because of my background ... or maybe because I saw Autumn like an angel just like Alyssa was to me.

"I have to go. He'll know I talked to you." She took a step forward, but I grabbed her wrist again.

"He has people watching you?" I whispered as I looked around the room.

She nodded.

"Paul and I can help protect you." I dropped her wrist, not wanting to scare her more.

"My husband's a powerful man in this city."

"I don't give a shit," I huffed.

"I have to go."

Before I could grab her wrist again, she walked quickly out the door.

NINE
Autumn

I WALKED ON SHAKY LEGS TO MY CAR AND PULLED OUT OF THE parking lot toward my house.

"I can't get you out of my head, Autumn. You have no idea what that means to me. And the fact that your husband hits you ... I want to save you."

I couldn't believe he'd been thinking about me. If he only knew that I couldn't get him out of my head either. I didn't know anything about Gabe but given he wanted to "save" me ... He made my heart stop. I never thought I'd need saving, especially from a man who I loved. But the more Rich hurt me, the more I felt myself falling out of love with him. Part of me questioned if he ever really loved me. Either way, I'd had enough.

As I sat at a red light, waiting for it to change, I kept replaying what had just happened. I closed my eyes briefly, remembering what he'd looked like in his black basketball shorts and green tank top that matched his eyes. I wanted to find out what his lips tasted like. How his body felt pressed against mine, his huge arms wrapped around me, and dammit if he didn't smell good too—like the warm sun on a summer day. *He was all man.*

As I drove, my mind switched to Rich. I still didn't have a plan on how I was going to leave him. I needed to get out of Vegas, not stay in it and look over my shoulder every day and fear for my life anymore. Given that Rich explained to me the night before he never "wanted" to hurt me, I decided to push the limits. Maybe it was stupid of me, but if he were really going to be the mayor of Las Vegas, then we couldn't hide the bruises forever.

I sent a text to him:

Me: *I'm going to stop by my parents' studio. Call my cell on your lunch. Love you!*

It was crazy to think that "pushing it" meant seeing my parents. I was to go to the gym, coffee and home every day. I was done having that leash. I was done being weak. It was only my parents, not someone who Rich didn't know.

As I pulled onto the street where my parents' studio was, a text from Rich buzzed my cell:

Rich: *Tell them hello for me. Love you too.*

I stared at the text as I sat in front of the studio. I expected him to call and yell at me, so I was stunned, shocked, baffled. Maybe Rich was really trying to change his ways. It was as if he knew I wanted to finally leave him and he was acting like the man I fell in love with.

I didn't reply. Instead, I threw my phone in my purse and went inside. The door dinged as I walked into the studio. Mom was behind the desk and she looked up.

She instantly smiled when she saw it was me. "Hey, what are you doing here?"

"Just came to say hi." I shrugged.

"Well, it's a nice surprise."

I leaned against the counter. "Where's Dad?"

"In the office—Dan!" she yelled. "Autumn's here."

Dad walked out, taking his glasses off and rubbed his face. "Hey, sunshine. I needed a break anyway. Editing makes my back hurt."

"I was in the neighborhood," I lied. "Just stopping by to say hi and also tell you that I'm throwing a surprise party for Rich."

"Oh?" Mom perked up. "What for?"

I debated telling my parents the truth, but if Rich found out that I'd told them, he'd be pissed. Call me rebellious ...

"Actually, it's a surprise party for the guests."

"I don't understand." Dad scrunched his eyebrows in confusion.

"You can't say anything—"

"Oh, it's a secret," Mom said, clapping with excitement.

"Rich is going to run for mayor and he wants to throw an announcement party."

"Really?" they asked in unison.

"Yep," I said with a fake smile.

"My son-in-law is going to be the mayor?" Dad asked.

I shrugged. "Maybe."

"When's the party?" Mom asked.

"In a month. You'll get the invitation this coming week. It's black-tie."

"This is exciting news." Mom beamed.

"I have no idea what it entails, but yeah ... it should be exciting." I gave a weak smile. "Anyway, Dad, I was thinking—want to go to the range this afternoon?"

"You want to go shooting?" he asked, taken aback. "You've never wanted to go with me before ..."

That was true. Guns had never been my thing. But given the circumstances, I figured it wouldn't hurt to learn how to shoot. I didn't intend to shoot Rich; I just wanted to learn to protect myself for when I did leave him.

"I know, but I'm bored and want to hang out with my dad if you can spare a few hours," I pleaded. "It will give you a break from editing."

"You're sure that you want to go *shooting*?"

"Yep, let's go." I smiled and waved my hand, motioning for him to follow me.

"All right." He smiled back. "Let's go to the range. Sarah, hold down the fort."

I'd never shot a gun before.

I didn't know what to expect. I'd watched people on television get *bit* by the gun when they fired it and that made me nervous, but I needed to do it. I needed to learn how to shoot.

"What do you want to shoot?" Dad asked as we looked into the gun case.

"I don't know," I shrugged. "Should I buy my own?"

"You want to buy a gun?" Dad's eyes widened.

"Maybe ..."

"All right, what's gotten into you?" He turned, facing me as his hip rested on the glass case.

"Nothing." I smiled.

"Sunshine ..."

A lie quickly entered my head. "All right. I want to learn to shoot so I can go with Rich sometime and impress him."

Dad's head tilted a little to the side as he thought about my answer. "You want to impress your husband?"

"Yeah." I shrugged again. I noticed I did that with all the lies I told. "Doesn't Mom do stuff to impress you?"

"When she cooks a new meal and it's delicious, yes. Not learning to shoot so she can come with me when I want to be alone and do something manly."

Telling Dad the truth was right on the tip of my tongue. I wanted to tell him. I envisioned him wrapping me in his arms and telling me everything was going to be okay and he'd help me—that he'd protect his little girl.

"It's not just for men, Daddy—"

Before I could lie some more, a clerk stepped over. "See anything you like?"

I had no idea what I was looking at. I didn't know what calibers meant, what size I needed, what type—I just knew what looked the most badass.

"I'm not sure I know what I'm looking at." I chuckled.

"What do you want the gun for?"

I looked out of the corner of my eye toward Dad then did my signature shrug. "Just to use here at the range."

"Well, women tend to start off with a revolver then grow into a semi-automatic pistol."

"If you're serious about learning, start with the semi-automatic. It holds more rounds," Dad interjected. My gaze drifted to his and his eyes narrowed at me. Dad was a smart man; he knew something was up.

"Okay, let's do the semi-automatic." I had no idea the difference except the look. The revolver looked like something from the twenties, but the semi-automatic looked more like something I could use.

"All right," the guy said. "I'd recommend the one with a longer trigger pull, so when you fire it, you know for sure you want it to go off. Fewer misfires."

I chose a silver and black 9mm, semi-automatic pistol that was compact enough to fit into my medium sized Coach purse. We went over the safety procedures, loading the gun, cocking it before it would shoot, how to clean it and how to go about getting a permit for it.

After I watched a short video, Dad and I shot a few rounds. Once I'd finally got a feel for the gun, I started to concentrate on the targets. Dad didn't say a word as I took in all the information and I was relieved. I didn't know how much longer I could lie to him.

"Remember when you'd take me to the arcade and we'd play Area 51?" I asked, trying to act as if this was just for fun and games.

He smiled. "Yeah, sunshine. I do."

"Remember how I would take both guns and try to kill more

aliens?" He laughed and nodded. "I wonder if I can get that good and be badass like that in real life."

He laughed again. "Are you trying to train for an alien invasion?"

I giggled. "No, but tell me that wouldn't be badass? I'd feel like Lara Croft or something."

"Rich would definitely be impressed."

"Hell yeah, he would." Just the thought of having two guns pointed at Rich as he tried to hurt me again sent a pulse of excitement through my veins—or maybe it was the fact that I was holding a gun and already felt safer. Whatever the case was, I was determined to hit the targets in the chest or head before we left.

After a few more rounds each, I finally reached my goal. It made me feel good—powerful—badass—stronger.

"Do you want to come back with me this weekend?" Dad asked as we drove back to the studio.

"I'm not sure if I can."

He nodded. "Just let me know. You'll be a pro before you know it if you keep practicing."

"I will."

"I'll file the paperwork for you to get the gun registered."

"Thanks, Daddy." I smiled. As we pulled up to the studio, my cell rang with Rich's daily call.

"I'll meet you inside," Dad whispered.

I nodded then quickly answered the phone before the third ring. "Hey, honey."

"Hey, princess. Having fun with your dad?"

I closed my eyes. He knew I was with Dad and not both my parents. I knew I needed to tell him where we went before he asked. "I am. Dad wanted to take a break, so I went with him to the range."

"He's good isn't he?"

I breathed a sigh of relief. He had eyes on me, but it didn't seem as if they went inside. "He is. He taught me how to shoot a few rounds."

"So you want to start going to the range?" I thought I could hear a smile in his voice.

Laughing I said, "Maybe. I did look pretty badass."

"I bet sexy as hell too."

"Well, that would be weird for Dad to say." I giggled.

"True. All right, princess. I'll see you when I get home. I'll be home by eight. Love you."

"Love you too."

After hanging up the phone, I walked inside and said goodbye to my parents before going home to start dinner. I needed to make sure it was ready when he got home so he'd stay in a good mood.

TEN
Gabe

AFTER AUTUMN HAD LEFT THE COFFEE SHOP, I HEADED BACK TO Club 24 and worked out with Jackson. I needed to run off some of my sexual frustration. When I'd stepped closer to her and whispered in her ear, I wanted to taste her skin. She smelled like heaven—in more ways than one. But what really got me was the feel of her soft skin, even if it was only her wrist underneath her oversized sweatshirt. Sure I feel the skin of soft women a few times a week, but there was something about the touch of Autumn.

After running for five miles, I stepped off and joined Jackson in the weights section.

"Maybe you should stop going to Starbucks," Jackson said while doing a bicep curl.

"P.J., when was the last time I've ever been this interested in a woman?"

"But she's married."

"To an asshole who hits her."

He shook his head. "You don't know that."

"I'm pretty certain. He even has spies following her."

His questioning eyes drifted to me as he set the dumbbell back on the rack. "Then how do you plan to even talk to her? You'll need to do that before you can convince her to leave her husband for you."

I thought for a moment, doing a few curls. "Let's not get ahead of ourselves. How can I be in a relationship with our profession?"

He chuckled. "Well, that's what you need to think about before you go running off, chasing this chick all over town."

I moved over to the lat bar, doing a few pulls. "I think about her all the time. I dream about her. Last night I dreamt about her and Alyssa—together."

"Sexually?"

"Almost." I smiled.

"Huh," he huffed, rubbing his chin. "I'm not an expert on dreams, but maybe it's your subconscious telling you that it's okay to let Alyssa go?"

I didn't respond. The thought was gut-wrenching, even if she was never coming back.

"Before you do anything stupid—or *more* stupid for that matter, you need to seriously consider the consequences if you pursue Autumn. She's married and you date women for a living."

"I know," I muttered. "If anything, I want to help her leave this guy. If she can't get past what I do for a living, then it's not meant to be. But at least she won't be in an abusive relationship anymore."

"You don't even know if that's the case."

"I know," I confirmed. "Trust me, I know."

That night, I did an experiment and fell asleep without drinking my daily dose of whiskey. I'd read once that, "Most commonly, dreams are a reflection of the minds natural subconscious process of organizing and resolving the information of the day." I still thought about Alyssa often throughout the day, but it felt as if my heart was finally trying to heal.

*Opening my back office on the computer, I read my date informa-
tion. I was to meet my client at the blackjack table at The Palazzo
where she'd give me a key to her room. Her name was Jennifer. She had
dark brown hair and light brown eyes, and she'd be wearing a white
tank top with studs along the straps.*

*I dressed casually in jeans and a black T-shirt, knowing this was
just for a fuck. Once I arrived at the hotel/casino, I walked to the card
tables in search of Jennifer. Her back was to me as I stepped closer, but
I knew it was her from the way her white tank top hugged her body.*

*The closer I got, the more I could hear her laughing with the men
at the table. I stepped up behind her, noticing she had a blackjack and
was waiting for the other hands to be dealt. I placed a hand on her
shoulder and she turned, knocking the breath from my lungs.*

"Autumn?"

"Hey, Gabe. Here's the room key. I'll be up in a few minutes."

*I stood there, not speaking and theoretically confused. She knew?
Autumn knew what I did for a living? How? When? I should have
asked her, but my words failed me. I stared at her as she placed a bet
and waited for her new cards. My gaze drifted to her arms where I
didn't see any bruises.*

*"Seriously, I'll be up in a few minutes." She ran her hand down
my bare arm and I took a deep breath, loving the feel of her skin on
my skin.*

*I nodded and glanced at the room key. I noted the room number
and walked to the elevators, not saying anything further to Autumn
as she continued to win. My head was spinning as I rode the elevator
up to the forty-seventh floor. After finding the room, I slipped the key
in and walked inside. The room was filled with candles that were lit
and placed sporadically around the large space. Rose petals were scattered over the bed and onto the floor and the room smelled like
vanilla.*

*The view ... Fuck, the view was perfect—perfect for my first time
with Autumn. The lights of the Las Vegas Strip lit up the entire street,
filling the room with a mixture of colors.*

As I stepped closer to take in the view, the door opened behind me and I turned, watching Autumn walk in.

"How—"

"Shh, no talking. I want to fuck you. I've wanted to fuck you since I first saw you." She started to strip out of her white tank top. "Gabe, you need to take your clothes off. This would work a lot better if we were both naked."

"I'm so confused," I stated.

"I'll explain after. But right now, I just really want to fuck you." Her bra went next then she started unzipping her jeans after kicking off her heels.

Before I knew it, we were both naked with her arms wrapped around my neck and her lips pressed against mine. She tasted good—so fucking good. Like vanilla ice cream.

"I've wanted to do this since I first saw you, too," I confessed. "Your eyes aren't light brown like you told my boss." I smiled against her lips, trying to get any info I could.

She pulled her head back a little then whispered in my ear, "Stop talking. I want you to fuck me against the window behind you."

"What if your husband sees?"

"Let him. I don't care anymore."

I stared into her hazel eyes for a beat. "Put your hands on the glass and wait for my dick then, angel."

Like most mornings, I woke up hard, but I didn't wake up panting. I didn't wake up in a pile of sweat, and I didn't wake up screaming. I woke up hard as fuck and aching for Autumn.

After taking my boxers off, I wrapped my hand around my dick while picturing her full lips as she leaned forward, parting to take my cock into my mouth. I groaned as my hand pumped a few times, a bead of pre-cum glistening the tip. I thought about her using her hand in place of mine while her tongue licked the underside and across the crown to taste my arousal.

My hand stroked faster, warming my shaft as I imagined her

warm, wet mouth swallowed my dick. My fist worked up and down, mimicking what I'd want her to do.

I stroked.

I pumped.

I twisted my hand, coating my shaft with my arousal.

I thought about the way she'd look up at me from between my legs. Her long, brown hair would tickle my inner thighs as she bobbed. Her warm breath would tingle me as she came up for air; her beautiful, luscious lips squeezing my dick as I was on the verge of coming into her mouth. I groaned my release, my cum squirting on my stomach as I continued to think about her.

I lay there still imagining her and thinking it was the best hand job I'd ever given myself.

After a quick breakfast, Jackson and I headed to Club 24. It was early, especially since he'd had a date the night before, but he wanted to go in case Autumn was there. He wasn't going to go as my wing-man, but as backup in case her husband's *spies* did anything.

Hopefully, his spies were required to remain in the distance and report shit to him because I had every intention of getting her alone. I wanted her to open up to me. I knew I might be pushing it since she knew nothing about me. If I forced her or came off creepy, she'd likely would never want to talk to me again.

"Are you going to *actually* talk to her if she's here?" Jackson asked, opening his passenger side door of my Yukon.

"I should right?"

"You need to play it cool. Yesterday didn't go as planned."

"Well, I talked to her," I reminded him as I opened the door.

"Congratulations. You've graduated middle school."

"Fuck you." I laughed.

We entered the gym, stopping at the desk to check-in, then like the day before, we split up in search of Autumn. Yeah—I was a fucking stalker, but I had good intentions. I was trained to protect and, deep down, I knew she needed protecting.

I spotted her on the treadmill and flashbacks of my dream crossed my mind. I was certain I would die if she turned and said she'd been waiting for me to show, but in all honesty, I wanted her to say that to me.

She glanced over as I stepped onto the treadmill next to her. I smiled then held my breath, waiting to see if my dream would come true. Instead her eyes widened, then she looked back in front of her.

Fuck ...

I started the treadmill with a brisk walk for a few minutes then into a steady jog. I watched her out of the corner of my eye, waiting for her to leave because she didn't want to be seen talking to me or around me. Instead, she continued to run until her three miles were over.

She stopped the treadmill and I glanced at her, still holding my jogging pace. She was looking at me, but quickly turned her head. I thought she'd leave since she was done, but instead, she stepped off the treadmill and stopped behind me. My feet faltered a little as I tried to turn my head to see her, but I couldn't.

After a few beats, she started to walk then stopped again. I could finally see her through the reflection of the mirrors in front of me. She looked as if she were lost in thought and arguing with herself.

Before I could stop the treadmill and talk to her, Jackson walked up. "Hey, Autumn. Fancy meeting you here." He smiled then looked at me, using the mirrors so our eyes could meet. He was up to no good.

"Hey, Paul. Good to see you again."

"My boy's not being creepy is he?"

I shot him a look as my blood started to boil. *What the fuck?*

She smiled. "No. Actually," she turned to me, "can I talk to you for a second? When you're done with your workout, of course."

"I'm done," I said, pressing the stop button and jumping off before the belt stopped moving.

I gave a nod to Jackson as I walked by, following Autumn. He smiled wide with approval and I wanted to punch him as I passed him, but I refrained. I knew he was trying to break the ice with her, but seriously—what the fuck? Fucking prick.

I didn't ask Autumn where we were going. Instead, I just followed behind her as she walked down a few halls and then into a vacant racquetball court.

"You want to play racquetball?" I questioned, looking around the high-walled room.

"No. If I have spies watching me, they can't hear us in here."

I nodded in approval. "Good thinking."

"Yesterday—"

I cut her off. "I'm sorry if I was too forward—"

"No," she shook her head, cutting me off in return. "Just—your words hit me hard."

"I'm sorry," I muttered. "I didn't mean—"

"Gabe, just listen to me. My husband doesn't hit me. He grabs me—"

"I knew it! That's not any better." I crossed my arms over my chest, spreading my legs wide as if I were ready to throw down. I was. I hated the thought of a woman being abused, especially the one standing in front of me.

"Please, let me get this out before I lose my nerve." She scrunched her eyes with a pleading look.

I gestured for her to continue. "Again, I'm sorry."

"The other day, I finally told my best friend about my husband. She's the only person I've told ... until now. I'm done having him control me. One minute he's screaming and hurting me, and the next he's the sweetest man I've ever met."

I chuckle with sarcasm, shaking my head. Her husband sounded like a piece of work and I couldn't wait to throttle the guy.

"The day you saw me at Starbucks," she continued, "I didn't realize that my bruises were showing. I've never forgotten to hide them before."

"I was meant to see them," I interjected.

"Maybe." She shrugged. "Something's going on. The day I told Brandi, I ran into you and now everything feels as if it's coming together. I bought a gun—"

"You bought a gun?" I asked, my arms still crossed across my chest.

"I don't plan to use it. I just bought it to have it."

"I can teach you how to use it."

"You know how to use a gun?"

I smiled. "I was in the army."

She paused for a beat, her eyes going wide.

"What?" I asked.

"So was my husband." She closed her eyes and I wanted to wrap her in my arms. Maybe she thought I was a spy.

"The army's a big branch. I doubt I know him."

"Right." She laughed. "Anyway, I think I do want your help. I know that seems weird—"

"No, it doesn't. Come stay with me and Jackson until we figure something ..." I stopped talking when I realized how crazy that sounded. "Sorry, bad idea."

"I can't just jump into leaving him. Things need to happen. If I just leave, he'll find me." She crossed her arms over her chest and looked away.

"Because he's powerful?"

"Right."

"Who is he?" God I'd love to know who this motherfucker was so I could show him a piece of his own medicine. Seeing Autumn hurting was breaking me. Sure I was attracted to her, but with my past, I wasn't sure if I could have a relationship. I knew, however, that

I wanted to at least be friends with her. Maybe even friends with benefits.

"It's better that you don't know and even better that I'm not seen with you."

"So you want to have a secret rendezvous?" I grinned.

Her face turned bright red.

"That's a yes," I flirted, my dick getting hard as I stared at her blushing face.

"I'm married."

"That's not a no, Autumn."

"Do you know what he'd do if he found out?"

"I'll protect you."

"You can't protect me at night."

I felt my heart clench in my chest. The thought of her going home to her husband every night, and the thought of him hurting her, felt as if I were being repeatedly stabbed. "You have no idea how much the thought of that hurts me."

"If I'm on my best behavior, he's fine."

I thought for a few moments before I spoke. "All right, here's the plan. Paul and I will come up with a way to help you. It guts me that you have to go back to this asshole, but I get it. We're going to figure this out. Every day we're going to have a secret rendezvous here at the gym because I can't get you out of my head, *and* I'm going to kiss you after I stop talking because I've wanted to do that since the first time I saw you."

I took the two steps toward her and cupped her face in my hands. Before she could stop me, I brought my lips to hers. My tongue ran across the seam of her lips and she parted, granting me access. I heard myself groan as my tongue took its first swipe of her mouth. Her lips were a little salty from her sweat given she'd just run three miles, but she tasted fucking good.

I expected her to pull back, maybe even slap me, but to my surprise, she didn't. She stepped closer, wrapped her arms around my neck, and deepened the kiss. My hands slid down her sides and along her curves; my fingertips brushed along the smooth skin on her torso as her shirt rose up a little.

I hated that we were in a room with fluorescent lights and I couldn't do anything but kiss her. I wanted every one of my dreams to come true. Before I could pick her up so her legs could wrap around my waist and I could push her against the wall, she stepped back, breaking our kiss.

"I can't do this. What am I thinking?"

"Angel, it's okay. I'm sorry, I did that."

She stared at me, not saying anything. She didn't move. Nothing.

"It won't happen again," I confirmed.

She ran her fingertips over her lips as if she could still feel my mouth on hers.

"Angel, say something."

But she turned and walked away.

ELEVEN

Autumn

LIKE MOST MORNINGS, RICH WOKE ME, TELLING ME IT WAS TIME to go to the gym. I had a little pep in my step as I got ready because I was hopeful I'd see Gabe. Rich asked me which tie he should wear to work and I chuckled; he only asked because of our previous fight. Biting my tongue, I picked the purple and black striped one that matched the purple shirt he was wearing.

After he'd left for work, I changed into my workout clothes, making sure I put on a long-sleeved running shirt to hide my bruises. *I'd never forget to hide them again.*

I hurried to the gym, and when I arrived I looked around the space, secretly hoping I'd see Gabe, but I didn't. Starting my usual run, I was lost in thought when I saw him approach out of the corner of my eye.

He didn't speak.

I didn't speak.

But my mind was going a million miles an hour.

How could I trust a stranger? Part of me felt as if Gabe was planted by Rich to find out what was going on. But then I remembered how we met. *Then* I remembered that it was still possible for Gabe to be a spy. *Then* I remembered how angry Rich was when he found out I even talked to Gabe. If Rich planted him, then I was certain he would try to manipulate me into telling him about Gabe, not walk into the house yelling and screaming.

101

I *had* to be right. Rich would kill me if I were wrong and Gabe was working for him.

When I woke up this morning, I'd never thought my lips would have touched Gabe's. I woke up thinking I needed to talk to him— that I needed to tell him what was going on because something told me that he wouldn't let it go that I had bruises.

And ... I was right.

For days, I couldn't get him out of my head. I'd never thought he'd feel the same way. I was married for Christ sake. But Gabe ... Well, Gabe obviously didn't care.

Now, I stared at him under the florescent lights of the racquetball court. I could hear rubber balls being hit against the walls in the next court over and I just stood there, running my fingers along my lips. His kiss felt nice—*like really fucking nice*, and I had to fight everything in me not to let it continue until I couldn't breathe.

If things were different ...

If I had already left Rich, then I wouldn't hesitate. But at the end of the day, I was married. Married to an evil man; a man I was certain would kill anyone who touched me, especially with his lips.

Did that prove Gabe wasn't working for Rich or was it part of his plan?

"Angel, say something," Gabe pleaded.

He'd said it wouldn't happen again and to make sure of that, I had to leave.

Turning, I ran toward the door. Before I could open it, Gabe's hand slapped against it, holding it shut.

"Don't run. I'm sorry. It won't happen again. I want to help you, Autumn, and you can't run for that to happen."

"He'll kill you," I whispered, looking down at the floor. I couldn't look up to meet his eyes because I knew I would stare at his lips, wanting them on mine again.

"He can try. But if I can survive Afghanistan, I can survive your asshole of a husband."

I took a deep breath, still not looking up. Before I could speak,

Gabe spoke again. "Let's just be friends. We can be friends, right? I'll keep my distance in public and when I need to talk to you, we'll come here." He motioned to the enclosed space with no windows.

I finally glanced up at him. I was already pushing the envelope so to speak with Rich and if I weren't doing anything wrong, he couldn't tell me who I could and couldn't be friends with.

"Okay." I nodded. "Friends."

"Friends who sometimes kiss."

He smiled and I wanted to smile back. I knew he was joking, but I wanted to agree. I loved the way his lips felt against mine. His kiss was tender and I hadn't had a tender kiss in a very long time. His lips were soft, and he used the perfect amount of tongue to give me a tease of what it could do on other parts of my body. If things were different, I wouldn't have stopped.

"Gabe—"

"I'm just kidding. I'll bide my time until we can get you away from him, then I can't make any promises."

Damn his smile! I had to look away, nodding again. "I better go. If you happen to show up at Starbucks, I'll see you there." I looked up at him after I stopped talking.

"It's a date." He smirked.

I narrowed my eyes at him.

"Just go, Autumn. I'll see you there."

Going to Starbucks when I had my weekly date with Brandi used to be my favorite day of the week. Now—I had other reasons to look forward to the coffee shop and it wasn't just one day a week.

As I sat in my usual chair, looking out the window, I replayed the morning at the gym. Did Gabe say he was going to wait for me? Did he say he wanted to be with me? Like actually be with me? We didn't know anything about each other. How could he say such a thing? If I didn't know better, I'd think he had women crawling all over him. He was gorgeous and strong and fuck that smile ...

Before I could finish my thought, Gabe and Paul walked in. Gabe met my eyes and smiled and I smiled back. I felt my face flame and I looked down at my coffee cup. I felt like a girl with a secret crush —*well, I was.* Gabe brought out my flirtatious side. The side that had been hidden for three years. I'd thought it was because I was married and that part of me had died because I didn't need to rope *them* in anymore. Maybe that was true. But the more Rich punished me, the more I wanted to fight back.

I pretended I wasn't waiting for Gabe and Paul to sit at the table in front of me. My focus was down on the table, reading on my ereader, when a folded piece of paper was placed on top of the screen.

Looking up, I noticed Gabe was still sitting at the table next to me. He motioned with his head for me to read the note.

A,

Since we can't talk in public, I decided that we should pass notes. Paul jokes that I'm still in junior high when it comes to you, so I might as well live it up. So tell me, what kind of coffee do you order?

Patiently Waiting,

Gabe.

I smiled as I read his note then reached into my purse for a pen to write him back on the same paper.

G,

I didn't even know they still made paper these days. I like your idea though. I always get a non-fat vanilla latte. You? Where'd you move from?

Patiently Waiting to Leave Him,
A

We passed a few notes back and forth while Paul laughed and shook his head at us. From an outsider's perspective you'd think that he was only talking to Gabe.

Before I knew it, I needed to head home and wait for Rich's call.

When I arrived home, I walked through the house, making a mental note of all the cameras throughout. I didn't know where the feed was being monitored from because I didn't see any room with a computer in it. That had led me to believe that Rich was monitoring my movements from his office.

After Rich's call, I checked the roast I was cooking in the crockpot and piddled around the house. I was bored to death. I hated feeling like a caged animal. I supposed some women would love to be a housewife where they were able to go to the gym every day, and get their hair and nails done as needed.

But I wanted to be able to come and go as I pleased.

Rich and I needed to have a talk. I was still going to leave him no matter what happened, but at least I could say I fought back.

Then a thought dawned on me. Rich assumed I hated him leaving bruises on my arms. Of course I did, but I never stood up for myself. Like I told him the night before, I'd never done anything for him not to trust me—

Except today when Gabe's lips happened to come into contact with mine ...

But that wasn't my fault.

I needed to start fighting back. Maybe not yell, scream and kick, but something that could be seen on the security cameras. Of course, Rich could just delete the footage, but it was worth a shot. It would show I was strong; strong enough to leave him. The more he let me have slack, the more I could put my plan into motion to leave him. He was being *nice* Rich right now, but *mean* Rich was bound to come out—soon.

Before I could text him that I was going to go shopping for a dress for his party, Lea knocked on the door.

"Hey, I have the invitations. We should get these out before five."

I glanced at the clock on the wall. We had three hours to get them done. "Wow, that was fast. Sure, come in." A part of me told myself I should text Rich and tell him Lea stopped by. But then I wanted to verify my suspicions that he was monitoring the security camera feed from his office. "Rich didn't tell me you were coming."

"I just got them in the mail and knew we were on a deadline, so I rushed over. I'm sorry if I'm intruding."

"No, not at all. I'm just sitting here reading." I shrugged while I led her to the kitchen. "Would you like something to drink?"

"Water, thank you." She sat down at the dining room table. "What are you cooking? It smells delicious."

"Oh, thank you. It's roast with potatoes and carrots."

"Rich is a lucky guy, coming home to a home cooked meal every night."

I fought the urge to laugh. If she only knew the consequences I'd face if I didn't have the meal ready. "It's no big deal. I have time to do it." I waved off her comment and grabbed her a bottle of water from the fridge before we got to work inviting people to Rich's party.

"Have you got your dress yet?" she asked, stuffing an envelope.

"Not yet. Haven't had time to go. Have you?"

"No, but most nights this time of year are nice nights to have a party. I'll probably have a sleeveless dress so I don't get too hot from running around."

"That's a good idea." I smiled. I wanted to wear a sleeveless dress or at least one with capped sleeves, but I could only do that if Rich didn't touch me again before the party. I needed time for my current bruises to heal. "I'm not sure what style I want yet. I've never been married to a mayor before," I joked.

She laughed. "Me, either."

Two and half hours later, all two hundred and forty-four envelopes were addressed. We could only fit approximately two hundred people on our property, but Rich wanted it full, so we invited more, knowing people wouldn't be able to make it.

After Lea had left, I waited for Rich to come home.

And waited ...

And waited ...

I woke on the couch, the morning sun shining through the glass windows that overlooked the golf course in the distance. I ran to the bedroom. The bed was still made like I had made it the morning before. I ran to my cell phone; no missed call from him.

I dialed his number and after five rings, it went to voice mail. I began to worry. I still loved him, but—if something happened to him ... No, I couldn't think like that. A few minutes later, I heard the garage open and I ran to the door, opening it.

Rich stepped out of his car. "Morning, princess."

"Morning? What the fuck, Rich? Where were you?"

"Obviously you didn't care enough to call me to find out," he hissed, walking passed me and into the kitchen.

"I was waiting for you and I just woke up on the couch."

"I know," he murmured.

"What? How do you know?"

"Autumn, I'm too tired for this conversation. I'm going to bed."

"But where were you?" I pressed.

"At work where I always am."

"Overnight?"

"Yes, overnight, Autumn! Don't question my actions."

"Fine, I won't." I stormed off toward our bedroom, but Rich grabbed my elbow, halting me.

"Are you talking back to me?" he hissed.

I stood still, his fingers biting into my skin. "No," I whispered. "I just don't like sleeping alone," I lied.

His grip didn't loosen. "I'm the man of this house, Autumn. I can come and go as I please."

"Okay." I shook my head. "It's time for me to go to the gym."

"Good," he grumbled, letting me go and loosening his tie—a navy blue one ... not the purple one I'd picked out.

Not wanting to press my luck even more, I changed, made myself a protein shake, and headed toward Club 24 hoping I'd see Gabe—someone who appreciated me.

TWELVE
Gabe

No WOMAN HAD EVER CAPTIVATED ME AS QUICKLY AS
Autumn had.

I'd known her for only four days and I was already addicted to
her. I was addicted to a married woman. Of all the women in the
world ... Even if she left her husband, there would be a lot of baggage
we'd have to deal with.

Shit, I was already thinking long term. Who does that? I needed
to step the fuck back and really take this friend thing to heart. I
couldn't fall for someone in only four days, especially when I hadn't
fallen for anyone in almost five years.

"Are we going to the gym?" Jackson asked, pouring a cup of
coffee.

"You know you don't have to keep coming with me, right?"

"I know." He shrugged. "I like going together. It reminds me of
the old days."

During the army, we were almost inseparable. We made sure
each other stayed in shape, and going to Club 24 together brought
back memories. When we lived in the L.A. area, we didn't live close
enough to each other to hang out every day. Plus we were both busy
with clients, so it was nice hanging out together again.

"I need to take a step back from Autumn. I'm falling for her too
fast," I confessed.

He paused mid-stir of his coffee. "If you were any of my other friends, I'd laugh at you. I'd tell you that you're fucking right, that you're being a sappy motherfucker. But given your past, Cap—"

"How does that make any sense?"

"Because you're finally opening up and living again."

"But she's married—"

"Not for long."

"And I barely know her."

"Let's be clear, you don't want to marry this chick, right? You just want to have more of a connection than sticking your dick in her."

I stared at him for a few seconds, thinking about what he was saying and what I wanted. Of course you couldn't know if you wanted to marry someone in only four days—that was crazy. What if meeting Autumn was supposed to help me start living again? I'd help her leave her husband and she'd help me heal the pain in my heart. "Right," I agreed.

"So step back. Stop flirting with her and just be a friend. Let's get her away from her husband."

"How are we even going to do that?"

I'd promised Autumn I'd help her, and I would. But I wanted to be like a barbarian and run in there and rescue her; not wait around while she put her ducks in order. Waiting around would lead to more bruises, and more bruises would lead to more anger from me.

"I've been thinking about this. I think she should do what a *normal* person would do and divorce him. She can't run off, especially since she said he's "powerful" and will find her." He put air quotes around powerful implying her husband wasn't. I had to agree. I mean, did he run a mob or some shit?

"And where does she go until the divorce is over and she can leave town?" I finished the last of my coffee then walked to the sink to rinse out the cup and put it in the dishwasher.

"With her friend we met the other day. She was worried about her, so I'm sure she'll take her in." He shrugged.

"And we can be with her twenty-four/seven to protect her?" I asked, finishing his thought.

"Exactly. We'll pick her up at her place and take her to the gym and Starbucks, then back home where they can have a security system installed if they don't already have one."

"And if she wants to go to more than just three places a day?"

"Then one of us will be with her." He shrugged again as if the plan would work. Theoretically, it would ... but could it be that simple?

"Like bodyguards?" I asked, crossing my arms over my chest.

"Yes!" He snapped and pointed his finger at me in agreement. "Exactly. I've always wanted to be a bodyguard." Shaking his head, he said, "Autumn's not getting shot on our watch, Cap." My eyes widened and he quickly sputtered, "Oh shit!"

"Right," I sighed with a slight nod.

"Cap—"

"It's okay."

"I didn't mean—"

"I know."

I did know. I knew Jackson was just fucking around. It had been five years since Alyssa was shot on our watch, but I was determined to never let it happen again. I needed to teach Autumn how to shoot her gun properly.

"Autumn bought a gun," I said, changing the subject.

"No shit?"

"Let's teach her how to use it properly."

"I like your thinking. I've been dying to shoot something."

"Me, too," I agreed.

When I was a kid, I'd visit my grandparents in Tennessee at their ranch, and my grandpa would take me into the backyard to shoot cans. I never thought that I'd want to fire a gun again after leaving the army.

But shooting was in my blood.

I hadn't been this happy in a very long time. Sure I was fighting with myself to hold back my feelings for Autumn. She was married and I'd only known her for four days. And I knew there was no way in hell she'd be okay with my profession.

Just like the day before, I found Autumn running on the treadmill when Paul and I arrived at Club 24.

"Hey," I greeted her, stepping onto the treadmill beside her.

"Hey." She frowned.

"What's wrong?" I asked, increasing the speed to a brisk walk.

She looked around the gym, probably searching for the so-called spies. "Meet me in our spot in a few minutes. If it's taken, I'll find an empty one." She stopped the treadmill and then started to walk toward the racquetball courts.

Out of habit, I looked around the massive gym wondering if I could spot the "spies". I didn't see anyone who looked as if they could kick my ass and I didn't see anyone who I recognized from being at both Club 24 and Starbucks—not that I was looking before. I made a mental note to start looking. After all, I was about to become a bodyguard for Autumn.

A few minutes later, I stopped my treadmill and went to find Autumn. I found her in a different court than the day before. She was sitting on the floor on the right side with her legs bent and her arms wrapped around them as she lay her head on her knees.

"What's the matter, angel? Did he hit you again?" I asked, sitting next to her.

She looked at me barely lifting her head. "He doesn't hit me, he just grabs me and ... no."

"Okay." I brushed a piece of her hair from her eyes. "So why aren't you smiling today?"

"He didn't come home last night."

"Hmmm ... Do you know where he was?"

She sighed and lifted her head. Leaning against the wall, knees still bent, she answered, "He said he was at work. He's *never* worked overnight."

"So ... you think he's cheating on you?"

Her eyes widened. "Maybe."

"All right. Well ... don't take this the wrong way, but why do you care? You want to leave him, right?" I matched the way she was sitting with my head turned toward her.

"Yes, but if I would have known ..."

I smirked. "Then you wouldn't have stopped our kiss yesterday?"

She snickered then took a few seconds before she answered, "Yeah."

I pondered what to say next. I wanted to lean over and take her lips again—taste her, but I needed to do the friend thing like I'd convinced myself to do earlier. "This may be good. I don't know how Nevada law works, but maybe you can get more money out of him if you can prove he's cheating?"

"You mean when I divorce him?"

"Yeah." I shrugged.

"I can't just divorce him. He'll never let that happen."

"He can't force you to stay married to him."

"No, but he could kill me," she sighed.

"Why do you keep saying that? Are you scared he will? Who the hell is your husband?"

"I'm not scared right now. I'm just nervous. I have a feeling his business isn't legal and he does harm to people. I've heard him on the phone several times. He has a guy named Remo who he sends after people. He tells me it's to scare them and collect money they owe, but something just doesn't sit right with me."

"And you still married the guy?"

"See, that's the thing. I knew none of that before we got married. He was the sweetest man I'd ever met—"

"Before me." I smiled.

She finally laughed. "Yes, before you. Anyway, after we got married, he slowly changed and then bam. He turned into the devil and made my life hell."

"So why didn't you leave him a long time ago?"

"He convinced me to quit my job, and he did something with my old car—sold it maybe ... drove it off a cliff, I don't know. But he bought me a nicer one and I'm pretty sure he put a tracker on it. He controls all of our money, and I'm given an allowance for coffee each day—"

"Okay, angel, I get it."

"Why do you call me that?"

"Call you what?"

"Angel."

I took a deep breath, remembering why I'd thought of her that way, then smiled. "The day Paul and I officially met you, I'd walked into Starbucks and I saw you sitting by the window with the sun behind you. It was as if you had an aura around you and it made you look like an angel."

She smiled, turning her head away from me. I could still see part of her cheek that was flush with embarrassment. I should be the one embarrassed, not her.

"I won't call you that if you don't like it."

"No!" she shrieked. "I love it."

I smiled again. "Good. Now, let me tell you what Paul and I have come up with for a plan."

I told her about the plan Jackson and I had talked about over coffee at the house. She shook her head the entire time, telling me no, but I pressed on insisting that she listen to me.

"It's not going to work. He'll drag me out of Brandi's house."

"Fine. Then you can stay with me and Paul. We have an extra room." I shrugged.

"I can't stay with you two!" she protested.

"Because we're strangers?"

She huffed. "Yeah. Exactly."

"Angel, people do it all the time. They find roommates they don't know and they live together."

"And some end up dead," she countered.

I chuckled. "I can assure you that Paul and I won't kill you. Your husband, on the other hand ..."

She paused, not saying anything. I figured in her position it was harder to agree to live with two guys since she was a woman.

"All right, angel. If it will make you feel better, how about we get to know each other while you get all your ducks in a row, like meeting with an attorney and stuff so you can get a divorce? While you do that, I'll teach you how to shoot properly, then once you leave your husband, you move in with me and Paul. You'll know us better by then and you'll know how to shoot us if shit goes down."

She paused for a few seconds, staring at me, then smiled. "I can't believe I'm going to say this, but ... okay."

I couldn't believe that she'd agreed. The original plan wasn't for her to move in with Paul and me, but the new plan just slipped from my mouth. Having Autumn live with us was either going to be really good or really bad. I was certain I wouldn't be able to just be friends with her. Once she was separated from her asshole of a husband and under my roof...

All bets were off.

THIRTEEN
Autumn

As I drove to the gym, I thought about Rich and how he didn't come home—and how he wasn't wearing the same tie he'd had on when he'd left that morning. Something didn't add up. If he wasn't cheating on me then why'd he change his tie?

The more I thought of him being with another woman while he was with me, the more my blood boiled. I was furious as I walked into Club 24. I thought running would help, but it didn't. I ran for a good twenty minutes until Gabe showed up and the only thing to get me out of my funk was his smile that made my insides turn to mush.

And how in the hell had I let Gabe talk me into moving in with him? I'll tell you how. It was that damn smile of his!

He convinced me that getting a divorce from Rich and moving in with Paul and him was the best plan, but the only way to ensure my safety was if Rich were in prison or dead. The latter was probably a no go, so I needed to find out what he did for a living and turn him into the police. I was certain he did things illegally. Maybe not lending money, but when client's didn't pay and they met Remo— well, he was the "handle it" guy, so I was certain he scared the shit out of people. In my head, I pictured him eight feet tall with the ability to lift a car over his head without breaking a sweat. In reality, that was impossible, but it still put fear in my blood when I thought about what he did for Rich.

"Wait!" I yelled as Gabe started to walk toward the racquetball door. "I just thought of an idea. I'm not going to Starbucks, but I'll meet you here tomorrow to workout, okay?"

"Where are you going?" He frowned.

"I'm going to pay a visit to my husband at his work." I was taking a gamble that was for sure.

"Is that safe?" he asked, crossing his arms over his chest.

"I'll just tell him I want to have lunch with him since I didn't get to have dinner with him last night."

"And what's the point of you going to his work?" He raised an eyebrow.

"To dig up dirt, duh! Get with the program, Mr. Green Eyes."

He gave a hard, belly laugh. "Mr. Green Eyes?"

I blushed, realizing what I'd said. "That's what I called you when I didn't know your name," I confessed, turning my head away from him so he couldn't meet my eyes.

"And why'd you have to refer to me before you knew my name?"

I looked up at him slowly. "I ..."

"Spit it out, angel. I'm dying to hear that you gossiped about me."

"I didn't gossip about you," I snorted.

"No? Then tell me why."

"I ..."

"Come on, angel. I told you why I call you angel. That was embarrassing for me."

"Not like this!" I protested.

"Enlighten me then."

He was smiling at me as if he knew. Fuck, he probably did. I walked closer to him. "I thought about you while I ..."

"Go on," he smirked with a nod.

I stepped closer and whispered into his ear. "While I got myself wet for my husband."

Before he could respond, I reached out, turned the doorknob and made a run for it. I looked over my left shoulder to see if he was following me before I ran up the stairs to leave. He was standing in the doorway of the racquetball court, staring at me with a huge smile.

117

Just before I took my first step on the stairs, I heard him say, "I'll remember that, angel."

My palms became sweaty the closer I got to Rich's work. Nervous would be an understatement. I'd only been to his office a handful of times in the last three years and that was only with him. His office was never on my *to-do list* for the day.

If my suspicions were correct, Rich might already know I was at his work. It frustrated me to think he had a tracker on my car, but I wouldn't put it past him. Hopefully, he wasn't monitoring whatever device he needed to watch to know where I was because I wanted to catch him in some sort of *act*.

Pulling into the packed parking lot, I found a space and hurried to the lobby door, noting Rich's car in a parking space in front. His work was in a ten story building he owned. His office took over the entire top floor while he rented each floor to other businesses.

I rode the elevator up, wiping my sweaty hands on my running tights in hopes they'd stop. As I stared at my image in the reflective steel door, I scolded myself for not changing before I'd arrived. I could already hear Rich yelling at me that this was his place of business and I had to look proper when I *showed* myself.

Instead of pushing the button for the ground floor so I could leave, I stepped off the elevator when it dinged and opened onto Rich's floor. As the doors opened, I was immediately greeted by his receptionist who sat behind a gigantic wood desk with a waterfall encased in glass behind her with the words: Jones Investments etched in the glass.

Rich's office was extremely modern with luxurious furniture in the waiting room. If I were a potential client, I'd be scared to sit on the white couch or chair in fear of getting something on them. Instead, I'd stand, looking at the abstract paintings on the walls and the fresh flowers that sat in a glass vase on the oval, glass table in front of the sofa.

"Mrs. Jones ... Ric—Mr. Jones didn't tell me you'd be stopping by. Can I get you something to drink?"

I smiled at Trina. "No, I'm okay. Is he with someone?" I motioned to his office that was at the end of the hall.

"No. Let me tell him you're here."

"Perfect. Thank you."

I waited as Trina buzzed Rich, telling him I was in the reception area for him. I had a half a mind to walk back and enter his office, but once again, I didn't want to press my luck too much.

"Autumn," Rich called from behind me. I turned, taking my eyes off of a painting of abstract colors that reminded me of the night he proposed. "What are you doing here?"

I studied him as he approached. He didn't look mad, but we were also in front of his employee. "I just left the gym and thought maybe you could take an early lunch?"

He glanced over to Trina, then stepped forward and kissed me on the cheek. "Sure, but we have to make it quick. I have a meeting with Remo in thirty minutes."

"Oh. Why don't we wait for him and we can go together? I'd love to meet him finally. It's been three years and I still haven't met most of your staff." I plastered a fake smile on my face, trying to hide my true motive for coming.

"You'll get to meet all of them at my party, princess."

"Right. I forgot we invited all of them. Well, let's go. I missed you last night since we didn't have dinner together."

I wished I could hang around. If things were done illegally, I'd bet money not all of his employees would be at his party since we also invited a lot of the police department.

"After you." He gestured for me to step up toward the elevator. I pushed the down button and it opened. "I'll be back in thirty. Tell Remo to wait in my office," he said to Trina.

"No problem, Bab—Mr. Jones." She caught herself again, this time her face turning beet red.

Why in the fuck would Trina think she couldn't call Rich by his first name in front of me?

As the doors started to shut on the elevator, I watched Rich and Trina make eye contact briefly before Rich turned to me. "You're lucky I'm in a good mood today, princess or I'd take you over my knee for wearing gym clothes to my work."

"Sorry. I just wanted to surprise you. I missed you," I lied.

"I shouldn't take a lunch this early, especially since I just got here about an hour ago."

I'd forgotten that Rich went to sleep once he got home this morning from his "all-nighter". "I forgot. Why are you here already?" I asked as the doors opened on the ground floor.

He gestured for me to exit before him. "Remo and I have a meeting with a client in thirty minutes."

"Couldn't you have rescheduled?"

He laughed. "I'm not in the business of rescheduling, princess. People won't know I'm serious about wanting my money back if I reschedule to sleep." He pressed the unlock button on his fob and we both slid into his Mercedes.

"What does Remo do to get them to pay exactly?" I asked as I buckled my seatbelt and looked over at him.

"Let's just say that once you meet him, you won't fear me anymore." He started the engine and began to pull out of the parking space.

I sucked in a breath. "You plan to have him start hurting me?"

He laughed. "No, princess. I'm just saying I look like a Ken doll next to him. You won't even see my muscles if I stand next to him."

"You can still hurt me," I murmured under my breath.

"I don't want to get into this, Autumn! I've said I'm sorry."

He said he was sorry for getting angry—not for hurting me. In my mind, they were two different things. "Fine, but you can't touch me like that anymore. I want to wear a sleeveless dress to your party. It's supposed to be a warm night."

"That's why I said I'd spank you. No one will see them on your ass."

I stared at him. Was he joking? Surely he was joking. He said he didn't like hurting me and even if it were only spanking my ass, it would still hurt. It would also leave a bruise if he did it hard enough.

"No spanking either," I whispered.

He cut his eyes to me. "Fine. Just don't piss me off," he hissed.

Why don't you stay at work every night then? "I don't mean to. I don't even know what I do." I turned, looking out the passenger side window as we drove down the street.

"We talked about this the other night ... Just fucking drop it."

And I did.

Rich and I ate at a little café down the street in twenty minutes before he had to return to work. I'd hope I'd at least see Remo in the parking lot. No such luck. My hasty trip to Rich's work was a bust.

Or was it?

Brandi met me at Starbucks for our weekly date a few days later. I was excited because I wanted to tell her about the plan. I wished I could call her and tell her when I found out, but like everything else, I didn't know what Rich monitored.

We sat at a table in the corner after we'd both ordered our coffee. I was anxious as my leg bounced up and down. I wanted to blurt it out, tell her everything, but I had to wait for Gabe and Paul to show up since they were part of the plan too.

I looked at the time on my phone, noticing that they had two minutes before we'd agreed we all would meet to fill Brandi in. Typical men; never early.

"Are you going to tell me why you have a nervous twitch?" Brandi asked, motioning with her head toward my leg that was still bouncing.

"I will once ..." I drifted off as I noticed the guys walk in. Gabe was wearing a navy blue T-shirt that hugged his muscular frame and I had to fight myself not to walk up and hug him while smelling his scent. There was something about him that made me feel safe. Deep down in the deepest part of my soul, I knew Gabe would never hurt me and would stop at nothing to help me.

Paul stepped in line to order and Gabe walked over to us. I watched him with a huge smile spread across my face that matched his as my fixed stare drifted down his chest to his waist that was hugged perfectly with jeans.

Damn I couldn't wait until I was no longer married.

"Angel," he greeted with a nod as he sat at the table next to us. "Nice to see you again, Brandi."

Brandi turned toward me, whisper-yelling. "Um ... What the fuck is going on?"

I looked around, not noticing anyone that looked familiar; a potential spy, then leaned forward and whispered, "We've come up with a plan."

"We've?" she asked, eyebrows scrunched as she looked from me to Gabe.

"Yeah. Me, Gabe and Paul." I shrugged. "But we have to keep it quiet because I'm fairly certain Rich has spies. I don't think they follow me into places, but just in case, Gabe and Paul are going to sit nearby as I whisper the plan to you."

Paul walked over, handing Gabe a cup of coffee and gave me a nod. Once he sat, I leaned forward again and told Brandi I'd divorce

Rich and live with the guys. The more I thought about the plan, the more I realized this was the way to go.

"You bought a gun?" Brandi asked after I finished talking.

I nodded.

"Like a real gun that shoots bullets?"

I chuckled. "Yes."

"Where is it now?"

After I'd bought the gun, I'd carried it in my purse for a few days, but I knew that wasn't the best place for it. Every room was monitored, so I couldn't just hide it randomly without Rich knowing. And I couldn't leave it in my car or with Dad or Gabe because that would defeat the purpose of keeping me safe from Rich. I knew he was going to lose his shit when he was served with divorce papers and if I wasn't at Gabe's when that happened, I needed to be ready.

"That was the tricky thing." I took a quick sip of my coffee. "I thought long and hard about it. It had to be a place Rich could never find, but where I could still get to it."

"Right. So where is it?"

I looked at Gabe briefly. He and Paul were staring at each other. They weren't talking, but I knew they were listening. I'd never told Gabe that Rich had security cameras in the house. He probably never thought to ask me where I hid the gun, assuming I hide it in my underwear drawer or in a shoe box in the closet like *normal* people.

"I had to make sure to cover my tracks since there's a camera in the garage. So as I looked for the Gorilla glue, I found some *hefty* Velcro and quickly waded it up in my hand and continued looking until I found the glue."

I paused and looked at all three. They all didn't say anything as I continued to whisper to Brandi. "Then I went into my closet—which I'm almost positive doesn't have a camera in it—and stuck the sticky side of a piece of the Velcro to the gun sleeve for the gun. Then I stuck it in the pocket of my black hoodie I was wearing that hid my bruises."

"I'm following, A, but if Rich watches the camera feed, won't he wonder why you needed the Gorilla glue?" Brandi asked, looking from me to Gabe as if to ask him if he were wondering the same thing.

"It was a coincidence really, but it gave me the idea for the Velcro. My laundry basket just happened to start cracking the same day, so I grabbed the basket, sat on the floor by the bed and glued the crack."

"Okay, go on," she said, gesturing for me to continue.

"While the basket was drying on the floor, I sat there as if I were waiting for it to dry while I *read* on my ereader. But really, I stuck a piece of the Velcro on the underside of the wood frame on my side of the bed. I don't think ... well I hope they couldn't see what I was doing." I shrugged. "Anyway, I slowly grabbed the gun in the holster and stuck it on the Velcro under the bed."

"You better hope Rich couldn't see that," Brandi warned.

"That was a few days ago. I've checked since and it's still there. I assume he watches the camera feed daily to make sure I'm not doing anything I shouldn't be doing."

"All this makes me sick to my stomach," she moaned, giving me a worried look.

I sighed. "I know."

"Autumn," Gabe called. I slowly turned my head, but he was looking at Paul. "I bought the same gun so you could leave that one there and still practice how to shoot."

It took me a few seconds to realize he was talking to me and not to Paul. "You did?" I asked, looking at Brandi.

"Yeah—"

"Wait ... how are you two even a thing?" Brandi asked, nudging her head toward Gabe.

"Walk with me and I'll fill you in," Paul said as he stood.

Brandi got up a few seconds later and walked over to where Paul stood by the merchandise. They talked for a few minutes as Gabe and I didn't say anything. Our next meeting was going to take place in the racquetball court because I hated not being able to talk freely.

A few more days passed and Rich was spending more and more time at work—or so he'd said. If his routine was changing, so was mine.

Me: *Hey! Rich isn't home and I'm bored. Want to go get a drink?*

I waited for Brandi to text me back. It didn't take long.

Brandi: *Can you?*

I sighed and responded back.

Me: *He can't expect me to stay locked up in the house while he's working. I do that enough already. One drink won't hurt.*

Brandi: *All right. I'll pick you up in twenty.*

I did a little happy dance as I made my way to my bathroom to do my makeup and change into something besides my pajamas. I put on a pair of tight, boot-cut jeans, a plain black tank top I'd paired with a long silver and black necklace with large beads. Since I hadn't been out with Brandi in what seemed like forever, I took it as a special occasion and slipped on my black Louboutins.

As I was putting my finishing touches on my makeup, Brandi texted that she was out front. I grabbed my purse and left.

"Hey!" I greeted, slipping into her car.

"I feel like we're teenagers and you're sneaking out of your parents' house." She put the car in drive and I turned around as she drove to see if anyone was following us. I didn't see any other cars and breathed a sigh of relief.

"Kinda feels like that to me too." I laughed.

As soon as we stopped at the stop sign down my street, I got a text from Rich.

Rich: *Where are you going?*

I rolled my eyes and responded.

Me: *Out with Brandi.*

Rich: *To where?*

"Rich is texting me. He knows I left," I grumbled.

"How?"

"I'm assuming from the cameras in my house."

Me: *To have a drink. You're not home and we wanted to have a girl's night.*

"Does he watch those twenty-four-seven or something?" she asked, scrunching her eyebrows.

I groaned. "Probably."

Rich: *The mayor's wife is NOT to be seen whoring it up in a club!*

Mayor's wife? He hadn't even announced he was going to run and no one would know who I was.

"Look what he just texted me." I read her the text.

Grunting she said, "Whoring it up in a club? Whatever."

Me: *I'm not. It's just a drink. I'll see you when we both get home.*

I knew I was really pressing my luck, but I was determined to show him he could trust me so I could have more leeway when it came to doing things. Then I'd be able to make my escape when he least expected it.

"Where do you want to go?"

"Blue Martini? I haven't been there in forever."

"Perfect." She nodded. "It's been a while since I've been there too."

Rich: *11:00 No later!*

Me: *Will do. Love you!*

I shuddered at my words of endearment. Of course I still loved him; he was my husband, and at one time we had something special. But with each passing day, the more he abused me, controlled me and yelled at me, the more I wanted to give my heart to someone who deserved it.

We arrived at the packed bar. There were no free seats, so we walked toward the wood bar to wait in the crowd so we could order a drink once the bartender noticed us.

I hadn't been at a bar like this since before I met Rich. I felt as if it was my twenty-first birthday all over again. I was excited, nervous, and anxious all rolled into one. I was used to staying home, making dinner for Rich, watching TV and enjoying a quiet night—after the wrath. I wasn't used to being in a packed bar where I was being checked out by every guy on the prowl.

Part of me wanted to hide my princess cut diamond ring and see what else was out there. I wasn't looking for a relationship. I just wanted to see what the single men looked like these days. I thought better of it though—until my gaze landed on the familiar green eyes I daydreamed about by the front door.

I grinned like a fool and he smiled back as he started walking toward us. He was dressed in jeans that hugged his hips and a button down light blue long-sleeved shirt.

"Gabe's here," I whispered into Brandi's ear even though the music was loud enough in the background that Gabe wouldn't have heard. "And Paul," I said when I noticed he was walking with Gabe.

"I told them we would be here."

"What? When? How?"

"Paul and I exchanged numbers the other day just in case I needed them to help you or something and we've been texting. We were texting when you asked me to go out, and then I mentioned we were here when we were driving here."

"Wait ... You and Paul have been—"

"Angel," Gabe greeted with a nod.

"Hey." I smiled. "What are you guys doing here?" *As if I didn't know.*

"Paul wanted to come have a drink."

"Did he now?" I crossed my arms over my chest and eyed Paul and Brandi.

"What's that look for?" Paul chuckled.

"We have to go to the ladies' room. Excuse us." Brandi grabbed my arm and pulled me away from the guys before I could protest.

"What the hell is going on?"

"Nothing. It's strictly platonic."

"You're married."

"So are you," she hissed, pushing the swinging door open to the ladies' room.

"I'm not texting Gabe," I corrected.

"A, calm down. Paul and I are just friends."

"Does Todd know?" I crossed my arms over my chest waiting for her reply.

"No, but nothing is going on. I swear."

"Just like nothing's going on with me and Gabe," I murmured.

She grabbed both of my shoulders in her hands and looked me straight in the eyes. "Just calm down. We're all going to have drinks. That's it."

"You do know that Rich is probably tracking my phone?"

She rolled her eyes. "Let him. I'd love to see those two kick his ass."

"You're not the one that has to go home to hell, B."

"If he puts a hand on you again, trust me, those two will be with me on your doorstep in a heartbeat."

I sighed. Rich knew I was going out, but I didn't think he'd show up. I was certain I would get in trouble when I got home for leaving the house, but I was hopeful I was wrong and my plan would work.

We walked back to the guys. Gabe smiled again when he saw us walking back to them and I noticed both guys had a drink in their hand when we got closer.

"You couldn't get us one?" Brandi teased.

"Come on, firecracker. I'll buy you ladies a drink." Paul swung his arm across Brandi's shoulders with his free arm and they both laughed while walking toward the bar.

Just friends ...

"Did Paul tell you we were going to be here?" I asked Gabe, stuffing my hands in the back pocket of my jeans.

He nodded. "He did."

"So ... You came to see me?"

"I barely get any time with you because you're always on the run. I wanted a few more hours." He took a sip of his drink.

"In public," I said. It was more of a reminder than a question.

"You know I couldn't pass up the chance, angel." He took a step forward and bent down toward my ear before he whispered, "I know it's not time yet, but since that kiss, you're all I think about. I'm trying not to come off too strong, but the longer you wait, the longer it will be until you know what else I can do with my mouth."

I choked on my spit.

Literally choked on my spit.

"Gabe ..."

"Mr. Green Eyes." He winked.

My face flamed. "Oh my God, I shouldn't have told you that!"

He bent to my ear again. "You're just wasting precious time, angel."

"How many drinks have you had today?" I joked.

He smiled. "This is my first one. I'm not drunk. I just know what I want."

My eyes closed involuntary. So much of me wanted to take Gabe up on his offer. I could picture his hips swaying with mine as we danced to the beat of the music playing around us, his cock hardening against my heat. It had been too long since I was seduced, and the words coming from his lips were sending shivers down my body and straight up want for him. I wanted him—bad.

I stared up at his lips when he stepped back. He licked them, enticing me to do something. Instead, I ran my thumb across the underside of my wedding ring out of habit and it brought me back to reality.

Before I could respond, Brandi and Paul came back with our drinks. Brandi handed me a vodka cranberry and I took a sip, trying to calm my nerves. I could feel Gabe's gaze on my face as I looked around. "I think a band is setting up," I spoke, barely removing my lips from my straw.

"Oh yeah," Paul agreed.

"They sometimes have live bands," Brandi confirmed.

"What's your favorite kind of music?" Gabe asked and I turned my head and looked up at him.

"I like a lot of stuff. Country, rock, some alternative, pop, R&B ..."

"Me, too." Gabe took a sip of his drink. "I grew up on country because my parents were from Tennessee, but when I was in the army, we'd listen to a lot of different stuff."

"You two were in the army together right?" I pointed between him and Paul.

Paul spoke up. "Yep, all nine years. We went through basic together and everything."

"Aw, you two have a little bromance going on," Brandi teased.

"I love you, man." Paul swung his arm over Gabe's shoulder like he had with Brandi. "You're my best friend." He said it in a teasing way, but I knew it was true.

Gabe shrugged Paul's arm off his shoulder and before he could speak, the band started to announce who they were.

"Good evening Vegas! I hope you enjoy the cover songs we sing and some of our originals."

The crowd cheered and we stepped closer to the stage as people surrounded us. The female singer nodded to her piano player and she began to sing a cover of *Many of Miles* by Sara Bareilles. Her voice was exquisite.

"Holy shit, I love this version of this song," Brandi said, swaying to the beat.

Before I knew it, my hips were moving to the beat as well. I looked over my shoulder to where Gabe was standing behind me and he smiled, looking down at my ass. I laughed, turning back around to the stage.

A few songs later, Brandi and I still swayed to the beat as I slurped my drink through my straw until it was empty. I didn't want to fight at the bar for another one so I stuck a piece of ice into my mouth instead. My gaze was fixed on the stage when I felt Gabe step closer to me, our bodies flush. I was going to step away—that would have been the right thing to do, but I loved the feel of him pressed against me.

He leaned down and whispered, "You know what they say about eating ice?" I turned my head slightly as I felt his breath tickling my ear. "They say it's a sign of sexual frustration ... I can help with that, angel."

Goose bumps pricked my skin. I didn't know if it was from his words or from the ice in my mouth, but it didn't matter. I knew he could deliver. There was something about him. Some guys you can read and know they only know the basics, but Gabe ...

I knew he could rock my world.

"I think that's an old wives tale." I laughed.

"We could find out."

I turned and slapped his arm playfully. "Behave."

"I'm trying, but you're shaking that ass in front of me."

I shook my head as I turned my attention back to the stage, but my brain was thinking about everything Gabe could do with an ice cube on my body. My body heat rose even higher.

"We need to go soon!" I yelled to Brandi.

She nodded. "One more song."

The singer began to sing a cover of Sam Smith's version of *How Will I Know* that was originally sung by Whitney Houston. Her sultry voice silenced the crowd, and all eyes were on her as chills coursed over my body.

Listening to the words, I thought about the man behind me and not the man I was married to. Gabe was promising me he'd protect me. Maybe he didn't want a relationship, but only sex. Deep down, I knew I wanted to see where our relationship would go. If I were single, I would explore it. Once I left Rich, I didn't want to jump into a relationship with Gabe. I wanted to take things slow and get to know him because I obviously married a man I didn't know.

I hadn't realized that I'd stopped swaying to the beat of the music as I listened to the words. When the song ended, we said our good-byes, but not for long because we'd see each other at Club 24 in the morning.

And I couldn't wait.

When I entered my house through the front door, Rich sat at the dining room table, a vodka martini sat in front of him. I swallowed hard—he was pissed.

I slowly walked toward him, not saying anything. His gaze was trained on my face. I was starting to think I should speak first—apologize, grovel, whatever. Before I could, he stood and I stopped dead in my tracks.

"Do you like testing my patience, princess?" he hissed.

"Come on, honey. I was tired of sitting at home."

"So you think it's okay for you to go traipsing all over town?"

"Traipsing all over town? We went to one bar. I had one drink—"

"You could have had a drink here!" he shouted.

"I wanted to hang with my friend," I whispered.

He stepped closer and I swallowed. "You really are testing my patience."

"I don't see the harm in going—"

He grabbed my arms with both hands and squeezed. "It's not a matter of—"

"Let me go," I groaned and wiggled. I knew I shouldn't because he'd only grab me harder, so I reminded him of why he shouldn't touch me. "Remember I said I wanted to wear a sleeveless dress to your party?" He let go. "And remember we talked about trust? I didn't do anything to make you not trust me."

He paused, looking down at my arms, then he rolled his neck as if he were trying to relieve the tensions. "Why do you think it's okay to do whatever the fuck you want to do?"

"Why is it not okay?" I took a deep breath to calm myself before he really did hurt me.

"I didn't say you could go."

"Come on, Rich. You weren't here and I was bored. I went out with my friend that you know."

"As well as many men I don't know."

"It wasn't like that," I lied. "Brandi and I went to have a drink and talk. The only difference was it wasn't coffee."

He studied my face and then ran his gaze down my body. "Is this going to be an ongoing issue?"

I looked him straight in the eye, trying not to roll mine. "There's no issue. I wanted to hang out with my friend instead of watching reality TV."

He thought for a moment, looking past me and then met my gaze before he spoke and crossed his arms over his chest. "I'm going to be spending a lot of time on my campaign. So help me God, if I hear about any man touching you, you'll pay. It *will* be your fault because you'll be in a place you shouldn't be in and therefore disobeying me. Once that happens, you'll never be able to leave this house except to accompany me to whatever appearance I need to make to become mayor. You'll only be allowed to use the pool for your workouts, and if you get fat, you know what will happen. Do I make myself clear?"

I swallowed down my need to object and nodded. "Yes, but if I get pregnant, I'm going to gain weight."

He reached up with his hand and tucked my hair behind my ear. Not removing his hand from my face, he cupped my cheek with a little too much force. "That will be under different circumstances and you'll still be required to stay healthy for our baby."

"Okay," I whispered.

"Now, be a good wife and go wait naked for me. I've had a long day and I need to relax."

FOURTEEN
Gabe

ONE THING WAS CERTAIN.

Autumn wasn't the weak person I thought she was when I'd first met her.

I'd like to think it was because of me—that I was her savior which made her stronger. But for that to happen, she needed to have the strength within her the entire time.

Checking my back office, I didn't have a date until the following Saturday. I was okay with that. I didn't need the money—I had enough saved from the past three years.

During the week leading up to my next date, Jackson and I met Autumn at the gym and then went to Starbucks. I wanted to go to the range and teach her how to shoot, but she needed to figure out how to go without her husband finding out.

Everything was platonic between us, but I'm not gonna lie, I watched her ass while she ran every single day. I'd watch her breasts bounce through the reflection of the mirror as we both ran side by side. And I'd watch her stretch. God—watching her stretch put thoughts in my head that I'd dream about. No joke. Each night, I dreamt about us together in bed.

And when I saw her at the bar, a few weeks back, I knew there was no getting her out of my system. After almost five years of drowning myself nightly with at least a half a bottle of whiskey before bed, I stopped needing it. Each night my dreams were vivid. They were of Autumn; they were of Alyssa *and* Autumn, and they weren't about the last day of Alyssa's life that used to haunt me.

The more I thought about it—the more I was convinced Autumn was an angel sent to rescue me.

My past was haunting me.

But now my future looked promising.

"Hey," Jackson called, coming into the living room where I sat on the couch watching TV. "The guys want to grab a drink. You down?"

I nodded. Guy time would be good. "Yeah. When?"

"Now."

I looked down at my jeans and blue T-shirt. I was ready. It was the middle of the afternoon and I didn't have anyone to impress.

We met the guys at Oak & Ivy, a whiskey cocktail bar in Container Park. The bar was narrow with wood lining all the surfaces, and there was only enough space to sit at the bar or outside. The copper lamp shades that hung above the bar gave everything a rustic feel. I'd never heard of the bar, but I fell in love as I walked in, noticing the forty-plus different kinds of whiskey they had to offer.

"You're a whiskey man?" Brad asked as we all looked over the menu as we sat belly up to the bar.

"The glass can be half empty or half full as long as there's whiskey in it," I replied with a smile.

"We're gonna be great friends." He laughed.

I settled on trying the Brown Sack Special, which was bartender's choice. I had no doubt the man dressed in his bow tie and suspenders could make me a drink to my liking.

"How are you two liking Vegas?" Vinny asked, looking from me to Jackson.

"Dude, the women ..." Jackson began, shaking his head. "This is my first night off since we got here last week."

"Same with you, Gabe?" Nick asked.

I shook my head. "Nope. I guess the ladies don't like the bald head." I laughed.

"That's kinda true," Vinny said, rubbing his bald head. "These fuckers get more dates than me." He motioned with his thumb to Nick and Brad.

"I'm not complaining. I've been helping out a friend."

"A girlfriend?" Nick asked.

"Nah—"

"He wants her to be," Jackson interrupted.

"Does she know what you do for a living?" Brad asked.

I chuckled and took a sip of the concoction the bartender placed in front of me. "Nope. Not sure how that's going to work out."

"It's not," Nick and Vinny said in unison.

Nick looked at Vinny. "We've both tried to have relationships, but they only last a few months before jealousy takes over. Women can't grasp that it's just work and we have no feelings for these chicks."

"Yeah, but I wouldn't be okay if she were an escort either," I countered.

They all nodded in understanding. I had no idea what I was going to do when I had Autumn in my house. Once she left her husband, I wasn't going to hold back how I felt for her. It was already hard enough seeing her every day and not being able to touch her as I wanted too. It felt like it had when I was with Alyssa.

I just hoped it didn't turn out the same way.

On Thursday after our daily Starbucks post-workout rendezvous, I checked my back office again to make sure I didn't have any dates besides the one for Saturday— I didn't. I also double-checked the instructions for Saturday's date.

Trista was hiring me to escort her to a black tie party. I was to be her boyfriend and eye candy on her arm for the night. The problem— I didn't have a decent suit to wear. Since working out five days a week, sometimes six since being in Vegas, I'd bulked up, causing my suit to be uncomfortable.

"Hey, want to go with me to the mall?" I asked Jackson as he sat on the brown leather couch watching baseball on our giant sixty inch flat screen TV.

He furrowed his eyebrows, turning his head toward me slowly. "Did you just ask me to go to the mall?"

I laughed, realizing what I'd asked. "Sorry, I just wanted to know if you wanted to go with me to get a suit for my date on Saturday."

He chuckled. "Yeah ... Cap. I'm gonna pass. Baseball is much more entertaining than seeing you strut your stuff."

I shook my head. Hanging out with Jackson every day was turning me into a chick. "What? You don't think my ass looks good in these jeans?" I asked, turning and sticking my butt out.

I had driven around for a good thirty minutes before Siri helped me find a good place to go. My plan was to go to the first store I saw that sold suits and get one that fit enough to get by for one night. I didn't need anything custom tailored.

However ...

My plans changed when I saw *her*.

Autumn was walking along the sidewalk of the outdoor shopping area, and I watched as she slipped into one of the stores. I crossed the street, following her. Even though I had just seen her a few hours before at Starbucks, I wanted to see her again. After all, we were *friends*.

I searched the store, looking for the women's department until I found her where she was looking in the dress section.

"Angel," I greeted, walking up behind her. "If I would have known you'd be here, I wouldn't have made an ass out of myself and invited Paul to come."

She jumped as if I scared her, holding her hand to her chest as she turned to look at me. "Oh my God, what are you doing here?"

"I have to get a suit for work." How could I tell the woman I was interested in I was going on a date with another woman ... a date I was paid for? I knew I needed to tell her. If she found out on her own, it would more than likely be the end of whatever we were and whatever we were going to be once she was *free*.

"I was starting to think you and Paul didn't have jobs." She laughed, looking around—probably for a spy. There wasn't anyone around but us.

I chuckled. "We have jobs." My gaze roamed her body as I took in her perfect frame in tight jeans and a simple black T-shirt and flip flops. I usually saw her in casual workout gear, but damn if I didn't love her in jeans as well. And the icing on the cake: She smelled like warm vanilla sugar.

"What do you two do then?"

"It's complicated," I answered with a shrug. "Why are you here? I thought you'd have to go home after Starbucks?" I asked, changing the subject. Luckily she didn't press the issue about my job.

She shrugged. "I did go home, but I wanted to go shopping. I've been pushing the envelope with my husband for weeks now."

"And everything's okay?" I asked with a raised eyebrow.

"Yeah," she answered, giving a tight smile.

I followed Autumn as she went from rack to rack, grabbing a couple of dresses. "When do you meet with an attorney?" I asked. Whenever she was going, I wanted to go and at least wait for her in the parking lot for support. If her husband's spies told him she was meeting with an attorney, there was no telling what would happen. I wanted to be there in case he showed up.

"I haven't found one yet. My luck, my husband knows all of them." She moved a few hangers, looking at different dresses as she spoke.

"I highly doubt that. When are you going to tell me what he does for a living?" I asked, crossing my arms over my chest.

"When I'm safely in your house."

I groaned, liking the sound of that scenario as it came from her mouth. "It's been a month, angel." A month too long.

"I know," she groaned. "This is part of *my* plan. Your plan can only work if my plan works."

"What's your plan? I thought my plan was *our* plan." I gestured between the two of us.

She grabbed a couple of dresses and started to walk toward the fitting room. "My plan is to push the envelope. Get him to let me go places other than just the gym and Starbucks. That way, when I find an attorney, I'd have more of an excuse to be in that area—wherever that may be."

I followed her as she walked, thinking of her plan. "Well, since you're here and I'm here, want to help me pick out a suit?"

"Sure," she beamed. "Just let me try these on and then I'll help you."

Sitting in a chair outside of the fitting room, I waited for her to pick which one she was going to buy. I thought about her naked as she changed from dress to dress.

I wanted to see her naked ... I wanted to help her change ... I wanted to zip up the back of the dresses as my fingers brushed along her smooth neck ... I wanted to be on the other side of the door, my head between her thighs as she moaned my name ... I wanted to bury my dick so far in her that we'd feel connected as one.

Fuck ...

I just wanted *her*.

This *friend* thing wasn't working out too well.

As I wondered what color underwear and bra she had on, she stepped out in a long black dress with a laced top, and all thoughts of her naked vanished. She was breathtaking as she twirled, looking at all angles in the floor length mirror. The dress had a slit that ran from her upper thigh on her right leg to the floor, exposing her smooth, toned leg as she turned.

Fuck, I was instantly hard.

"The bruises are gone," she said, looking at me through the reflection of the mirror.

My gaze darted up from her ass to meet her staring eyes. "I'm not looking at your arms, angel."

She huffed with a smile. "Gabe! We're friends, remember?"

I stood, walking toward her. When I reached her, I stepped flush with her body, bringing her ass back so she could feel how hard I was.

"I can't help what you do to me—friend or not." I saw her swallow hard as our gazes met again in the mirror. I rested my chin on her shoulder and started to glide my hand up her thigh. "I'm not sure how much longer I can wait," I confessed, whispering in her ear. "I think we should revise what we are. I'm thinking—friends with benefits."

She took a deep breath, my sight lowering to her chest as her breasts moved up and down with the movement. My hand continued to slide up her thigh, and just as it was about to slip past the slit, she caught my hand with hers.

"You have no idea how much I want to say yes. I do. I really, really do. But if you're right and I get more money if my husband's cheating on me, then I can't cheat on him."

I groaned out of frustration. "Next week, angel," I whispered into her ear. "You better find an attorney or I will."

She nodded her head and I stepped back, breaking our contact. My dick was like stone, and I had a half a mind to take her behind one of the fitting room doors and fuck her while she watched in the mirror.

Fucking friend zone bullshit!

"I'm having a hard time controlling myself. I'll be in the men's department looking at suits." I turned on my heel, adjusted myself, then went to find the men's department.

FIFTEEN
Autumn

Rich hadn't laid a hand on me all week because he was rarely home. When I'd see him, he'd tell me he was busy with his campaign manager and getting ready for his big announcement.

I honestly didn't see the big deal about announcing at *his* party at *his* own home that *he* was going to run for mayor. It wasn't as if it were going to be televised and he needed to make a long speech for Christ sake.

He hadn't touched me all week … not even for sex. But he also hadn't bothered to tell me when he was or wasn't coming home, so I still felt like a prisoner at night.

I was finally able to get him to let me go shopping. He didn't like it, but I told him that I was bored since he wasn't coming home often. Plus, I still needed to get my dress for his party. So far, *my* plan was working.

Gabe happened to be shopping at the same store and damn if he didn't look fine in a suit! I was instantly turned on when he walked out of the fitting room, asking me if the simple black suit with a white dress shirt and black tie looked all right. I wanted to answer his question by throwing him against the wall and letting him pleasure me with his hard cock—the hard cock that pressed into my backside as he whispered into my ear, soaking my panties when I was in my dress.

Gabe was right; I needed to find an attorney fast because this whole friends thing sucked ass.

Fridays were bittersweet. Rich worked and I went to the gym to meet Gabe, but then I'd have to wait an entire weekend before I saw Gabe again. When I walked into Club 24 the morning after dress shopping, I could still feel Gabe leaning into me as he'd said, *"I can't help what you do to me."*

I shivered as I recalled his words.

It felt amazing to be wanted again—to be desired. It had only been a few weeks, but I was starting to think about Gabe a ton. I hated that I could only be with him for a couple of hours a day. I wanted to go to the gym, Starbucks and then on a date with him. I didn't want to go home and wait for Rich—*if* he came home for the night.

Just like every morning I went to the gym, I waited for Gabe to arrive. I began to warm up with a brisk walk on the treadmill where he knew to find me. Usually, after they arrived, Paul went his separate way and Gabe picked a treadmill next to me that wasn't being used. We'd run together without talking, stealing a few glances here and there. Knowing he was there to see me felt good—really good. I was starting to have feelings for him, especially after *feeling* how much he wanted me the day before.

Today, instead of jumping on the treadmill, Gabe handed me a folded piece of paper. I smiled, looking from the paper and back to meet his green eyes. Without a word, he turned and walked away. I furrowed my eyebrows as I opened the paper, trying not to trip as I continued to walk on the treadmill.

Angel,

I wanna get sweaty with you.
Meet me in a racquetball court.
Mr. Green Eyes

That whole "trying not to trip" thing, went out the window. I tripped over my feet and clung to the rails of the treadmill, trying not to fall and make a fool out of myself. After steadying myself, I stopped the machine and wiped it down, not knowing what I was doing. I was still married, but I wanted to see what Gabe meant.

I took hesitant steps as I looked around, wondering who was watching as I walked down the stairs to the racquetball courts. I finally found Gabe in the last court, leaning against the wall in his black workout shorts and a black fitted tank top that showed off his strong arms. His legs were crossed, and he held two racquets in one hand and a blue ball in the other.

So he meant get sweaty by actually playing racquetball ...

"I don't know how to play," I admitted, closing the door behind me.

He shrugged with a smirk. "Me either."

Walking the few steps to where he stood, I said, "But you want to play?"

He pushed off of the wall, reaching out to hand me a racquet. "Figured it would be fun."

I chuckled. "All right. Do you know the rules?"

"Rules are made to be broken, angel." God his fucking smile was plastered across his face and I wanted to run up to him and kiss him again.

I bit my bottom lip and smiled. "Not in sports. That's called ... cheating." I hesitated on the words as a slight pain pinged my heart. "All right," I shrugged and reached my hand out to take the racquet that was slightly smaller than the ones I've seen for tennis. "I go first."

He laughed and tossed me the ball. I bounced it then swung the racquet and hit the blue rubber ball against the far wall. It flew passed my head and bounced near Gabe where he swung and hit it on a different wall. I went for it and missed.

"Point for me." He nodded a cocky nod.

I glared at him. "How do you even know you hit it on the right wall?"

He shrugged. "I don't, but we can play that whoever misses it, loses the point."

I tilted my head a little, still giving him my evil eye. "You'll hit it over my head. You're stronger than me."

"In that case, it will hit off the back wall and come right back to you." He laughed and tilted his head to mimic mine.

I stared into his green eyes and he stared back, not saying anything. A slow smile crept up his face and I huffed. "Fine. But that was warm up, so you don't have any points."

He chuckled then jogged to where the ball sat on the floor near the front wall. "If I lose by one point, we tie." He tossed me the ball again.

"Whatever," I giggled and bounced the ball and swung, hitting it against the front wall again.

We went back and forth, laughing and I ending up losing. I knew I'd lose, but I had to give it a shot. At one point, I envisioned it as Rich's head and I hit it as hard as I could. It bounced from the front wall, straight to the back wall and then bouncing and hitting a side wall. Gabe hit it on the same side wall and I swung as hard as I could again and missed the ball completely.

"Letting off steam, angel?" He laughed.

"You have no idea," I panted, trying to catch my breath from running around to chase the ball.

Something switched in Gabe's head. I don't know what it was, but he started to lighten up on his swing and I was able to hit the ball instead of missing it.

"Letting me win, Mr. Green Eyes?"

He shook his head with a smirk on his face. "Not at all."

I chuckled. "*Right.*"

We continued again as I panted all over the court, trying to catch up to the ball and hit it. The more I swung, the more I could feel my stress leaving my body. Rich could stay at work every night for all I cared. It was better that way. Sure he could still monitor me on the cameras in the house, but I wasn't walking around on eggshells.

After some time, I finally gave up. Sweat was running down my back and I could barely catch my breath. Lying on the floor on my back, I sighed. "I like getting sweaty with you."

His laugh could be heard around the room as it echoed, then he lay beside me, both of us staring up at the ceiling with florescent lights. "I figured we should at least pretend to play since we come in here sometimes."

I sighed, my breathing starting to even out. "I have to go soon."

He looked over at me, turning his head. "Yeah, it's about that time. Are you almost ready to leave him?"

I turned my head to face him. "Let's not talk about the plan. Let's talk about you. Tell me about yourself for a few minutes before I leave."

He turned and stared back up at the ceiling. "Well ... as you know, I was in the army—served for nine years. I always wanted to serve my country because my grandpa did."

"Why'd you stop?"

I started to think he hadn't heard me because it took him a few seconds to answer. "Got tired of the sand and shit."

It felt like there was more to the story, but I didn't press him. I knew a lot of soldiers suffered from post-traumatic stress disorder, and I didn't want to force Gabe to tell me until he was ready. We were becoming good friends; he'd tell me when he was ready—I hoped. "I bet. I can't even imagine seeing what you must have seen."

"Yeah ... Sometimes it haunts me."

Trying to lighten the mood, I asked. "Have you ever been in love?"

He didn't speak for a few beats again. "That's a story for a rainy day."

"It doesn't rain that often in Vegas." I laughed.

"Right," he mumbled. "Time for some coffee." He stood and held his hand out for me.

Call it a woman's intuition, but I knew there was something he was hiding and didn't want to talk about. I hoped once we were able to spend time with each other outside of Club 24, he would open up and tell me. I was already starting to care for him. Any man willing to help a stranger leave her abusive husband was a hero in my book and worth having as a friend—a *hot* friend with benefits.

"You look cute, princess," Rich said, putting gel in his light brown hair as I did my makeup. We were getting ready for his big party, and I just wanted to hurry and get the night over with. But instead, I had to play the perfect trophy wife with perfect hair, perfect makeup, perfect nails and the perfect dress.

When I'd tried on the black floor length dress at the store, I wasn't sure if I wanted to wear something so sexy. The slit was high— so high that if I sat down in an *improper fashion*, you'd see more than what Rich would deem acceptable.

But when I stepped out of the dressing room, I saw how Gabe looked at me, and I knew I had to buy it. And when I slipped it on after my shower, all I'd thought about was how his hand had slid up my thigh, seeking my pussy.

God, his touch. His touch sent shivers down my spine and I knew —I just fucking knew if we slept together he'd make sure I came first. None of the bullshit Rich did now, only thinking of himself. Gabe would please me, show me tenderness and then fuck my brains out after he made me come with his fingers and mouth.

But the person I was looking at in the mirror as we got ready for the party, wasn't Gabe—it was Rich. And he only cared about two things: getting himself off and getting me pregnant.

"You look cute, princess." Not beautiful. Not gorgeous. Not stunning. Cute as if I were a five-year-old girl getting ready for my first day of school. I was a woman dammit. A twenty-nine-year-old woman! How about sexy? Breathtaking? Good enough to eat?

I smiled back at him and prayed that I could fake it long enough for the plan to take full effect.

Be strong, Autumn!

Rich was dressed in a black suit with a red dress shirt and black tie. I used to find the way he looked in his suit intoxicating but now, as I stared at him through the reflection of the mirror, I felt nothing for him.

I was surprised how quickly feelings could change. It was as if each time he left bruises, a sliver of my heart died and eventually had vanished completely. I didn't think there was a rhyme or reason as to why people fall in and out of love, but physically hurting someone was likely reason to fall out of love. I wished that I wouldn't have been blind when I met him.

We met, we got engaged and married, all within less than a year. I should have known it was a recipe for disaster. Everyone was under his spell: me, my parents, Brandi ... Rich was a manipulator through and through.

But here I was, getting ready for his party and I was "cute". Well, la dee da.

"Thank you. Red looks powerful on you." Rich wanted all the power he could get.

"I want people to know who's in charge tonight, and red *shows* power. Thank you for realizing, princess. You just gave me the boost of confidence I needed for this evening."

I smiled as I applied a coat of mascara. "You're my husband. I know you like I know the back of my hand."

He chuckled. "Are you almost ready? People should be arriving soon."

"I am," I replied. "I just need to put my heels on and then I'm good to go."

He stepped to my side as I put down my mascara tube then grabbed my chin with his hand, forcing me to look at him. "It's been a long week. After everyone leaves, I want you to keep the heels on and nothing else while I fuck you. You're to be wet and waiting for me and not wet by the feel of your own hand. I want you thinking about it all night because I'm going to fuck you so hard that if you're not wet —well," he smirked, "then you're going to *bruise.*"

I gave him a tight smile. "I like the sound of that. I'll be wet and waiting."

Our house was decorated exactly as I'd envisioned. The inside had several small, counter-high cocktail tables scattered for people to use to mingle and eat. The lights were dimmed with candles lit on each table, giving everything an intimate feel. Soft music played on our sound system wired through the entire house plus the backyard.

Outside, poles had been set up to line the patio with white lights draped across from one to the other. More of the cocktail tables were placed around the area and around our pool that sat beyond the patio. A fire pit was set up in the center of the patio. It was a nice night, but a lot of our guests were nearby, grabbing a few minutes of warmth before moving on to get a refill of drinks or more food.

Rich introduced me to everyone I didn't know as they arrived. I kept expecting the one person I wanted to meet face to face to arrive, but as the house filled, Remo was a no show.

"You're breathtaking, sunshine," Dad said when he arrived, kissing my cheek.

I blushed. At least someone thought so.

"Autumn, honey. Everything looks lovely," Mom gushed, looking around as she spoke.

"Thanks, Mom. Lea, our event planner, and I arranged everything."

"Dan. Sarah. Please enjoy our open bar. Once everyone has arrived, we'll join you." Rich gestured toward one of the bars we had set up.

"Don't have to tell me twice." Dad laughed. Just as Dad passed, he whispered, "Sunshine, everything okay?"

I scrunched my eyebrows in confusion. He nodded his head slightly toward Rich when he wasn't looking and then it dawned on me. Dad knew there was a real reason I wanted to buy a gun. He was fishing for answers other than the lie I told him about impressing Rich by being able to shoot. I should have known better. Dad had twenty-nine years of practice catching me in lies.

I gave a tight smile then whispered, "Yes."

"If you need to go back, I'll go anytime. Just let me know."

"I will." I nodded, knowing he was referring to the gun range. I gave him a quick hug before they walked off to get a drink.

We greeted more people, then walked outside to where my parents were talking with some of Rich's cop friends.

"There's a lot of people here," Dad said, looking around.

Rich smiled. "All the important ones."

My heart dropped to the pit of my stomach as I watched another couple walk in. Our gazes met and I wanted to run, lock myself in my bedroom closet in the dark and cry myself to sleep only to wake up and realize it was just a dream.

But it wasn't a dream.

Gabe was arm in arm with a woman I'd never seen before. He didn't smile and I didn't smile. I stood there gawping as he stared back, unable to take my gaze off of him. So many thoughts ran through my head. How was it possible he was here? Who was he with? Was that his girlfriend? He'd never told me he had a girlfriend. And the most piercing question:

Did he know Rich?

I heard Rich mumble, "It's about time she showed up. Come along, Autumn. There's someone else I need you to meet."

I couldn't move. I mean, how could I? I wondered if Gabe was hired by Rich to be a spy ... he was always there. The gym, Starbucks, and when I'd told Rich I wanted to go dress shopping, Gabe just happened to be at the same store in all of Las Vegas.

What the fuck?

"Autumn. Come," Rich grunted with a snap of his fingers as if I were a dog—as if I was his little bitch.

Fuck ... I was.

I took a hasty step, reaching for Rich's hand so he could lead me toward Gabe and the mystery woman. As we moved closer, I decided to face this motherfucker head on. I straightened my back and walked with confidence toward Gabe, ready to pull him aside when Rich was busy and chew him out.

With just a few steps to go, Gabe turned his back on me. *As if that would work asshole!* I was furious, but I couldn't let Rich know. I'd know soon enough if Gabe was a spy. Rich would love watching my face as he introduced me to someone he knew I already knew— and spent time with.

"Trista! Can you believe it? The night's finally here," Rich beamed, hugging the woman with Gabe.

"I know!" Her smile widened and Rich stepped back.

"Trista, this is my wife, Autumn. Autumn, Trista's my campaign manager."

I shook her hand, plastering on a fake smile. "It's nice to meet you."

"I've heard so much about you," she gushed. "Let me introduce you to my *boyfriend*. Gabe, sweetie, this is Richard Jones and his wife, Autumn."

Gabe slowly turned. "Major," he nodded to Rich.

"Holy shit, if it isn't Captain Gabriel Hastings. I haven't seen you since—"

"Since we both left Afghanistan," Gabe finished Rich's sentence, sticking his hand out to shake Rich's.

I watched as they apparently got reacquainted with each other. My head was spinning. *So Gabe didn't know Rich was my husband? But Gabe had a girlfriend this entire time?*

"You two know each other?" Trista asked.

"I was his commanding officer," Rich answered.

Gabe's gaze fell on mine and we stared at each other again. I could tell something was wrong. His lips were pressed tightly together, his hands clenched at his side, and a vein was protruding from his neck.

It felt as if the floor was going to give way and swallow me whole. In fact, I wanted that to happen. I never expected Gabe to have a girlfriend. He'd never mentioned it, and he said he wanted to be with me after I was away from Rich. Was he just biding his time until then?

The thought of Gabe with another woman turned my stomach, but he had to know I was sleeping with my husband. And now that he knew who my husband was, he had a visual just like I had now with him and Trista.

"Sweetheart, let me get you a drink before Major—"

"Gabe, we're done with that. Call me Rich."

Gabe gave a tight smile with a nod. "Sounds good. Let me get you a drink before Rich and I catch up." He leaned over and pressed a kiss to Trista's cheek.

I wanted to break down and cry. This wasn't happening.

Trista nodded her head and said thank you. Rich turned to me, silently asking me to get him a drink as well.

I nodded back with a smile. "I'll go with you," I said as I fell in step with Gabe.

He looked over his shoulder then whispered as he leaned closer to me. "You mean to tell me that your husband is Major Dick?"

"Why do you care? You have a girlfriend," I hissed.

"She's *not* my girlfriend," he groaned.

"She just introduced you as her boyfriend, Gabe."

"I'm her date, not her boyfriend."

"How—"

"You need to trust me, angel."

I paused as we stepped in line for the bar. I loved when he called me angel, but now ...

"Please," he begged, "she's not my girlfriend. She wanted me to come with her tonight, so I came. I had no idea we were coming to your house."

"I didn't know you and Rich knew each other," I mumbled.

"Oh, we know each other all right. And since I know he hurts you—"

"No!" I shrieked, then lowered my voice back to a whisper. "Please, don't do anything. There are cops here and all of his friends. I don't want anything to happen."

The line moved up a step. "You have no idea how badly I want to go over there and beat the living shit out of him, Autumn," he groaned. "I care too much about you. And now that I'm face to face with him and have wanted to kick his ass for years—"

"Please," I whispered.

"If I would have known this entire time your husband was Major Dick, I would have come up with another a plan. A plan where he ended up not breathing."

We took another step forward. "You can't. We need to stick to *our* plan."

"Fuck our plan, angel. When Paul finds out who your husband is, he'll agree with me. We didn't call him Major Dick for nothing."

We stepped up to the bar and ordered our drinks. I needed a

drink. *Bad.* My heart and head were hurting and I didn't know if the pain would ever go away.

"By the way," Gabe started to whisper in my ear. "You know how much that dress turns me on. You're breathtaking in it, but I want to see it pooled on the floor of my bedroom."

SIXTEN
Gabe

Trista picked me up for our date in a black limo which made Jackson jealous. I didn't expect to be picked up in a limo, but Trista had said she planned to drink and didn't want to drive. I wasn't going to complain. I liked riding in style.

As we drove to our destination, she filled me in on our plan for the evening.

"As you know, you're supposed to be my boyfriend. I told my boss I had a boyfriend and I need to keep up that appearance." She took a sip of the champagne I'd poured her.

"Sure, no problem."

"Awesome. So just enjoy yourself and when asked—"

"I'm your boyfriend." I smiled.

"Exactly."

"Don't worry. I'm a good boyfriend." I winked.

I could see a hint of red on her cheeks. "I'm just nervous. My boss is going to run for mayor and I'm his campaign manager. Everything has to be perfect tonight."

"Mayor? That's awesome. Don't worry. I gotcha, sweetheart."

She took a deep breath. "Okay. Good."

When we arrived at the large brick house on a golf course, I took Trista's arm and led her in through the front door.

"We're a little late, so ..."

I heard Trista talking, but it was drowned out the moment I saw *her* standing next to *him* in the dress I'd dreamed of taking off *her* the night before.

Have you ever walked into a room and saw the person you loathed standing with the person you wanted more than anything in the entire world?

That was my reality.

Autumn was standing by Major Dick.

The moment her eyes met mine, I felt as if I were living one of my nightmares. This couldn't be happening. Major Jones ...

Fuck.

Autumn's last name was Jones. Realization hit me like a ton of bricks. My heart broke, my blood started to boil, and I wanted to run as fast as I could and knock Major Jones on his ass. I wanted to punch his face until he could no longer move.

"My boss is coming," Trista whispered.

As soon as she said those words, I realized that Autumn and Major Jones were walking toward us. Fuck my life. Not only was Major Jones Autumn's husband, but he was my date's boss and I had to pretend everything was normal—that I didn't know who Autumn was.

Taking a deep breath, I turned away from them, trying to calm down before I blew. I could feel Autumn's scrutinizing eyes trying to burn a hole in the back of my head.

"Let me introduce you to my *boyfriend*. Gabe ..."

Fuck. My life just got worse. I had to say Trista was my girlfriend ... I closed my eyes and turned around slowly. This wasn't happening.

I plastered on a smile while Major Dick—I mean, *Rich* and I got reacquainted. Autumn was silent as she watched. I knew she wanted to yell at me, but I was just as shocked as she was. I hadn't seen Rich in years. But he was still the sly prick I knew from all my years in the Army.

When he realized who I was, he pretended as if we'd never had words before. God, almost five years later and he was still getting under my skin. I didn't want to act as if we used to be best friends. I wanted to pull Autumn out the front door and take off in the limo, never to see Major Richard Fucking Jones again.

I needed to get away from him before I throttled him. I told Trista I was going to get her a drink, and luckily, being the asshole that he was, Rich made sure Autumn went to get him one too. I'd never have my woman get me a drink just so I could stay and talk shop. I'd get my own fucking drink *while* talking shop and I'd get my woman a drink while I did so.

As Autumn and I walked toward the bar that was set up, she confirmed Major Dick was, in fact, her husband. The same guy who continues to hurt her repeatedly. The same guy who had spies following her. The same guy who has security cameras around the house to monitor her every step. The same guy who I wanted to kill before I knew who he was. The same guy who I was certain I'd kill if he ever laid another hand on her.

Doing damage control, I tried to explain to Autumn that Trista wasn't my girlfriend, that she was just my date. She didn't believe me, but I begged her to trust me. Somehow—she did.

"Fuck our plan, angel. When Paul finds out who your husband is, he'll agree with me. We didn't call him Major Dick for no reason," I'd told her after she'd told me she wanted to stick to *our* plan.

We ordered four glasses of champagne after Autumn took two shots of Patron. I didn't blame her. I couldn't imagine being in her position. She probably thought I was playing her the entire time— that I was a spy for Rich. She blushed as I told her how beautiful she was tonight and I wanted to see the dress on the floor in my bedroom. She was like a drug—I wanted to consume her and become addicted to her.

"Was any of it true?" she asked as we started to walk back toward the front door where we left Trista and Rich.

"Was what true?"

"Everything you've said to me. How you feel ... the way you—"

"It's all true, angel. Not was—is. I had no idea who your husband

ANYTHING Like Me

COPYRIGHT

was and I want to run out of here with you in my arms and never look back," I confessed quietly.

"I can't believe this is happening." She took a deep breath and my heart ached as I saw how close she was to tears. I didn't want to see her cry. Sure this was a nightmare situation, but now that I knew who I was dealing with, Rich was going to pay. We were no longer in the army and he was no longer my commanding officer—we were equals.

"Everything's going to be okay. I promise."

She snapped her head toward me. "How am I supposed to walk up to Rich and pretend that everything's okay?"

"The same way you do every day."

"But every day it's because of you, and now I have to be across from you and pretend we just met and watch you and Tris—"

I grabbed her hand, loving the feel of her warm, smooth skin as I halted her just before we rounded the corner to the front door. "I'm doing Trista a favor. She told Rich she had a boyfriend and she didn't want to show up without a date. I'm just her date. You need to believe me."

We stayed staring at each other for what seemed like hours as I watched her question everything she knew about me in her head. Finally, she sighed. "Okay."

"It's not easy for me either, angel. I want to rip Major Dick's head off right now."

"Please don't," she begged.

"If he does anything to you tonight I will."

She took a deep breath. "He won't. He has an image to uphold."

I nodded. "We should get back to them."

She gave a tight smile as we turned the corner. Trista and Rich weren't standing there. "Um ... where'd they go?" Autumn asked, looking around.

I shrugged. "Don't know."

"We need to find them before Rich gets mad."

"Angel, he won't get mad in my presence. I can guarantee that—"

"No, but he will tonight when we're alone. He likes to remember things before bed."

I sucked in a breath, imagining the way Rich would grab her when he was mad. The way he'd punish her with sex. I hated all the images in my head, and I hoped my imagination was extremely vivid and not realistic.

"If that happens, tomorrow you're not returning home and honestly, I can't guarantee he will either."

Before Autumn could protest, Rich spotted us and motioned for us to come to them. They were standing outside near the fire pit, talking to people. After we'd handed them their drinks, Rich leaned over and whispered into Autumn's ear.

Acid rose from my gut as I watched him get close to her. I wanted to rip his fucking throat out and throw it into the fire in front of us. Instead, I stood there sipping the acidulous champagne, hoping the little bit of alcohol would calm me. Autumn nodded, then Rich walked a few feet and stood on the hip-high brick wall that lined the patio, clicking his champagne glass with a fork to get everyone's attention.

Autumn stepped closer to me so I was sandwiched between her and Trista. My arm was pressed into Autumn's as we made room for everyone to gather around. Reaching around with my hand, I moved it until I found hers then laced her fingers with mine. I needed her touching me. I wanted to comfort her, show her that no matter what, I was there for her. We were in this together.

Part of me hoped Rich would see. I wanted to see his face when he realized his wife he controlled was faking. That she was strong and was going to leave him. I wanted to watch his face as I left bruises all over his body like he did to her, then again as she left with me.

Fuck the plan.

I started to lean over and whisper in Autumn's ear that we needed to leave—that I couldn't take this shit any longer. I wanted to save her, and leaving her in this house with him was not something I could do. I was trained to protect, and I wanted to shield her from the hell she was living.

Before I could speak, Rich started his speech, his eyes scanning the crowd. I pulled back from Autumn. "Family and friends," Rich began. "Some of you approached me this evening, telling me you'd thought this was a surprise party. When I agreed that yes, this was indeed a surprise party, you all looked at me as if I'd lost my mind. I can tell you," he chuckled, "that I have not. This is, in fact, a surprise party, but the surprise isn't for me. It's for you."

People started to look at each other in confusion. I just rolled my eyes. God he was a douche.

"The surprise is I have an announcement. After months of consideration, I've decided that I'm going to run for mayor!" He smiled a cocky smile.

Gasps could be heard all around and Autumn squeezed my hand —hard. I'd forgotten Trista had told me her boss was going to run for mayor. Was this what Autumn meant when she'd said he was power-ful? Did he have cops in his back pocket? I wouldn't put it past him to corrupt people. He was a master manipulator; I'd watched him work first hand at getting his way with everything during our time in the army.

After the crowd had stopped clapping, Rich spoke again. "Thank you, everyone. Now please, enjoy yourself this evening, and when it comes time to vote, don't forget this face," he said, taking his pointer finger and drawing a circle around his face.

"See what I mean?" Autumn whispered. "A lot of these people are cops, or people who have pull in the city. I'm sure they're even on his payroll."

"I'm not scared of him," I whispered back.

Before Autumn could speak, Trista stepped in front of me. "Honey, let's go get another drink."

I gave Autumn a tight smile before I looked at Trista. "Anything for you, sweetheart. I'll get it. You stay here and enjoy the fire."

SEVENTEN
Autumn

SWEETHEART? HEARING GABE CALL HIS PRETEND GIRLFRIEND sweetheart did the same thing to my stomach as when Rich called me princess. I wanted to fucking hurl.

I couldn't wait for the night to end. I wanted to be at Club 24 in our racquetball court and be able to talk freely. To be able to laugh as he tried to cheer me up like he always did.

Gabe left me and Trista standing on the patio as I waited for Rich to speak with people. A few seconds later, Rich walked over with his receptionist, Trina. Her gaze adverted mine, but I knew something was up. She couldn't be here only for the party. I had to give her credit; took a lot of balls to come into my house. If it were a month ago, I'd be pissed. But now that I had Gabe, I didn't care.

"Trista, come with me. I want to introduce you to some people who we need to get on our side."

She smiled brightly as if she wanted to please Rich any way she could. "That's what I'm here for."

All three walked off, Rich not acknowledging me, and I was left standing by the fire pit alone. I looked around for my parents, Lea or Gabe, but I didn't see any of them.

As I stared at the orange flames, my heart felt as if it was finally starting to calm down after everything was sinking in. While Rich gave his speech, Gabe grabbed my hand and held it. It was as if he knew I needed the contact. Instead of only his hand, I wanted him to wrap me in his arms and tell me everything was going to work out.

He told me as much, but I wanted the warmth of his body pressed against mine. I felt safe with Gabe, and if I were in his arms, I would feel safer because he wouldn't let Rich touch me again.

Instead, I was standing alone while my husband tried to win over people to get their votes. I watched as he spoke and everyone laughed. I couldn't hear what was being said, and honestly, I didn't care. Come Monday morning, I was finding an attorney and filing divorce papers. Gabe was right; I should have done this a long time ago, but now I had support. I had support from Brandi and Gabe and Paul. I wouldn't need immediate money. Gabe and Paul were offering me their house, and I knew they'd feed me.

As I stared at Rich, I thought about how people would react when they found out he was getting a divorce. More than likely, they would never know the reasons, and I was confident he'd still run for mayor and feed off of being *lonely*. He didn't care about me. All he cared about was himself and wanting to keep up appearances.

Thank the stars above I wasn't pregnant with his baby!

"Want to slip away?" I stilled at the words being whispered into my ear until I realized it was Gabe.

Turning slightly I said, "You know I can't. He'll be pissed if I'm not in eyesight. Plus, there are cameras everywhere."

"I know, angel. Wishful thinking I guess." He shrugged.

I gave a weak smile. I should leave with Gabe—leave Rich wondering where I'd gone—make him worry about me and then *bam* —divorce papers.

"I'm going to go give this glass of champagne to Trista. If she doesn't want me to be with her, I'm going to come back. If she does—"

"I understand," I sighed with a weak smile and watched him walk away again.

After everything that had happened during the night, I hadn't been able to enjoy how handsome Gabe looked in his suit. It hugged all the right places, and when I say all the right places, I mean *all the right places*. Damn, his ass was perfect as the black slacks formed around what I assumed was a hard muscular backside. With the slight contact we'd had, I could tell everywhere was stone hard. And at the gym, I got my fair share of his sculpted arms and legs. I'd yet to see his stomach, but if it were anything like the rest of him, I knew it was rippled to perfection.

"Why the long face, sunshine?" I turned to see my parents standing next to me with concern in their eyes, bringing me out of my lust-filled daze.

"What? Nothing's wrong," I said, trying to pretend everything was okay.

"Don't you think we know when something's wrong with our daughter?" Mom asked with a slight tilt to her head.

I turned to them fully, ready to make up more lies, when a big, burly man ran past me. *Remo?* The man ran toward Rich.

"What's that all about?" I heard Dad asked.

I shrugged, not saying anything as I watched Gabe pull Trista to the side. I briefly thought Gabe and Rich were about to start throwing fists when I saw Rich wasn't looking at Gabe. He was looking at another man. A man I'd never seen before. And shielding Trina with his arm to move away from the angry man.

Rich and the man were toe to toe, and the man who I thought was Remo was within a few steps. My eyes darted to Gabe's and he was staring back at me. I gave him a questioning look and he shrugged, then grabbed Trista's hand and started to pull her toward me.

My sight fell back on Rich. Just as the man he was arguing with was about to throw a punch, the burly man stepped between them, blocking the blow. The man's fist collided with the burly man's chest, then he was hunched over, holding his hand as if he were in pain.

"We're gonna go," Gabe bellowed next to me.

I looked up at him, wanting for answers.

"Something's going on and I don't want Trista here. Do you want to come with us?" he asked.

"I ..." I looked between him and my parents. "It's that serious?"

"That guy who's yelling at Rich," he pointed in the direction of the swarm of men, "is making threats. You shouldn't be here, Ang ... Mrs. Jones."

This was my chance. My chance to slip away. Could I do it? My heart began to pound as I became anxious about the possibility.

"Come to our house, sunshine," Dad suggested.

I nodded. "Okay."

The five of us started walking toward the white French doors that led inside the house. I wanted to tell my parents if I went to their house my new plan wouldn't work because Rich would find me and bring me back home. In the few seconds we had to make a break for it, I needed to slip away with Gabe. I couldn't say anything because Trista would hear and tell Rich.

Fuck!

"Go get the car and then I'll be ready. I need to find Lea," I added, dodging people as they walked quickly out the door.

Out of the corner of my eye, I saw a circle of people standing where Rich had been. I was certain he was still there, dealing with the man who had crashed his party. Luckily, there was a ton of cops at our house and I'd recognized a few in the crowd of people. Whoever it was had picked the wrong night to threaten Rich—but the right night for me to escape.

I stepped around the corner to the kitchen to find Lea when I felt a hand grab mine, halting me. "Angel—"

"This is my chance, Gabe. I can slip away and hide from him while I file for divorce."

"Wait. What?"

"I don't want to go to my parents. I want to come home with you and put our plan in motion. It's perfect."

"Are you sure?"

I smiled. "I'm positive."

Lea went to rush past me and I grabbed her arm. "Hey, you need to go home. Shit's going down. I'll send you the money—"

"What about cleaning up?"

I shook my head. I didn't care how the house was left. Rich could clean it up or hire someone. "Don't worry about it. Get your staff out fast. I want everyone out."

"How are we going to get you to my house?" Gabe asked when Lea walked away.

I thought for a few seconds and then an idea came to me. "I'm leaving everything here because I'm certain Rich can search it," I said while walking toward a drawer in the kitchen. "Write your number on this and I'll call you to come pick me up after I explain everything to my parents. I'll be at their house."

He gave me a concerned looked. "Are you really sure about this?"

"Yes!" I shrieked. "We need to hurry."

He wrote his number on a piece of paper I'd gotten from the drawer while I ran to my room, grabbing my gun and my purse. I put the gun in my purse and threw my cell phone on the bed before going back to the kitchen where Gabe was waiting. He handed me the piece of paper and we started to run toward the front door.

The plan was in motion and I was scared shitless.

Gabe gave me one last look before slipping into the limo where Trista was waiting and I slid into my parents' SUV.

My heart felt as if it were pounding out of my chest as I kept looking over my shoulder out the back window, making sure we weren't being followed. I couldn't believe I'd left everything behind. I hoped once I'd filed for divorce, my attorney could get a few of my childhood photo albums back at the very least. I didn't need the clothes, the jewelry, my cell phone—all of that was replaceable.

"Now do you want to tell me what's going on?" Dad asked, pulling onto the freeway.

"I will once we get to your house."

"Autumn, this is scaring me," Mom sobbed.

"It's going to be okay. I promise." I reached over and placed my hand on her shoulder where she sat in the front seat. I didn't know for certain if everything was going to be okay, but it had to be.

We sat in silence as Dad drove to their home. I looked down at my hand where I had the piece of paper with Gabe's number written on it. I wished I had my phone. I wanted to hear him tell me everything *would* be okay and I wanted to be in his arms—safe.

Dad pulled into their garage and we all got out and went inside.

"There are some clothes in your old room that you can wear," Mom advised, turning on a few lights.

I looked down at my dress. I hadn't thought about changing or grabbing clothes. "Thank you. Let's all change and then I'll tell you everything." I started to walk down the hall toward my childhood room. "Dad." I called out, turning around.

"Yeah, sunshine?"

"Make sure all the doors and windows are locked and turn the alarm on."

He gave me a concerned look before he nodded his head and started walking the security system. I turned and headed back toward my old room. My head felt as if it were spinning and my heart was still beating fast. I didn't know how long we had, but I knew I needed to tell them what was going on. Once Rich found I was gone, he'd more than likely check at my parents' house first.

I pulled a few drawers out of my old dresser and found a pair of black yoga pants and a purple tank top. After getting my dress off, I slipped into the clothes and then went to the closet where I found an old pair of running shoes. I didn't know why Mom never threw my old clothes out, but at that moment, I was thankful.

Walking back down the hall, I sat on the couch.

"Well?" Dad questioned impatiently.

I took a deep breath, ready to tell them everything that was happening when I realized we needed to leave. No telling what Rich would do if he came to the house looking for me. "Actually, I have a better idea. We need to go to a hotel."

"What?" my parents asked in unison.

"I don't want you here where Rich can get to you."

"Autumn. You need to tell me what's going on!" Dad barked.

I jumped from my seat. "I will, but we don't have a lot of time. We need to go."

"Autumn!" he yelled again.

"Dad, please. You need to trust me."

"Jesus Christ, young lady. You need to tell me what the fuck is going on right now!"

"Rich isn't the man you think he is!" I yelled.

They both stilled and I imagined them holding their breath, waiting for me to tell them why.

"Look, I'll tell you everything when we get to a hotel far away from here. We need to be somewhere where he can't get to you and hurt you."

"He can't hurt us," Dad grunted.

"There's no doubt in my mind once he finds out that I left without a trace and I'm going to divorce him, he'll hurt you to find me."

"This is ridiculous," Dad grumbled.

"Please trust me. I've known Rich for almost four years."

"Let's just listen to her," Mom pleaded. "All of this is scaring me. I thought we were leaving your house because someone was making threats to Rich, not that you—"

"I know," I cut her off. "I've wanted to leave Rich for a while. We need to leave now." I stood, walking toward the garage door.

After my parents stared at each other for a few seconds, they finally agreed to go to a hotel. They packed a bag in a hurry and we took off for the strip. I convinced them it should be a hotel with a lot of people and not a little hole in the wall motel Rich could easily get into.

We stopped at the bank on the way, getting cash for a room because I didn't want Rich to trace their credit cards. I knew Dad wanted to wait to do anything until I told them everything, but he just nodded and did as I said.

After leaving the bank, we agreed on the Luxor hotel. My parents couldn't afford a few nights in one of the hotels closer to the center of the strip, and the Luxor was close enough for there to still be a ton of people around.

"We need a room for four nights," I said to the front desk clerk.

"Four nights?" Mom asked. "We can't stay for four nights!"

I turned slightly to her. "Mom, you gotta trust me."

Dad rubbed his forehead and I turned back around to the clerk. "Sorry. We need a room for four nights with a king sized bed if you have it."

"Where are you going to sleep?" Mom asked.

"I'll tell you everything once we get to the room."

Dad paced as I checked in, and Mom sat in a chair, her leg bouncing up and down. I wondered what the front desk clerk thought. We were all dressed in sweats, walking in to check in for four days without a reservation at eleven o'clock at night and paying in cash.

We rode the elevator up to their room. Once the door was closed behind me, I went to the phone and called Gabe.

"Hey. It's me," I sighed.

"Oh my God, angel. Are you okay?" Hearing Gabe's voice put me at ease. I wanted to break down and cry, telling him how scared I was, but I had to be strong in front of my parents. I couldn't let them know how truly bad it was. Dad already suspected, but if I stayed calm then he would too.

"Yeah, I'm fine. I'm at the Luxor with my parents."

"I thought you were going to their house?"

"We did, but I was scared for their safety when Rich comes looking for me—"

"Good thinking."

"I'm going to tell them everything. Can you come pick me up?" I turned to see my parents staring at me.

"Yeah, I'm on my way."

I rattled off the room number then hung up. "Okay," I groaned, turning around to face my parents.

"Who was that?" Dad asked.

"Sit. I'll tell you everything."

They sat on the bed while I sat in a chair and proceeded to tell them the truth about my marriage and about Gabe. Dad's arms were across his chest as he waited for me to start. Mom worried her lip and my heart was once again beating so fast I was certain it was going to fly from my chest and slam into the wall as it tried to escape.

"That was Gabe," I started.

"Who?" Dad asked.

"The guy from the party who told us the guy was threatening Rich tonight."

Dad's head tilted a little as he recalled who I was referring to.

"He's my ... friend and he's going to help me get away from Rich."

"Why do you need to get away from your husband with another man?" Mom asked.

I paused for a moment, searching their faces. Taking a deep breath, I decided I should tell them the truth so they knew how serious everything was. "Before Rich and I got married, everything was perfect. It wasn't until after our honeymoon that he started to hurt me."

Mom gasped, covering her mouth, and Dad groaned, bringing his arms down to his lap, fists clenched.

"It started off with a grab once in a while. I can't even remember how it started or why. I just know I did something to piss him off. It got to the point where he'd grab me so hard I'd have to wear long sleeves to cover the bruises."

I paused, swallowing the lump forming in my throat as I saw Mom on the verge of tears. "I hid it from everyone because I was scared of him. He started saying stuff that led me to believe he had people following me to make sure I did what I said I'd be doing for the day. I had to make sure I checked in with him when I wanted to go anywhere but the gym and to Starbucks. The first few times he *allowed* me to go to Starbucks, I made sure to grab onto it as one of my *approved* places. I needed to go somewhere other than the gym and home. And you know what? That's where I met Gabe a month ago. I know it's only been a month, but he's helped me come up with a plan to leave Rich. And tonight ... tonight I found out that Gabe knew Rich in the army—"

"Can you trust this Gabe fellow?" Dad interrupted.

I paused for a moment. I really hoped I was right. "Yeah, I can."

"You barely know him," Mom protested.

"I know, but we all thought we knew who Rich was and he turned out to be the devil."

"What happened at the party tonight?" Dad asked.

"I don't know." I shrugged. "I do know Rich's job isn't what we all think it is."

"How do you know?" Dad asked, crossing his arms again.

"I've heard him on the phone and he's said stuff around me. I don't know for a fact, but I think he hurts people when they don't pay him back the money he loans them."

"Like a loan shark?"

I snorted. "Yeah, like a loan shark."

"Fuck." Dad groaned.

"How is this possible?" Mom sobbed.

"How do you explain criminals? You can't. They are just bad people and somehow Rich fooled us all."

"I'm going to kill him!" Dad groaned as he stood and started to pace.

"Don't do anything stupid. Let me handle this," I protested.

"You're my daughter. I'm supposed to protect you."

"I know, Daddy, but I've thought a lot about this and it's best to just divorce him and move on with my life."

"If he's as bad as you say—he won't let you just divorce him," Mom advised.

"I know he won't," I sighed. "But I think he'll be less likely to do anything now that he's announced he's running for mayor."

"Aw fuck!" Dad groaned. "I forgot he's running for mayor."

"Tonight didn't go as planned. I didn't know I'd leave him tonight, but I saw an opportunity to slip away without him knowing and I took it. Gabe's been a part of the plan and I didn't know he was going to be at the party. Tonight has been exhausting and crazy and scary and any other terrifying words you want to use. I'm sorry I'm making you stay in a hotel, but I can't take the risk of Rich hurting you," I cried.

"Sunshine ..." Dad stopped pacing and reached for my hand for me to stand so he could wrap me in his arms. "I'm tough. It's going to take a lot more than some ex-army major to bring me down."

I smiled briefly. "Rich has people who work for him. Did you see that big ass dude storm in when shit went down?"

Dad nodded.

"I think that's his muscle."

"You forget I'm a good shot."

"And you forget Rich is too."

"Oh my God, I can't take this. This can't be happening," Mom said, starting to freak out as she paced back and forth at the foot of the bed.

Before I could say anything else, there was a knock on the door.

"Go hug Mom. I'll let Gabe in."

EIGHTEEN
Gabe

I REPLAYED THE MOMENT AUTUMN LEFT IN HER PARENTS SUV over and over in my head as I waited for her to call. I hated not being able to go with her, but I had to tend to Trista as part of my job. She'd hired me for four hours and while shit hit the fan early, I still had an obligation to make sure she was all right and safe.

The partition was down between the front and back of the limo, so I leaned forward and spoke to the driver. "Go to Trista's house first, then drop me off."

He nodded his head.

"Gabe, it's really okay," she said.

It wasn't. I'd never expected this night to turn into anything but me going on a date for work. Little did I know that tonight would be the night my angel told me the words I wanted to hear.

"I want to come home with you ..."

I texted Jackson a brief message that the plan was in full force and to clean up the house before Autumn got there. Of course, he'd texted back wanting to know what was going on. I'd explained I was still with my client and I would call him on the way back to the house.

I dropped Trista off at her house. We didn't have sex. There was no way in hell that would happen with everything going on. I knew if I wanted to be with Autumn, my days as an escort were numbered. I didn't have any desire to be one anymore. I had no void to fill with mindless sex. I wanted to know everything there was to know about my brunette angel, and if she felt the same way, I wanted to be with her as soon as possible.

Instead of calling Jackson as I'd said I would, I waited until I was home to tell him everything. I didn't know the limo driver, and with my luck he might work for Rich. Jackson was waiting for me on the couch when I entered. I smiled as I walked in noticing he'd lit candles. I knew Autumn held a special place in his heart too. Not the same way as she did in mine, but I knew he wanted to impress her.

"She's not with me." I laughed.

"Where is she?"

"She had to take care of her parents. She should be calling soon for me to go pick her up."

"What the fuck happened?"

I sat on the opposite side of the sectional sofa we had. "I walked in with my client and Autumn was standing next to Major Dick. It was surreal, man. I thought I was having another nightmare."

"I bet. When you texted me that Major Dick was Autumn's husband, I wanted to go over there."

"I'm just glad she's out of there now. Major will get what's coming to him. I'll make sure Autumn lets everyone know who their wannabe mayor really is."

I pulled my phone out of my pocket, making sure I hadn't missed a call from Autumn. I was beginning to worry, I hadn't heard from her yet. I gave Jackson a run down on what had gone down that evening and how Autumn saw an opportunity and left with her parents. Then I went to my room to change out of my suit and wait for Autumn to call.

I was beginning to become anxious, wondering why she hadn't called, when finally my phone rang with a local number. I breathed a sigh of relief when I heard her voice. She was at the Luxor Hotel and Casino and wanted me to come pick her up there.

The night went from good to shocking to heated to crazy to worried and now to one of the best nights of my life.

"I want to come home with you ..."

Smiling as I jumped into my SUV, I cranked the engine and then left to rescue my angel.

I sped down the clustered streets of Las Vegas as fast as I could. I still didn't know my way around that well, but I knew where the Luxor was and I couldn't get there fast enough with all the tourists. Jesus, it was almost midnight and the streets were still packed with taxis. Vegas was definitely the city that never slept.

I glanced out of the windshield into the night sky as I got closer to the light beam shooting straight out of the top of the pyramid of the Luxor. The closer I got, the more my heart pounded in my chest. I felt as if I were on a rescue mission again.

Of course, this mission was different. I wasn't in the sand. I wasn't with my crew and there wasn't anyone injured. But the thought of saving Autumn made my heart swell. We might not be together tonight, but once we've slept together, I wasn't going to let her go. I wanted to wrap her in my arms and never let her leave. When I was a kid, I'd thought my fate was to serve my country until I couldn't walk any longer. Over time, my destiny was broken. Now my future was to protect the angel who I was certain was sent to me by my guardian angel above who I'd lost five years before.

I finally reached the Luxor. After parking, I made my way to the room number Autumn told me she was in. My palms became sweaty as I raised my hand to knock. I didn't know why. I wanted this. I wanted her, but everything was sudden.

I knocked and waited a few seconds. It opened and my angel was standing there no longer in her beautiful dress I wished I could take off of her. Instead, she was in yoga pants and a tank top that showed off her curves. Her brown hair was pulled into a ponytail. She was stunning.

"Hey." I smiled, instantly calming when I saw her.

"Hi." She grinned back and reached for my hand.

I pulled her to me instead and hugged her for a few seconds. I finally had her in my arms and I was reluctant to let her go. "I was worried about you, angel," I mumbled into her head as it lay against my chest.

"I'm okay."

I looked past her and saw her parents staring at us. Whispering I said, "You have no idea how much I want to kiss you right now." I felt her smile against my chest and then I let her go and walked past her toward her parents.

"We haven't been formally introduced," I said, sticking my hand out to her father. "I'm Gabe."

He took my hand in his. "Dan. And this is my wife, Sarah." He nudged his head toward the woman who looked like a slightly older version of Autumn.

"It's a pleasure," I said, shaking Sarah's hand.

After closing the door, Autumn leaned against the dresser. "Like I was explaining, Gabe apparently knew Rich from the army."

I nodded. "He was my commanding officer," I explained.

"Tell us about him," Dan suggested.

Before I could tell them how much of a dick he was, Autumn spoke. "Not tonight. We're all tired and I want you both to relax and get a good night's sleep. I'll be back tomorrow and we can talk about everything. Try to stay in the room as much as you can." She turned to me. "Do you have a credit card I can use so they can get room service? I had them check in with cash."

"Of course."

"You don't need to do that," Dan protested.

"It's not a problem, sir."

"I want you two to be safe. And this way you can order in and not have to go downstairs where Rich can look for you."

"How will he know we're here?" Sarah asked.

"I don't know if he will, but I'd rather not take the chance," Autumn explained.

"It's not a bad idea," I chimed in. "He shouldn't connect me with Autumn, so he'll have no reason to trace anything of mine."

"Oh my God," Autumn gulped. "He'll see you gave me your number on the video cameras in the kitchen."

"Shit," I murmured. "I didn't realize that while—"

"I know. Me either. Everything happened so fast."

"Can you still keep her safe?" Dan asked.

"Without a doubt, sir."

"Please, call me Dan. If you're going to protect my daughter, we can be on a first name basis."

I smiled. "I'll protect her."

"What do we do?" Autumn asked, looking up at me with wide eyes.

I thought for a moment. "We can get a pre-paid credit card."

"Ahh. Why didn't I think of that?" Autumn pouted.

"It's been a crazy night."

Everyone nodded in agreement.

"Let me go get one and I'll be back," I suggested.

"I'll go with you."

"They probably just have them downstairs—"

"I want to go," she cut me off. "You two can shower and stuff while we deal with the card and put it on the room. We'll be back."

They agreed and we left the room to see if anything was open at this time of night. It was Vegas, after all. If I had to drive somewhere, I would.

"Everything's going to be okay." I grabbed her hand and held it tight.

"Hope so. I can't believe this is happening. It's as if I'm having a—"

177

"Nightmare?"

"Exactly."

I nodded. "I felt the same way when I walked into your house and saw you with Major Dick."

"I can't wait for this to be over," she groaned.

I pressed the down button to the elevator. "It's only the beginning, but I'm going to protect you, angel."

She gave a tight smile. "Thank you."

I brushed a piece of her hair away from her eyes that had fallen loose from her ponytail. "I hope you don't get sick of me because I'm going to be with you every step of the way."

"If I do, I'll go hang out with Paul." She laughed.

"He's excited for you to stay with us."

The elevator dinged and we entered.

"Really?" she asked.

"Yep. You won't even be able to tell that my house is a bachelor pad. He cleaned and lit candles so it smells nice now." We stepped into the empty car.

"That's hilari—"

I grabbed her face with my hands and silenced her with my mouth just like I had the first and only time we'd kissed before. I couldn't watch her mouth move any longer before I refreshed my memory with the way she tasted. She backed up, pressing into the back wall of the car, and wrapped her arms around my neck.

My hands stayed cupped to her face as my tongue slid into her mouth, sweeping a few times as it gathered her flavor. Touching, tasting and smelling her all at once was what I'd been dreaming about for so many nights. I wanted to stay against her forever. My dick started to stiffen as she moaned, kissing me back. I couldn't wait to be buried inside her, our bodies covered with sweat as I watched her come apart beneath me.

The elevator came to a stop and we broke apart, not saying anything as I grabbed her hand again and led her out into the lobby. We found a small store in the Luxor that was open twenty-four hours and I paid for a pre-paid credit card with cash. Afterward, Autumn put the room on the card and we went back to tell her parents we'd return tomorrow.

"Thank you," Dan said, sticking out his hand. I took it and we shook. "Please take care of my little girl."

"I will. She means a lot to me."

Autumn smiled warmly at me then said her goodbyes.

Holding her hand, I drove us to my place. It was going to be strange seeing her in my house. I'd wanted her there since the first day I saw her, and now everything was coming along as we both had hoped.

"You doing okay?" I asked, kissing the back of her hand.

She smiled. "Yeah. Now that my parents are taken care of, I'm wondering what Rich is doing. He's probably at their house now."

"Don't worry about him. Paul and I got you, angel. Tomorrow we'll make sure your parents have everything they need for a few days, and on Monday I'll go with you to talk to an attorney."

"I hope I can get an appointment that soon."

"If you can't, I'm sure I can find us something to do at my house." I winked. I felt her hand tighten in my own. "I'm just joking. I know it's going to take you some time. I'm not gonna lie though, seeing you in your dress tonight made my dick hard again."

"Rich said I looked cute as if I was a five-year-old," she mumbled, looking out the passenger side window.

"I can assure you that you didn't look like a five-year-old." I chuckled. "Rich is just a dick."

She turned her head back to look at me. "Are you going to tell me why you call him Major Dick?"

"I will, but we're almost to my house. How about I tell you in the morning after we get some sleep like you told your parents?"

She groaned. "Yeah, I'm exhausted. I'm not sure how much more information I can take tonight."

I pulled into the driveway of my house and we walked hand in hand through the front door. The candles were still lit and Jackson was on the couch watching TV.

"Auttie, it's about time you got here." Jackson rose and engulfed her in a big hug.

"Auttie?" I asked.

"It's my new nickname for her. Shut up."

I rolled my eyes. "Whatever, man."

"Thank you for having me." Autumn hugged him back. "I really appreciate—"

"Nonsense. Like I told Gabe, I've wanted to be a bodyguard. And to think I might kick Major Dick's ass ..."

"No, I get to kick his ass," I joked ... well, half-joked.

She sat on the couch and Jackson and I followed suit. "No one's kicking anyone's ass. I don't want to see him again until I'm in court."

"What about your stuff?" Jackson questioned.

"It's just material things, except the photo albums from my childhood I'd like to get."

"We'll go tomorrow," Jackson suggested.

"No!" Autumn shrieked. "It's too soon."

"Angel, it's better we get all your stuff now before he can destroy it."

"But—"

"He's right, Auttie. All three of us will go get your stuff, and you can tell Major Dick to fuck off and that you're filing for divorce. If he tries anything, we'll kick his ass. We've wanted to do it for years, and now that we know he's your husband, I sure won't be holding anything back."

"I won't either," I agreed. "Don't worry, he won't touch you anymore."

"I hope not," she sighed.

"One of us will be with you every time you step out that door." I pointed to the front door.

"He has muscle. Didn't you see that big ass dude run into the party tonight?" she asked, looking at me.

I saw the guy. He *was* big. Most of the time, those guys are slow and prey on scrawny dudes that can't fight back. I wasn't scared of him one bit. Once I got the upper hand, I'd be able to knock his ass out.

"You don't need to worry about us, angel. We got you."

"I hope you're right."

I saw her eyes start to close as she leaned back on the couch.

"Let's get you in the shower and then into bed, okay?"

Her eyes opened and she nodded with a weak smile. "Okay."

I took her hand to help her stand from the couch and started to lead her down the hall toward the bathroom in my room. Both Jackson and I had a shower in our room, plus there was a guest bath as well. I probably should have had her shower in the guest bath, but there was something about knowing she was in mine.

"I'll be in the living room when you're done, and then I'll show you to your bedroom." I kissed the top of her head and started to walk away.

"Wait. I don't have any clothes to sleep in." I walked to my dresser and pulled out a pair of boxers and a T-shirt for her. "Thank you."

"No problem. Tomorrow we'll make sure you get your clothes too."

She nodded and closed the bathroom door.

"Well, this shit just got real," Jackson remarked as I walked back into the living room.

"Yeah," I exhaled, sitting on the couch. "Crazy ass shit."

"Are you really sure we can take the big ass dude Autumn's referring to?"

"No doubt. This guy is huge, but just remember, light as a feather. We'll be able to take him. Let's hope it doesn't come to that though." I rested my head against the back of the couch as I thought about the evening. I was exhausted. "That reminds me." I lifted my head. "I'm going to put that gun I bought in the glove compartment in case we need it for tomorrow. If Autumn comes out, just tell her I left something in the car. I don't want her to know and freak out."

"Yeah, sure. No problem."

When I walked back into the house after putting the gun in the car, Autumn was still in the bathroom. I didn't hear the water running, so I waited for her in the living room until she was ready to come out of my room. She walked out dressed in my boxers and T-shirt and I smiled. I liked seeing her in my clothes. *I wouldn't mind seeing her out of them either.*

"Come on, it's been a long night." I reached for her hand to lead her to the guest bedroom. I wanted to bring her to my bed, but I knew she needed time to digest everything. She said goodnight to Jackson and then we walked down the hall. "Get some sleep. If you need anything, you know where to find me."

She nodded. "Thank you for everything."

"Anything for you, angel." I kissed her softly after tucking her in bed, then turned out the light and closed the door.

We continued to fire. I didn't know how many enemy troops there

were. I couldn't see with all the sand in the air, but we kept firing until the wind wasn't blowing and all the enemies were down.

"Everyone good?" I asked. I turned around to see one of my medics down. I couldn't tell who, but my heart stopped.

"Jackson!" I hollered as I ran to the down medic.

When I reached her, I fell to my knees, flipping her over —Cochran.

"No!"

"It's okay," Cochran mumbled, choking on her blood. "I like her. She'll be good for you."

"Who?" I asked, brushing her hair from her face.

"Autumn."

I awoke with a start, panting.

My door slowly opened and I could barely make out the figure entering. "Gabe?" Autumn called out.

"Yeah, angel. Are you okay?"

"Can I sleep with you?"

I smiled. "Come here." I pulled the covers back and she crawled in, moving until her back was flush with my chest. I wrapped my arms around her and held her, no longer thinking about my dream as a nightmare.

It was an epiphany.

NINETEN
Autumn

Every time I closed my eyes, I saw Rich's angry face. I knew the wrath was coming. Every scenario was playing through my head as to what he was doing in the moments after he realized I was gone and what he was currently doing.

Was he searching for me? Did he go to his office to check the security camera feed? Did he know Gabe was helping me? Did he go to my parents' house? Did he even realize I'd left? Did he care that I was gone?

As I lay in Gabe's guest bed, I started to freak myself out. I envisioned Rich crawling through the window ... hiding under the bed ... in the closet. I envisioned him breaking down the front door and getting to me before Gabe could. I couldn't take it any longer. I felt safe in Gabe's arms and I wanted to be there.

Pulling back the covers, I climbed out of the queen sized bed and down the hall to where I'd showered. I knew it was Gabe's room when he pulled out the boxers and T-shirt for me to wear. They smelled like him. Even though I tried to focus on his scent to fall asleep, I couldn't whenever I closed my eyes.

I slowly opened the door and called out to him. He was awake and let me crawl into his bed. The moment he wrapped his arms around me, my body touching his bare chest, I felt safe again. It felt right.

"You sure you're okay, angel?" he whispered against my shoulder.

I nodded. "Yeah. Just don't want to be alone."

"I got you." He wrapped me tighter in his arms and my backside nudged into his hardening cock.

Instantly my stomach dropped as he poked me. I didn't move away. Instead, I fought with myself. I wanted to be with him, but I was still married. I was married, but I'd left Rich tonight. In reality, I'd left him a month before in my head and heart—just not legally yet.

I needed to look toward my future now. All the pain I'd endured. The hurt, the fear, the lies—everything was now behind me. I was strong. I was a warrior and I deserved to be happy again. Gabe made me happy. Maybe he was only meant to save me from Rich and then down the road, we'd go our separate ways. I'd cross that bridge when I got to it, but here and now, I wanted him.

Most of all, I needed to erase Rich's touch. I knew that wasn't possible, but I didn't want his touch to be the last one on my body anymore. I wanted to know what it was like to taste more than just Gabe's kisses. I wanted to know what it was like to be touched in a way that felt nice again. The last time Rich and I made love, it was awkward. I'd still pictured Gabe even though Rich was gentle. I wanted to be able to leave my eyes open and the man staring back at me was the one I wanted to be with.

The night was a whirlwind and I was taking back my life finally.

Turning over in Gabe's arms, I lay on my back, his hand draped over my stomach. Without saying a word, I put my mouth to his.

"Angel ..." he mumbled against my lips.

"It's okay. I want this," I moaned.

He pulled back, breaking our lips apart. "Are you sure?"

"Yeah," I whispered.

Pausing, he stared into my hazel eyes and I waited. "Okay," he finally whispered, and without any more hesitation he returned his mouth to mine.

He tasted like a hint of mint as my tongue licked his. My heart was beating fast and my panties were damp with anticipation. His mouth moved slowly as if he enjoyed the way I tasted as much as I enjoyed him. All of our previous kisses had been rushed and cut short, but not this one. This was slow and passionate.

He broke our mouths apart again. "One last time to back out. I won't be able to stop when I have you naked."

I smiled. "I'm sure."

He lifted my shirt, pulling it over my head and tossing it on the floor. I was left with a bare chest, his chest brushing against my breasts as he hovered over me. I could barely see his silhouette in the dark room, only making out a few features as they were highlighted by the moon through the blinds.

"You have no idea ... no idea how much I've wanted to taste every inch of you."

I didn't respond. I tried to form words as he lowered his head and his mouth took a nipple inside. I tried. I really did, but none came to mind expect a slight moan as his wet tongue circled my puckered nipple. God it felt good to have his mouth on my skin.

His tongue did circles as his hand cupped my other breast in his palm. My body relaxed as currents washed over me and straight to my core. I'd always imagined Gabe would fuck me against a wall, a door, a car—hell, even on the counter at Starbucks. What I'd never imaged was the way he'd take his time exploring my body. While I'd thought I wanted him to rock my world, this was much better.

His mouth moved to my other breast being kneaded by his palm while that hand slid down my body and dipped into the waistband of the boxers I was wearing. The tip of his finger ran along the seam of my panties and I wanted to wiggle beneath him to make his hand move farther down. I was aching, wet, and so aroused, the slightest touch on my clit would probably send me over the edge.

Instead, his tongue worked my nipple and his finger teased my skin just above my coarse hair. I was panting, my head tilted back as I enjoyed his touch and waited for that moment when his fingers brushed against my center.

"Gabe ..." I called out.

"Shh. I got you."

I knew he did—in more ways than one, but the anticipation was killing me. I wanted him inside me, rocking against me as my legs held him close. I wanted to feel him. Hell, I wanted to run my hand along his stomach and confirm he had the rippled abs I'd envisioned. Instead, he was out of my grasp and I was laying with my hands to my sides, trying to fight the urge to slide up the bed so his hand would slip into the lips of my pussy.

Just as I was going to lose the battle with myself, his hand inched lower and I sucked in a breath, ready for it.

"How many times do you want to come, angel?"

My eyes flew open. "Wha ... What?"

"How many times do you want me to make you come?"

"Um ..." I was tongue-tied. Rich only let me get off once—if that.

"One, two, three—"

"Three," I blurted. I wasn't even sure that was possible. I was exhausted from the night's events, but thinking about Gabe making me come three times had me wide awake.

I felt him smile against my stomach. "Three's a good number for our first time."

I gasped when he said those words. One time was good. Two was better than good and three was going to be the most I'd ever had in my entire life in one night—shit in a row even. But more than three? I couldn't even imagine how that was possible.

"It's possible." He chuckled.

Did he read my mind?

"I—"

"Shh. Just relax."

I nodded and his hand teasing me at my panty line left my skin. I wanted to protest—kick, scream, cry. He lifted himself up, leaning back on his heels as his hands started to pull my boxers and panties down my legs.

"The more you relax and let me pleasure you, the better it will be. Trust me. I got you."

I nodded again, biting my lip as I watched his bald head slip between my parted thighs. The moment his tongue took its first swipe, my body jerked as pleasure rippled through me. He started off slow as if he were drinking my arousal with every lick. His tongue would swipe, one, two, and on the third time, circle my clit. I moaned.

"That's it," he cooed. "Just relax, angel."

I didn't know why he kept telling me to relax. I was relaxed. Fuck, I was so relaxed as his tongue continued to lick and taste, my back arched, my head tilted back as I enjoyed the pleasure. He worked my pussy to the point where my orgasm crept up on me and I didn't realize I was going to come until I was jerking with the wave as it tore through me.

"One down."

I had no idea how I was going to do that two more times. I hadn't come that hard in years.

My pussy continued to pulse as the aftershocks of my orgasm dwindled down. While I lay to catch my breath, Gabe got off the bed and went to the bathroom, opening a drawer and then returned, the bed dipping beneath him as he settled between my legs again.

"God, baby. You tasted so fucking good."

I blushed, still in a daze. His mouth came down on mine again and he kissed me for long seconds, the taste of mint gone and replaced with myself.

"Stay relaxed, angel. And no matter what, trust me."

I nodded in agreement, not realizing what he meant. I trusted him immensely and no matter what he wanted to do, I was certain I'd do it.

"Now that I've tasted you, it's time to feel how warm and wet you get around my fingers."

"Okay," I moaned.

He slipped a finger in slowly, my core still pulsing a little and then he slipped another finger in. Like his tongue, he started off slow. His fingers going in and almost completely out and then he increased his speed as my arousal coated his fingers allowing him to glide effortlessly.

Before I knew what was happening, his hand pressed against my stomach, my eyes opening with concern.

"What—"

"Trust me, angel. Stay relaxed and focus on the feel of how good my fingers are working your tight pussy."

"I—"

He shushed me again. "Trust me."

His fingers continued to pump, hitting the spot that did things to my insides and caused me to moan. I forgot about his hand on my stomach, focusing on his fingers and how good they felt inside me. I faintly registered that I might need to pee, but this wasn't the time. I wanted to feel the orgasm run through my body again.

It was as if Gabe had a special touch. He knew which buttons to hit and he was sure enough hitting them each time his fingers went inside and curled slightly. I knew within seconds I was going to come again. This time it didn't sneak up on me. Instead, it was intense as it started from my head and continued down my body. It felt as if I was going to explode from the inside out.

"Oh my God," I moaned. "Faster, I need to come now."

His fingers increased and so did the pressure on my stomach. My legs started to shake. I *needed* to come. It felt as if at any moment I would, but I didn't. His fingers continued their pleasure and I started to squirm, needing more friction and thinking that would send me over the edge.

"Relax," he whispered.

I tried. I really did. My hands were all over my breasts, squeezing them, playing with my nipples. My legs were still shaking. Just as I was sure I was going to come, Gabe removed his fingers and rubbed on my clit. My pussy was throbbing, aching with the need to ...

"Fuck!" I moaned as a rush of arousal gushed from my pussy, instantly filling the air with my scent. My body was on fire, I was shaking, *and fuck*, that was more intense than the first one.

"That's my girl."

"Holy shit," I exhaled. "Did I just—"

"All over my hand and the towel I laid out."

I hadn't even realized he'd gotten a towel while he was in the bathroom. "That's so embarrass—"

"Fuck no, it's not. Do you know what it does to a man's ego if he can make a girl gush like that?"

My face flamed. I was thankful we were in the dark because I was already embarrassed.

"Don't be embarrassed. It's the hottest thing, and I wish we weren't in the dark because I want to see it, not just feel it."

I was thankful we were in the dark, yet Gabe wanted to have a spotlight on me as I came. What do you say to that? I'd never squirted before and I wasn't certain I could ever do it again, but holy fuck did it feel awesome. I felt as if I could fly if I wanted to. As if I had all these magical powers because the pleasure was so intense that I was certain that since I had a taste of what Gabe could do to me, I wasn't going to stop wanting it.

"One more time, angel, and then we sleep."

Again? Oh right ... three times.

My body was in pure bliss. I'd never experienced anything that intense and I felt limp, wanting to simply roll over and sleep the night away. At the same time, I was still aching with the need to feel Gabe inside of me.

He left the bed again, this time I noticed the towel as he took it and threw it in the bathroom. He returned, standing next to the side of the bed, his boxers gone and his hard length sticking straight out at me.

Taking my eyes off of his cock, I brought my gaze up to his abs and sure enough, there were eight sets of them. The sight instantly turned me on again. I didn't think it was possible, but I was once again aroused and aching for his dick.

He slid a condom on and then climbed into bed again, my legs parting to allow him access.

"I'm going to try to make this slow, but I'm so ready to come, you have no idea."

I smiled. "It's okay. I've imagined you'd fuck my brains out before tonight even happened."

He smiled as he slowly inched inside me.

"Well then, angel, hang onto the bars in the headboard because I'm going to do just that."

And he did.

TWENTY
Gabe

I'D NEVER WOKEN UP WITH A WOMAN IN MY ARMS.

Before the army, it was a bang 'em and leave 'em kinda thing. With Alyssa, I'd never gotten the chance because we always had to cover our tracks in a hurry. With clients, I never had an overnight date like some of the guys. But now with Autumn, it felt nice, right—perfect as my eyes opened to see her smooth naked skin disappearing under my blue sheets.

I wanted to lay in bed, staring at her as she slept. She was finally relaxed and as she dreamed, she looked peaceful. I wanted her to stay that way because I knew she'd have a bumpy road ahead of her.

What I never expected was for her to climb into my bed and seduce me. It didn't take much convincing, but I was surprised, and once I had her naked, there was no turning back. I expected her to be resistant and not relaxed enough our first time, but she surprised me. It was as if she was made for me.

Dreaming about the way her pussy would taste or feel was nothing compared to the real thing. She tasted like cotton candy as her arousal melted in my mouth. The way her cunt tightened around my dick as I pounded into her was like a ride I never wanted to get off. God ...

Hearing her moan sent shivers straight to my cock. It was aching so bad to be buried deep in her while I fucked her with my fingers and made her gush all over my hand—I was surprised I didn't come when she did.

Thinking about what we had done the night before was making my cock throb. I wanted to take her again, hear her call out my name, and then go with her to her house and see Major Dick's face as he noticed how thoroughly fucked she was.

Instead, I slowly rolled out of bed and after throwing on a pair of sweats, I started to open my bedroom door but stopped. After everything she'd gone through the night before, I didn't want her to feel as if I'd left her.

Walking back toward the bed, I knelt down and brushed her hair away from her eyes. "Angel," I whispered.

"Hmm?" she responded, not opening her eyes.

"It's almost eleven. You can stay asleep as long as you'd like, but I'm going to make coffee. Okay?"

She nodded but still didn't open her eyes. I smiled because even though I was exhausted, I had a feeling she was more so. I wasn't able to hold back last night once I was inside her, and we went at it until she was almost asleep with my dick still inside her. There were two things I knew helped fight off nightmares. One was fucking until you couldn't keep your eyes open, and the other was downing a bottle of whiskey. Needless to say, we both slept well—I was sure of it.

I made my way to the kitchen for coffee where I found Jackson eating an omelet. He eyed me with a grin as I poured myself a cup of coffee. That fucking smug look on his face was driving me insane and I wanted him to spit it out.

"Go ahead," I sang, pouring vanilla creamer into the black liquid.

"I'm surprised you're able to walk this morning."

"So you heard?" I asked as I sat down across from him at the table and leaned back with my arms over my bare chest.

"How could I not? My room's right across the hall."

I shrugged with a smirk. "What can I say?"

"If you make women scream like that each time you fuck 'em, I'm surprised your clients aren't booking you every night." He chuckled.

I stilled. I'd thought I'd have more time until Autumn left her husband. Hell, I thought I'd have more time until we were together.

Were we together? There was no way she'd want to be with me if she knew what my job was.

"Fuck dude!" I hissed. "I gotta quit."

"Whoa, slow your roll."

"She's gonna flip when she finds out who our employer is," I groaned, running my hand down my face.

"She just left her husband. Give her time to adjust."

"Right." I nodded. Last night could have just been for the sex. "I was thinking though ..." I stood and went to the cabinet to look for pancake mix, "we can't do this forever. And if Autumn wants to start a relationship with me, I think I want to try."

Jackson set down his fork on his plate with a clink. He watched me as I read the box of pancake mix on how to make them. "And if she doesn't?" he finally asked.

I shrugged. "Maybe I'm ready to date. Like really date."

He nodded his head and picked up his fork. "Good, but don't quit until you find a girl. We have bills to pay."

I chuckled and shook my head, ready to tell him I could survive three years without a job with the money I had saved. Before I could, I heard the door open to my bedroom. I turned and grabbed the other ingredients in the fridge I needed to make breakfast.

"Mornin', Auttie," Jackson snickered behind me.

"Mornin'," she replied.

I took a few moments to grab the ingredients before I stood and turned around. When I did, I swallowed hard when I saw Autumn sitting across from Jackson as if she was meant to be there, still wearing my clothes. "Mornin', angel. Sleep well?"

She smiled, looking out the window toward the front yard. "I did. Thank you."

I waited for Jackson to chime in to give her a hard time about the fact that he heard us, but he didn't. "Like pancakes?" I asked.

She looked back at me, her hair framing her face as if she ran her fingers through it to brush it. "Who doesn't like pancakes?"

"I'm a waffle man," Jackson shrugged and stuck a bite of egg into his mouth. Chewing while talking, he said, "I love how the syrup stays in each square. You get the perfect ratio in each bite." Autumn and I stared at him, not saying anything. "What?" he asked, looking from me to her.

She giggled and I responded with a chuckle. "You're an idiot."

"It's true," he confirmed.

I turned around toward the counter and placed the ingredient down then went to get a bowl. Afterward, I made her a cup of coffee. It wasn't Starbucks, but vanilla creamer worked just as well.

I placed it in front of her. "Thank you." She smiled up at me, her hazel eyes shining from the light coming in the window.

"You're welcome." I returned back to making the pancakes.

"Let me help you. It's the least I can do," Autumn spoke, scooting the wood chair back against the tiled floor.

"I can make you pancakes," I protested.

"But you're letting me stay here—"

"I can cook."

"You can?" Jackson asked.

I shot him a look, glaring my eyes. "I can cook. I just don't since you do."

"Asshole," he muttered under his breath.

I chuckled. "Relax, angel. I'm making you breakfast and then we can go see your folks then go to your house and get your stuff."

"Yeah—I still don't want to face Rich." She crossed her arms over her chest and looked out the window again.

"Auttie, we've both been waiting for the day to nail his ass," Jackson said, pointing his fork at her.

"What did he do to you two anyway?"

Jackson looked over at me and I took a deep breath and nodded. "Let me make these pancakes and then we'll tell you."

Autumn got up and started to go through the cabinets as I whisked the pancake batter.

"What are you doing?" I asked.

"Going to set the table and get us something to drink."

I chuckled. "I'm tryin' to take care of you, woman."

"It's not a problem. This way we can eat faster."

I shook my head. "Okay."

Jackson finished his breakfast and played on his cell phone while I finished the pancakes. I served Autumn before we began to eat the delicious, fluffy goodness with no holes for syrup.

"So I'm not sure how much you know about the army or military for that matter."

She shook her head. "Rich barely told me anything about the army other than he was a major."

"Figures," Jackson mumbled.

"I'll try to tell you this in a way you'll understand. Major Dick moved up in the ranks quickly because to his commanding officers, he was always respectful to them. He manipulated everyone and people loved him."

"Like he did to me and my family and friends," she sighed.

"Sounds like it. And to the soldiers under him—"

"He was a dick," Jackson chimed in.

"But that doesn't mean you hate the guy so much you want to kick his ass," Autumn said, cutting another piece of her pancake with her fork.

"Right," I agreed. "Like I was saying ..." I glared at Jackson, silently telling him to let me tell the story. "Before we were deployed to Afghanistan, we were stationed together. Our whole crew. Me, him, Jackson and everyone else." I left out Cochran, not wanting to talk about her just yet. At the time my story took place, Alyssa and I hadn't started dating yet. We were only training together as a crew. "On Fridays we had what we called a safety breach during final formation. Major Dick would give his speech saying don't do this and don't do that over the weekend. There were also places where we weren't allowed to attend and they were on what was called a blacklist—"

"Why?" Autumn asked.

"In Afghanistan, they were places that could potentially have enemies lurking around. At Fort Hood, they were mainly places soldiers could get into trouble."

"Like?" she asked, leaning back in her chair.

"Like strip clubs." I smirked.

She smiled and nodded. "Right."

Jackson cut his eyes to me and I continued. "So on this one Friday, Major Dick said to not go to this particular strip club in the area. I can't remember the name."

"Sweet Tarts," Jackson recalled.

"Yeah." I laughed. "That was what it was called. Anyway, we weren't supposed to go there because it was on the blacklist, but it was the only one in the area and we were a bunch of soldiers who had already been to war a few times and didn't think some random ass strip club would be a problem. I mean, we wanted to see tits and ass like most guys." I chuckled.

Autumn shook her head and laughed. "So you guys went?"

"Yeah," I confirmed. "We went and watched a few strippers do their thing while we drank our first drink and then this guy," I pointed to Jackson, "wanted to get a lap dance—"

"Oh, shut up. You wanted one too, asshole."

I laughed. "All right, fine. We all wanted a lap dance. So we go to the semi-private room where they do them and when we walked in, guess who we all saw getting one?"

"Rich," Autumn whispered.

"Yep. Major Dick, getting his very own lap dance," I confirmed.

"So he's a dick because he went to a place he told you all not go to?" she asked.

I shook my head. "No. We all backed out of the room, but he saw us anyway. Seeing as though he saw us, we figured we should enjoy the time before we got into trouble. So we watched more of the pole dancing while Major Dick stayed in the room and got his dance. Afterward, he left, not saying a word. We thought he didn't say anything because he could get into trouble too.

"Thinking we were in the clear, we all got lap dances and then decided to call it a night. When we walked out into the parking lot, Major Dick was standing by our car. We walked closer and then he let us have it. He started going on and on about how he was driving by and saw our car in the parking lot and he couldn't wait to tell his commanding officer."

"He said he wasn't there?" she asked.

Jackson snorted. "Asshole denied it and said no one would believe anyone but him because he was a higher rank."

"It was his word against ours," I continued.

"So what happened? Did you get into trouble?"

"See that's the thing. Monday we go in and he doesn't say anything. He hung that shit over our heads until the day we left for Afghanistan. Every day he was a dick to us. Telling us that if we didn't do what he asked, he'd rat on us."

"But he never did?" she asked.

"Nope. We were furious, and he knew he was untouchable."

"Just like he thinks he is now," she murmured.

Both Jackson and I laughed. "He thinks he is, but he's nothing but a piece of shit, angel."

"I don't want anything to happen to you two."

"Nothing will," Jackson confirmed.

"I just want to get you your things and *if* he tries to start something, then I'll step in," I reasoned.

"I know. I just want this whole nightmare to be over with," she sighed.

So did I.

TWENTY-ONE
Autumn

My parents seemed to be taking this "on the run" situation as a mini-vacation. I didn't blame them. All morning, while they waited for me to come check on them, they stayed in bed and ate room service. By the time I arrived, they looked relaxed. I hadn't realized they haven't taken a vacation in many, many years—even if it was still in the city we lived in.

Paul came with us and helped my dad feel as if they could keep me safe no matter what the future held. He was hesitant at first, but none of us wanted him to get involved—not even Mom.

Gabe convinced them we were just going to go in and get some of my things. If Rich were there, Gabe and Paul would assess the situation. None of us knew what Rich was doing or how he was feeling about me leaving. I was sure he was pissed ... maybe even worried.

Rich needed to not be home so I could make a clean getaway.

Driving to my house was nerve-racking, to say the least. Paul let me sit in the front while Gabe drove. The SUV was silent as I stared out the window, my heart pounding with each mile we got closer. I didn't want to go back—I didn't want to see Rich again. I wanted to wait and let the court or our attorneys decide how to divide everything up. Once the boys mentioned Rich could destroy my things, it made me realize he could hurt me further by ripping up my childhood memories.

Rich was like a ticking time bomb. Whenever I did something to piss him off, he'd explode out of nowhere. I had never recalled a situation where I knew I fucked up and *deserved* to be yelled at—except for leaving him.

"It's going to be okay, angel." Gabe grabbed my hand, lacing our fingers and held it while he drove.

I continued to stare out the passenger side window, not saying anything until we pulled into my driveway. "You're not going to leave my side, right?" I looked at Gabe before we all opened our doors.

"Of course not," he replied.

"I won't either, Auttie." Paul reached forward and squeezed my shoulder. I didn't know what made these two men move from L.A. to Vegas, but I was grateful. Maybe it was perfect timing ... or fate.

Reaching into my purse, I grabbed my keys and nodded. We opened the car doors and after stepping out of the SUV, we began walking up the stone path to the front door. With each step, my heart thumped. It was as if it stilled because I had no blood pumping until I took a step. I was certain it wasn't beating the normal sixty to eighty beats per minute.

Before we stepped up to the door, Gabe reached out and took the keys from my hand. I hesitated before releasing my grasp on them. "Let's just leave," I suggested, looking into my reflection of Gabe's sunglasses.

"We're here already. I'll go in first and see if Rich is in there. Paul can stay with you."

I nodded and Gabe unlocked the door while I stood, looking out at the street every two seconds thinking Rich would pull up at any minute. Paul draped his arm over my shoulder and pulled me to him, making me feel as though he were my shield. Gabe walked inside and every second that passed felt as if it took hours.

Finally, Gabe came out and told us that Rich wasn't there. When we entered, all the tables from the party were still set up, empty glasses sat scattered around and everything looked intact until I entered my bedroom to grab some of my clothes.

Gabe grabbed my hand, halting me before I rounded the corner to go to my room. "Your room doesn't look like the rest of the house."

I turned my head toward him. "What?"

"It's not pretty."

I nodded, preparing myself for the worst and after he let go of my hand, I continued to my room only to stop mid-stride when I saw clothes scattered in the entryway. I gasped and covered my mouth as I stepped in further. There was a hole in the wall, my cell phone lay on the floor, shattered into pieces as if Rich threw it against the wall. The lamps on each nightstand were knocked over and onto the floor, their lamps shades smashed and each light bulbs crushed.

Every drawer in the nightstands and dressers were thrown, the clothes were strewn around the room. Everything I had on top of the nightstands, the dressers and on the en-suite bathroom counters were on the floor. Most of the stuff broken, the glass from the picture frames and my perfume bottles.

And lastly as I walked into the closet, I stopped, avoiding stepping on all my clothes that were tossed from their hangers. I turned, ready to head back and to the guest bedroom to see what Rich had done in that room. Instead, the moment my gaze met Gabe's, I froze, a lump forming in my throat.

"It's only material things, angel. Everything can be replaced," he reminded me, stepping toward me and catching me as I crumpled to the floor, tears running down my cheeks.

I tried to speak—to tell him I understood, but everything I'd once used or thought was pretty was now destroyed, and it was all because of my hasty decision to fly.

"It's going to be okay," he cooed, running his hand down my back and bringing me closer to him until there was no space for air to seep through between us. "I know you want to stay here on the floor and cry ... I get it. But since Major Dick isn't here right now, we should get what is salvageable and get out before he comes back."

He held my head to his chest as my body shook and tears continued to stream down my face. Sniffling, I finally stood.

Paul walked in a second later. "All the other rooms look okay, Auttie. I found these bags," he lifted a few duffle bags and a piece of luggage, "in the garage. There's also only one car in there. I'm assuming it's yours?"

I nodded, assuming the same, and turned back toward my closet. Gabe followed and we picked up all the pieces of clothing and stuffed them in the bags. I didn't have time to see if they were ruined; I'd do that once I was back at Gabe's.

"Can you fill those up with all the clothes that will fit? I'm going to go to the spare bedroom. There are a few boxes in there with my albums and stuff."

They both agreed and I left the room. Grabbing a chair, I stood on it and reached for the boxes on the top of the closet.

"Why don't you get your *boyfriend* to help you with those boxes, princess? Or is he not man enough to help you with the heavy stuff?"

I stilled at the words that rolled off the tongue of the man I didn't want to see.

Before I could turn around, I heard Gabe say, "I'm assuming you're talking about me, asshole?"

Rich was leaning against the doorframe, his arms crossed over his chest. He turned when I did as Gabe came up behind him.

"Tell me, Captain, did you think stealing my wife would somehow destroy me?"

My body tensed as I waited for Gabe to answer. I felt like a giant as I looked down on them from the chair I was standing on. My heart started to race as I looked on and my palms became sweaty. I wanted this to be a dream—to wake up in Gabe's bed again and stay there until I met with an attorney.

"I can't steal something that doesn't want to be with you any longer," Gabe barked.

Rich chuckled, still leaning on the wall. "Did you seek her out to get to me?"

"What?" Gabe asked, jerking his head slightly back in shock.

"You can't tell me it's a coincidence you two know each other and you're helping her?" Rich pointed his thumb toward me.

Gabe chuckled. "You're so full of yourself, even after all these years."

"You always wanted to get me discharged."

"This has nothing to do with the army, asshole. This has to do with Autumn!" Gabe snapped.

"And what about you, Lieutenant?" Rich asked Paul.

"I don't have to tell you shit," he hissed.

Paul stepped forward next to Gabe. I hadn't seen him until he did so. Then I saw Remo come around the corner and take a step too. I felt like I was trapped in the room. The only exit was the doorway that all four men stood in.

Rich snickered and turned his gaze back to Gabe. "I've been waiting for the day to fuck up your world."

Gabe stepped closer, getting in Rich's face. "My world? Your wife is leaving you."

Rich laughed again and looked over at me, pointing his thumb in my direction and said, "Her? I don't give a shit about her. There'll be others."

It felt as if time stood still as I tried to process what Rich had said.

Gabe grabbed Rich's T-shirt with one hand and stepped even closer, noses almost touching. "What the fuck does that mean?"

Rich shoved Gabe back a step. "You should know me by now, Captain. All my moves are calculated."

Gabe shot his gaze toward me and I stared back, unable to say anything. "Enlighten us, *Major*," Gabe hissed.

"Fuck off," Rich spat.

"Then tell me!" I yelled. All heads turned in my direction.

"Why should I tell you anything, cunt?"

I sucked in a breath as Gabe grabbed Rich's shirt again. Paul blocked Remo with his entire body the best he could and Gabe yelled, "Don't fucking call her that, asshole."

"I can call my *wife* whatever the fuck I want and I suggest you let go of me before my man here takes action." Rich nodded in Remo's direction.

"I'm not scared of either one of you."

Rich snickered again and Remo went to take a step to move around Paul toward Gabe, but Paul wouldn't let him pass. I stepped off the chair and begged for Rich to tell me what was going on. "Just tell me what you mean. If I'm replaceable, why are you even fighting us?"

"Because!" Rich yelled, snapping his head toward me. "It takes time to make the plan work. It's been four years with your ass and you're still giving me a hard time."

"What plan?" I pleaded, a tear rolling down my cheek.

"You think your tears are going to work? I don't love you, *princess*." Rich shrugged out of Gabe's grasp and Remo went to step around Paul again, but he blocked him.

"Then let me get my things and I'll leave you," I sobbed.

"That's not going to work for me. See ... you're part of the plan. I need a wife to win votes, and I'll be damned if I'm going to let your training go to waste."

"If you think I'm going to let her stay here, you have another thing coming," Gabe growled.

"Try something. See what happens when Remo knocks you out. You two assholes will be brought out to the desert and you'll never see her again."

"No!" I gasped, covering my mouth. This couldn't be happening. This wasn't the plan—my plan. Gabe was sent to protect me. He promised.

Gabe's gaze landed on me again, and as he spoke, he backed up and never looked away. "All right, let's go. Let me see what Major Dick has to offer," he hissed, beckoning for Rich throw the first punch.

I saw Rich's mouth curve, and before I knew it, Gabe landed a punch on Remo's jaw, sending him back a step. I didn't think anyone was expecting it. I jumped at the sudden movement and it felt as if my lungs collapsed and I couldn't breathe. This was all my fault.

As Remo tried to gain his balance from Gabe's unexpected blow, Paul rammed him, sending him to the floor. Rich rushed toward me, grabbing me by the hair and bringing his arm across my neck. I grabbed his forearm with both hands, trying to breathe as he tightened his hold.

Paul's gaze darted to me and he ran, ramming into Rich's side, and sending us slamming into the wall. Rich's grip loosened at the contact and as hard as I could, I elbowed him in the stomach. He hunched over, trying to catch his breath as Paul punched him in the face.

The room felt as if it were getting smaller. I couldn't breathe. I couldn't speak. I couldn't cry. Four men fought, each of them with a different agenda. Gabe was dodging Remo's punches, blood seeping from his lip as if Remo had landed one, though Remo looked worse as blood trickled from his nose and cheek.

I was certain they wouldn't stop until someone was dead.

I ran through the doorway, dodging Gabe and Remo, who were spinning around. I expected Remo to attack me, but Gabe landed another punch on Remo's face. Running as fast as I could, I opened the passenger side door of Gabe's SUV and reached for my purse. Pulling the gun from its sleeve and setting it on the seat, I started to look in the console for anything that could give me the upper hand. I didn't know what I was looking for. I had a gun I'd only used once and I was scared I'd miss.

There was nothing in the console. Then I opened the glove

compartment and saw the gun Gabe bought. After grabbing both guns, I ran back into the house.

"Stop!" I shouted, but no one did. "Stop!" I repeated. Still nothing. "Stop!" I yelled once more and cocked one of the guns. Nothing. I cocked the other. At the sound of the gun being cocked, they all stopped and looked at me. I pointed one of the guns at Rich and the other at Remo. "I said stop!" I barked.

"Angel ..."

"What are you doing, princess?" Rich asked, narrowing his eyes.

All four men were heaving, trying to catch their breath as I stood fuming, my arms shaking with adrenaline. "Don't call me that!" I snapped, glaring at Rich.

I saw Gabe and Paul out of the corner of my eye, slowly starting to walk toward me. My gaze met theirs briefly, and then darted between Rich and Remo.

"Give me one of the guns," Gabe whispered.

I shook my head, not wanting to give Rich or Remo a chance to act.

"Okay ... I'm going to take it. Just keep looking at these assholes." He reached out slowly, taking the gun from me, my gaze never leaving the other two men.

"Give the other gun to Paul," Gabe whispered.

Paul reached out and did the same thing Gabe did to get the gun. My hands dropped to my sides and I waited for more instructions. For a split second, I felt in charge. I wasn't going to shoot anyone. I just wanted them to stop fighting and let me leave. If Rich never loved me like he said ...

"You never loved me?" I asked as I remembered what he'd said.

Rich laughed and wiped a drop of blood from his lip. "I loved how you let me fuck you whenever I wanted."

Gabe growled next to me and my teeth clenched at the hateful words.

"So from day one you came up with this master plan?"

Rich rolled his eyes and laughed.

"Answer her!" Gabe spat, moving the gun a little as if to remind Rich he was held at gunpoint.

I saw the slight change in Rich's face before he spoke. Before he laughed as if this were a game, but maybe there was something in Gabe's tone told Rich that he wasn't playing around. I just wanted answers, to get my shit and leave.

"Yes. When I saw you at the bank the first day, I knew you were the perfect woman to be my trophy wife." He paused and I looked down at the floor trying to process how my life was apparently a sham. "I made you fall in love with me, making sure I did everything women wanted out of a man."

I lifted my gaze back up to his. "Why did you become controlling after and not stay sweet? If you had, I would have stayed with you forever. I loved you."

"I thought you were weak—too weak to ever leave me."

"Why not find someone who you could actually fall in love with?"

He chuckled. "When you have power and money, you get all the pussy you want. I didn't need love."

I nodded, feeling as if I gotten all the answers I needed. I didn't want to break down and cry and show Rich how much he was hurting me. The last four years of my life were a lie. I didn't need to ask him if he was cheating on me the entire time. He obviously was.

Gabe and Paul continued to point the guns at them as I went to the closet and retrieved the two boxes I wanted. They weren't heavy and if they were, I'd still load them into Gabe's car myself. I didn't want Rich or Remo to do anything. I wanted out.

Walking passed Rich with the last box in my hands, I stopped and stared him in the eyes. "You're an asshole," I hissed.

"I've been called worse, princess." He grinned.

Narrowing my eyes and without hesitation, I kicked him in the balls.

"You bitch!" he groaned, doubling over.

I didn't respond. Instead, I walked outside and put the last box into Gabe's SUV. They walked backward until they got to the front door and I heard Gabe warn, "Just let us leave and this doesn't have to go any further."

"Whatever," Rich replied.

I was going to find an attorney and fast because I was determined to take him for every penny he had. We'd see how much pussy he could get when he was broke and bunking with his man Remo.

TWENTY-TWO
Gabe

As we drove away from Autumn's house, my heart rate returned to normal. When she came back into the house with the guns, I became nervous. I wasn't uneasy as I fought off Remo—he was slow like I'd thought. What made me tense was Autumn having two guns in her hands and the possibly of hurting herself. She'd told me before that she'd only been to the range once. There was no way she'd be able to aim both guns and hit Major Dick and Remo if something were to happen. Using one gun with little experience was bad enough.

I'd expected Rich to follow us. Instead, as I looked in the rearview mirror, there were no cars behind us. I hadn't realized that Autumn had her gun with her nor that she'd find the one I put in the glove compartment. I was prepared to knock both Major Dick and Remo out and then leave with her stuff. I was certain I could take Remo. Yeah, he was big, but one cheap shot in the nuts and a right hook and he would have been out.

I was hoping that was the case because I really wanted to kick Major Dick's ass. Autumn went all Lara Croft on us instead and now Jackson sat silent in the backseat, I was silent and Autumn was silent, each of us probably thinking how crazy the situation was.

"You okay, angel?" I asked, reaching for her hand.

She only nodded, not saying anything and not looking away from the side window. She let me lace our fingers and I couldn't wait to be home and wrap her in my arms. Major Dick was a complete asshole and said things that shocked *me*. I couldn't imagine what was going through her head and I had no idea how she wasn't crying or at least yelling. I'd be yelling, hitting shit ... probably would have shot him in the nuts instead of kicked him.

We drove in silence until we arrived at my house. Jackson and I grabbed Autumn's stuff while she went to her room and closed the door.

"Should I go in there?" I asked Jackson as we set her stuff down in the living room.

He shook his head. "Just give her time."

"Right." I nodded.

We sat on the couch, both of us with our heads back. I was replaying everything over and over in my head. The moment I heard Major Dick's voice when I was packing Autumn's clothes, I became angry. And for him to accuse me of seeking out his wife to get to him was downright idiotic.

"Do you think Autumn thinks we planned this so we could get back at Major Dick like he said?" I asked, staring up at the stark white ceiling.

"Nah man. She knows he's a liar."

"I hope so. I really like her." I sighed.

He raised his head and looked at me and I looked over at him. "I know you do."

We were quiet again. I knew what it felt like to want to have time alone. After Alyssa had died, I didn't want to talk to anyone, not even Jackson. It was as though you needed time to process everything. Of course Alyssa dying was a different situation, but I'd think if she were to tell me she'd never loved me, it would have been worse.

"I have a date tonight," Jackson groaned. "I should cancel and stay with you two just in case."

I shook my head, looking up at the ceiling again. "We should be fine. Nothing links us to this house. The lease is under Saddles & Racks."

"All right, but if you need me, you call me right away."

I nodded. "I will." I paused for a few seconds and then said, "Speaking of work, I think I'm going to tell Doug that I'm out."

Paul sat up fully. "You want to quit?"

I sat up, my arms on my knees. "You know I just did this to fill a void."

"I know, but what are you going to do?"

I smiled my first smile in hours. "What about some sort of self-defense course, but we also teach them how to use guns properly?"

Jackson turned his head, looking past me as if he were thinking. "When you say "we"—"

"Yeah. You and me." I motioned between us.

"Hmmm ..."

"Think about it. You don't even have to quit S&R. But if I want this to work out with Autumn, then I need to have another job. I could always go back."

"That's true. Look into it."

Ever since Autumn told me how she'd bought a gun and I promised I'd bring her to the range to teach her how to use it properly, I'd had the idea of teaching women how to shoot. Of course, I didn't get the chance to show Autumn. If I hadn't been there today, I couldn't imagine what would have happened. Maybe she did it because I *was* there—made her feel safe, but not knowing how to use a gun properly could have turned into an atrocious situation.

Not only did I have the idea that if we taught women to shoot they could defend themselves against abusive spouses like in Autumn's case, but they'd feel better about living alone or even walking to their cars at night.

The real issue at hand though was if I should tell Autumn about my job or just quit and not tell her anything.

The sun was starting to set when Autumn came out of her room and into the living room where I sat and watched ESPN.

"Hey, you okay, angel?"

She nodded. "Can I get some water?"

"Of course," I said, starting to sit up.

"I got it. If I'm going to live here, I should learn where everything is."

"Okay." I smiled. Hearing Autumn say she was staying after everything that happened during the day, put me at ease. I was scared she'd believe Major Dick about me and Paul having some sort of vendetta against him.

She came back into the room with a glass of water and sat on the opposite side of the couch. I didn't know what to make of it. I'd expected her to sit next to me and at least lean her head against my shoulder so I could comfort her. She was being distant and I didn't know if it was me or everything else going on. I wanted to ask but didn't. After everything worked itself out with Major Dick, then we'd figure us out. That would give me enough time to quit S&R too.

"Can I use your phone? I should call my parents."

"Of course," I answered, and handed her my cell phone that was sitting on the coffee table.

She looked up the number for the Luxor and then I waited as she called and told them she got her clothes and things and was with me. She didn't tell them about the fight or that she pulled two guns on them ... or even that he said he'd never loved her.

I knew very little about Autumn, but from what I did know and what I felt like when I was around her, I couldn't imagine someone *not* falling in love with her. Even if Major Dick married her before he fell in love with her, they were together for almost four years. I was certain even he couldn't be that blind to what she had to offer.

"I will. Just one more day ... No, I'll be fine." Autumn sighed and gave me a weak smile as she talked on the phone.

I went into the kitchen to give her space and looked for something to make for dinner. I wanted to take her out to eat, like a date, but that probably would have been weird. And despite what Jackson thought, I *could* cook. If he were here and not on his date, I'd prove it to him.

"My parents said thank you." Autumn came into the kitchen and sat at the breakfast table.

"They're doing okay?" I asked, resting against the counter with my arms crossed over my chest.

"They are now that I called. I should have called earlier."

"I'm sure you were emotionally drained."

"Yeah." She nodded.

"Do you want to order pizza and watch a movie or something tonight?"

Her eyes lit up and I smiled. "I haven't had pizza in four years. Rich wouldn't—"

"Let's not talk about what he wouldn't let you do, angel. You're with me ..." I trailed off. I was going to say she was with me now *but was she?* She just left her husband and I hadn't been in a relationship in five years. "I mean, you don't need to do what he says anymore."

"Right ... Okay, let's order pizza!"

"What kind do you want?"

"Anything except olives and anchovies."

I chuckled. "All right. My favorite is bacon and jalapenos."

"Oh my God, that sounds fucking delicious."

"It is. I don't have it often though."

"Then it's like we're both celebrating." Her smile was intoxicating and I wanted to step closer to her and take her lips with mine.

I laughed. "Sounds good to me." I ordered the pizza and we sat on the couch—again not next to each other—as we watched ESPN. "Do you want me to change it?"

"No." She shook her head. "I'll let you control the TV for the night. Once I'm all settled in, I can't promise that I'll let you guys watch sports twenty-four-seven."

"It's going to be like that?"

She shrugged. "You wanted to live with a girl."

"I wanted to live with you," I blurted before I realized what I had said. Jesus, it was as if I couldn't think before I spoke around her.

"Then you're going to have to deal with it," she teased, sticking her tongue out. My eyes darted to her mouth and I licked my own lips, thinking about kissing her. "And no using my—"

I couldn't take it anymore. I sat up on the couch and leaned over, silencing her with my mouth. My hand went to her nape behind her long brown hair as our months moved together.

"—bathroom," she finished when we pulled apart.

I laughed. "I won't use your bathroom."

"Good."

"Do you want to talk about last—" I was cut off by a knock at the door. Autumn instantly tensed. "I think it's just the pizza."

"Right." She chuckled. "Rich wouldn't knock."

I paid for the pizza and set it on the coffee table. "What do you want to drink?"

"Anything strong."

"I have whiskey, tequila, rum ..."

"Whiskey and Coke?"

"A woman after my own heart." *Jesus fucking Christ. Me and my tongue.*

She didn't respond. I went into the kitchen to make our drinks. I was struggling with talking about the night before. I wanted to know what she was thinking—if she wanted to do it again. I sure as hell did, but at the same time I knew she was going through a lot.

I decided to turn the TV anyway and changed it to re-run of a cop show when I returned with our drinks.

"Holy crap, this is good." She beamed.

"Told you. It's spicy and who doesn't love bacon?"

"Very true. Ranch would make this better."

Yep ... She was after my heart. "We have some."

She stood and I didn't say anything about her going to get it. She wanted to feel as if this was her house and I wanted that too.

"I should call Brandi too, but her number was on my phone and I don't know it by heart." She started to put a dollop of ranch onto her plate.

"Actually that reminds me." I dug into the pocket of my jeans. "I took the Sim card from your phone. I bet it will work in mine."

"You're a genius!" she gushed as she stood to hug me.

"So what you're saying is we make a good team?" I smiled while holding her in my arms.

She looked down into my green eyes with her arms still wrapped around my neck. "Totally."

"Good." I smiled and gave her a quick peck on the lips.

She pulled away again and I swallowed my confusion down with a sip of my Jack and Coke. "Here," I said and handed her the Sim card and my phone. I turned my attention back to the TV while she switched the Sim cards out.

"I should probably use your phone after I get her number. I'm not sure if Rich is tracing my phone. He shouldn't since he broke it and plus I don't know if you can with Sim cards."

"I don't either, but no problem. You can use it."

"Thank you. And thank you for everything."

"I told you that I'd protect you, angel. I meant it."

She sighed. "I know, but I can't believe I pointed a gun in my husband's direction."

"Are you ready to talk about it?"

"Let me call Brandi first. I'm not going to tell her everything yet. Just that I left Rich and we got my things."

"Okay. I'll make you another drink."

"Thank you." She smiled and I left the room. When I returned she was on the phone, so I left her to take a shower, trying to wash the day away.

TWENTY-THREE
Autumn

EVERY TIME GABE KISSED ME, I WANTED TO DO MORE. MY heart was broken and even though I had my façade up, I didn't want him to only be a rebound. After a thirty-minute conversation with Brandi where I briefly told her about what had happened with Rich, I looked around for Gabe and he wasn't in the room.

Talking to Brandi put me at ease. Sure I'd been with Rich for four years, but why should I be sad? I had a man in the next room that since day one had shown interest in me, but ... so did Rich. *"Most guys aren't like Rich,"* Brandi reminded me. She was right. My heart would take time to heal, but if Gabe kept his word, then he'd help me put my heart back together again.

I faintly heard the water running in his room. Before I realized it, I was walking toward his bedroom. The night before when I was *with* him it had felt right, and even though I'd been withdrawn since we arrived home, I needed him to tell me everything was going to be okay.

I wasn't sure why I waited until he was in the shower. Maybe part of me wanted to see his naked body in the light since I didn't see it the night before. Or maybe my heart was telling me it was time to open up and let him comfort me. I knew he'd been trying to, but every time, I heard Rich's words in my head.

"You think your tears are going to work? I don't love you, princess."

I knew I was already falling out of love with Rich, but to hear him that he'd *never* loved me, was as if he took my heart from my chest and crushed it into a million pieces. For a month, Gabe had been like glue for me; making me laugh, smile, feel happy, feel wanted—cherished and I needed him now.

Walking into his bedroom, I closed the door behind me and stripped off the black yoga pants and purple tank top I'd been wearing for almost twenty-four hours. When we returned home from getting my clothes, I was too emotionally exhausted to even change into something clean. At some point, I fell asleep only to wake up and realize it wasn't a dream. Everything happened and my entire marriage was a sham.

The door to the en-suite bathroom was open and the water was still running. The steam from the shower was seeping out into the bedroom, and when I rounded the corner to step inside, I could faintly see Gabe's reflection through the foggy glass doors of the shower.

The mirror was foggy as well and before he saw me, I slipped over and wrote him a note on the glass.

Patiently Waiting,
You're more of an angel to me than I am to you. Thank you for everything.
-Your Angel

When I opened the glass door to the shower, Gabe stood in all his glory. He was under the spray, the water running down his entire body. I tried not to stare, but really, how could I not? His entire body was perfect. Every bulge, every ripple, every smooth surface. My gaze drifted over his body as I watched the streams of water run down his broad chest, his rippled abs, his hips that lead to *that* V, his hardening cock, his massive thighs, and to his feet before going down the drain between us.

I slid in, closing the door behind me.

"Angel ..." he whispered hesitantly.

"I said you couldn't use my bathroom. You never said I couldn't use yours." I smiled and bit my lower lip.

He chuckled. "I guess I didn't."

"Brandi says hi."

"Does she now?" he asked, the water still cascading down his body as he stood underneath the head of the shower with his back turned toward the tiled wall.

"She also told me to get out of my head because what's done is done and there's no going back."

"I'm not sure it's that easy."

We switched places in the shower and I tilted my head back to get my brown hair wet. "Maybe not. He's not broken up about it, so why should I be?"

"Because you loved him. You can't just shut that off."

I tilted my head forward, staring at him. He looked back at me and I saw it in his emerald eyes. He'd loved before and like most first loves, they don't work out. "You've been in love before?"

His eyes closed for a few beats before he responded. "Of course I have. I want to talk about you though. This isn't about me."

"Will you tell me about her sometime?"

"You want to know about my first love?"

I nodded. "I do. You know about mine. I'd like to know about yours."

He thought for a moment. "Okay, but not tonight." He reached for my hand and pulled me away from the spray of the water and wrapped his arms around me as I leaned on his chest, his chin resting on top of my head. "I want to talk about us. Not knowing is killing me, angel."

"I want to take it slow—"

"Of course."

"And what happened last night can't happen again for a while."

"Says the girl standing naked in my shower."

"Touché." I chuckled, still leaning into his hard body. "Okay, but not every night."

"Can't make any promises, angel. Especially when you crawl into my bed and walk into my shower naked."

"All right, all right. Just promise me that you'll always tell me the truth."

He pushed me a little until I was no longer leaning on him. "I'm not him. I've never lied to you."

A lump started to form in my throat remembering almost everything Rich had told me over the years. "It's going to be hard. You know?"

"I'm a man of my word. You should know by now."

A tear ran down my cheek, mixing with the shower water and running down my face. "Hope so."

"You'll see." He pulled me into his chest again and he held me. My tears started to flow, mixing with the shower water again. I wasn't sure if I was crying happy or sad tears. I just knew I couldn't stop them. "Want to watch a movie in my bed?"

"Is that code for sex?" I grinned, pretending I wasn't crying.

His chest shook as he chuckled. "Only if you want it. I promised you a movie and I want to continue to hold you."

"Okay," I nodded. "I probably can't sleep alone again either."

"That's fine with me. I liked waking up to you next to me."

I liked falling asleep in his arms. The way he wrapped his arms around me, bringing me into him until our bodies were touching. The warmth radiating from his body kept me warm. The way he kissed my forehead when he thought I was already asleep before he drifted off. And most of all how safe and comfortable I felt being in his arms. If I didn't know any better, I'd think I was already falling in love.

The next morning, I woke up in Gabe's arms. I didn't want to get out of bed, but I needed to get a new phone and call around to find an attorney. Knowing Rich, he had already retained an attorney and was probably going to serve me the papers at any moment. I wanted to be prepared for when it happened.

"Don't go. You're all warm and soft," Gabe murmured into my neck with his arms wrapped around me.

"And you're ... hard." I laughed.

"Another reason for you to stay."

"We're supposed to be taking this slow," I said, reminding him of our conversation in the shower the night before.

"This is slow. We didn't do it yesterday. We both fell asleep watching the movie."

I snickered, not saying anything.

"You smell good too," he whispered along my neck as he kissed it. "Did I ever tell you I love the smell of warm vanilla sugar?"

I drew my head back. "You know what my lotion is called?" When I put it on after the shower, I was in my room, not his.

"I just know the scent."

"How?" I questioned, chuckling.

He groaned, rolling over to his back. "I just do."

Silenced filled the air for a few minutes and I watched as he stared up at the ceiling. After a minute or so, he turned his head to face me. The moment our gazes locked, my heart tightened and I knew. "Your first love?"

He was silent again, staring into my multicolored eyes. With all first loves, there was a tragic story. Gabe knew mine and maybe one day he'd tell me his, but I knew it wasn't today. "Yeah," he finally said and rose from the bed.

I stayed in bed while Gabe left the room. He was the one who brought up the smell, and I was the one to bring up how he knew about it. I didn't know it was such a big deal, but apparently it was. I could tell he was still hurting. I didn't know when they broke up or how—I may never find out. Hopefully, since Gabe had dealt with his own share of heartbreak, he'd be able to help me with mine.

I found Gabe in the kitchen and we had breakfast and coffee. I thought about going to Club 24, but I was worried Rich would show up. The more I stayed away from my usual haunts, the less likely I'd see him. Afterward, we left to get my post-Rich life started by trying to get me some money.

Paul was still asleep when we left the house. Gabe mentioned that he had a date the night before and probably got in late. I still didn't know what the two did for work. It was Monday morning and they both weren't working. I asked Gabe again, but he only said he and Paul took time off to help me. He mentioned something about having clients with specific needs. Before I could get more details, we pulled into the parking lot of the bank where I'd thought Rich held our bank accounts.

I filled out the withdrawal slip and stood in line. I didn't know the account number ... didn't even know if I was on the account. Since I had worked at a different bank for many years, I knew if I wasn't on the account then I wouldn't be able to pull out any money.

"I'd like to withdraw money from my account, please." I handed the teller my driver's license and the withdraw slip. "I don't know the account number. It's under my name and my husband, Richard Jones." I smiled.

She took the slip and my ID and proceeded to type in things on the computer. "I'm sorry, I don't see an account under your name."

"It's under my husband's name, right?"

"I'm sorry but I can't give you that information."

I gave a tight smile. "Thank you." I turned around to leave, but instead turned back toward the teller. "Actually, can I do a cash advance on my credit card?"

"Of course," Jill confirmed. "It's a five thousand dollar maximum."

"Perfect. Let's try that." I didn't know how much of a limit my credit card would allow. I wanted to get the most I could get. I wasn't sure why I hadn't thought of it sooner.

I was able to withdraw the five thousand dollars and we left and went to my old work. I wanted to see Brandi too. When we arrived, Brandi beamed when she saw me. After helping a customer, she came over to us.

"So ... Guess I missed one hell of a party?" She laughed and sat down in a blue cushioned chair across from us.

"You can say that again." I shook my head, still not believing everything that had happened. "You should be glad you weren't there."

"I wish I was there because I would've helped you."

"It's okay." I looked over at Gabe and smiled. "This guy happened to be there and my parents helped me."

"That's crazy you showed up with Rich's campaign manager. What are the odds?"

"Small world." Gabe chuckled with a nod.

"Especially since you know Rich," Brandi said.

Gabe groaned. "Don't get me started."

"Anyway. What are you doing here?" Brandi asked. "Shouldn't you be in hiding?"

"Autumn's not hiding," Gabe hissed. "She has me and I dare Major Dick to try something again."

"Again?" Brandi asked, giving me a questioning look.

"Remember he showed up yesterday?" I asked. I hadn't given her every detail when I talked to her the night before on the phone, but I had told her he showed up at the house while we were there getting my things.

"Yeah, but you didn't tell me that something went down."

"Nothing really went down," I groaned. "Words were exchanged and that's it." I leaned back in the plush chair and crossed my arms over my chest.

She held up her hands in front of her. "I understand. You don't want to get into it now, but I want to know details soon. I know you didn't tell me everything last night."

"I'll tell you soon." I gave a tight smile.

"Okay, good. So what are you doing here?"

"I need you to withdraw the max from one of my credit cards as a cash advance and then open a checking account for me."

"Sure. No problem." She stood, holding out her hand. "I'll go do that right now."

I handed her my credit card and driver's license. While she was gone, Gabe let me use his phone to search for an attorney. I figured there was a slim chance I could get a same day consultation, but I wanted to have one booked before I was served with papers from Rich.

Growing up, I never thought I'd get a divorce. I'm sure no one does. My parents had a loving marriage and after thirty years of marriage, they're still going strong. You go into every marriage with thoughts of staying together forever—except Rich apparently. Who knows, maybe he did want to stay married to me forever and have his *pussy* on the side. The night Rich proposed I envisioned growing old with him, having children with him and being together until our last breaths.

It seemed as if everything changed in a blink of an eye.

Now a part of me feared I'd never trust a man again. Gabe was right, he had never done anything to put doubt into my head, but I barely knew him. I was already in a relationship with Gabe and it had only been two days since I'd officially left Rich.

"You okay?" Gabe asked.

I turned my head toward him. "Yeah, I'm just reading about divorces in Nevada. Apparently Nevada's a no-fault state and it doesn't matter that Rich cheated on me the entire time or that I basically cheated on him with you—"

"You didn't cheat on him. You left him and he knew you left him."

"I guess we can look at it that way. Doesn't matter though." I shrugged.

Gabe nodded and I continued searching on his phone. I found a few websites that said it would only take two to three weeks to get divorced if we didn't contest anything. I hoped that was the case because Rich owed me. My luck though—he wouldn't want to give me a dime other than what he was obligated to in spousal support. I'd be okay though. I didn't need his *filthy* money.

Gabe and I left the bank after Brandi opened a new checking account for me and gave me a temporary debit card. Afterward, Gabe drove me to get a new cell phone and then I called a few attorneys and made a consultation for Wednesday. I'd wanted something sooner but apparently, not only were a lot of people getting married in Vegas, but they were also getting divorced.

I programmed Brandi's number and my parents' number into my phone—my parents' numbers were the only ones I knew by heart. While we drove back to Gabe's house, I called the Luxor to check on them. They were fine and ready to go home.

"Parents are good. They're going home tomorrow. I think it'll be safe."

"Yeah," Gabe murmured. I looked over to him as he drove, silently questioning his response. "So ... Paul just sent me a weird text."

"About what?"

"He said the cops are at our house and he has to go to the station for questioning."

My eyes became the size of silver dollars. "Questioning for what?"

"He didn't say, but he did say he thinks they are waiting for us too."

I swallowed hard. "You think Rich called the cops on us?"

"And said what? That we kicked his ass?"

"No." I shook my head. "That we held him at gunpoint."

He huffed. "Let him. It was self-defense, angel."

"Oh my God, this is turning into a nightmare." I leaned my head back against the headrest, taking a deep breath while I closed my eyes wanting to scream or cry. "I should have just left town."

"You're not running from him. You're not hiding from him either. I'm here to protect you."

"He probably talked his cop buddies into arresting us."

"Even if that's the case, he needs proof."

"He has the camera feed."

Gabe huffed again. "Feed that shows we were there getting your things, then he came in and started a fight—"

I snapped my head toward him again. "You threw the first punch."

He was silent for a few minutes as if he was trying to recall what had actually happened. "Yeah, I did."

"What if his plan is to get you and Paul locked up and then come after me?"

I was on the verge of tears, a lump forming in my throat. Rich couldn't win this war. This wasn't fair. This wasn't right. He was an atrocious man—a criminal—an abuser and I didn't deserve to live in fear.

TWENTY-FOUR
Gabe

"WHAT IF HE'S PLAN IS TO GET YOU AND PAUL LOCKED UP AND *then come after me?*"

The closer I drove to the house, the more I wanted to turn around and drive off with Autumn and never look back. Fucking Major Dick! I didn't know if I was driving into my demise or if it was just another hurdle I needed to face when it came to Autumn. I didn't want to lose her. If I was behind bars, and so was Jackson, there was no way for me to protect her.

"If the cops arrest us, I want you to take my car and go get your parents. Leave town."

"I can't just leave you," she protested.

"Just leave until this blows over. I'll call you. I have your number now." I smiled, trying to put her at ease when in fact I was nervous as fuck.

"And if they arrest me?"

"It's going to be okay." I reached for her hand and held it in mine. "They can't hold you. You didn't do anything, and once they see the feed, they'll know that. I have some friends in L.A. you can stay with. Take my phone and get the numbers for Bryce and Cayson."

She nodded and grabbed both phones. By the time I pulled into the driveway, she was done and an unmarked police car sat on the street in front of my house.

"It's going to be okay." I grabbed her hand before she could open the car door. "Whatever happens, we're going to be okay."

She sighed and I pulled her toward me, before giving her a kiss. I didn't know when I'd get to do it again and I wanted to ingrain it into my memory just in case. The kiss wasn't like our usual ones. The way her mouth moved against mine was hesitant as if she wasn't sure what I was saying was true.

I didn't know my fate; I'd assaulted Rich, but Autumn—she'd be okay. If she stuck to the plan, she could be in L.A. and I knew my boys, Bryce and Cayson, would take care of her.

I grabbed her hand when I rounded the hood of my Yukon and we started to walk to the front door but were stopped by a detective.

"Mr. Hastings. Mrs. Jones. I'm Detective Evans and this is Detective King." He motioned to himself and his partner. Both men looked to be in their late fifties with peppered colored hair. They took off their sunglasses as they approached and I stared at them.

"What can we do for you, detectives?"

"We'd like you to come in so we can ask you a few questions about an ongoing investigation."

"Questions about what?" I prodded.

"Mr. Hastings, it would be better if you came by the station."

I crossed my arms over my chest, my legs spread a little trying to show them I wasn't scared when in reality I was. The more I thought about it though, the more I realized they weren't looking to arrest us. If Rich filed charges against me or even Autumn, I'd assume they'd arrest us right away and not *ask* us to go to the station.

"Now?" Autumn asked from behind me.

"Yes, Mrs. Jones. The sooner, the better."

"We'll follow you." I grabbed Autumn's hand to lead her back to the car. "I'm not sure what's going on, angel, but if Rich called his cop buddies or the regular cops, I'd assume they would have arrested me."

"Every scenario is running through my head," she groaned.

"Mine too," I admitted.

I used to think the only excitement my life saw was when I was with a client. One time I'd escorted a client to a female strip club. I was all for it. Trista and I met up with two of her female friends and they watched me get attention from the strippers. They thought it would be a turn on. So did I. But when we walked into the strip club, at least two of the strippers were pregnant and the thought of a pregnant stripper trying to entice me had the opposite effect.

"No. Just no!" Allison commented as we sat around the round dance floor with a pole in the center running to the ceiling.

I barely heard her over the music that blared, but it made me laughed. "They need the money for their babies."

That night I'd thought I'd officially seen it all—now I might be seeing the inside of a jail cell for the first time. Fighting with Major Dick, guns being pulled, and now on the way to the police station tops the most excitement I've had in five years.

TWENTY-FIVE
Autumn

W E FOLLOWED THE DETECTIVES TO THE POLICE STATION. I T WAS a request on their part, but I didn't want to add running from the law on my list of shit I was stressing about. When we arrived, I went with Detective King and Gabe went with Detective Evans to small offices.

I'd always pictured people being interrogated in a large room with a steel or wood table in the center, a two-way mirror that watched the interview from and being asked if I wanted something to drink so they can run my prints. I'd seen it enough on TV to think that was how the system worked. In reality, I was led to a tiny room with a small rectangle wood table that barely fit in the room. There were only two chairs next to it and a video camera hung in the corner that pointed down on the table.

"Can I get you a bottle of water?" Detective King asked.

I looked up into his grey eyes as I sat nervously in the uncomfortable metal chair placed in the corner at the end of the table. "I'm good for now. Thank you."

"All right." He nodded and shrugged off his black suit jacket, hung it on the back of the chair and then sat down diagonal from me. "Let's get started. I have a few questions."

"Okay," I replied, nervously fidgeting with my hands in my lap.

"Where were you last night?"

"With Gabe at his house."

"The entire night?"

"Yes." I nodded.

"And what time did you arrive at his house?"

I thought for a few moments. "I'm not exactly sure. Sometime in the afternoon."

"And where were you in the morning?"

"You want every detail of where I was yesterday?"

"Yes." He nodded.

I tilted me head a little as if to question what he was getting at. "I woke up at Gabe's house, we went to visit my parents and then I went to my house."

"What kind of relationship do you and Mr. Hastings have?"

I blinked at him. "Why does it matter? What is this all about?"

"Mrs. Jones, just answer the questions."

"We're friends."

He leaned back in his chair, setting his hands in his lap. "You're not romantically involved?"

"What does it matter?" I questioned with irritation in my voice.

"It just helps with our investigation."

"Investigation with what?" I was trying to stay calm. I didn't want to upset the detective, but I also hated not knowing what I was doing there.

"I'll get to that after you answer my questions."

"Yes, Gabe—I mean, Mr. Hastings and I are romantically involved."

"And you're married?"

I sucked in a breath. "Yes. Technically I'm married, but the last time I checked it wasn't illegal to have an affair." The words slipped from my mouth before I could process what I was saying. Maybe Rich had hired these detectives to find out how long Gabe and I were seeing each other. I didn't know what good that would do, but it was the only thing I could think of.

"It's not. When was the last time you saw your husband?"

I crossed my arms over my chest and leaned back in my chair to match Detective King. Of course, this was about Rich. "Yesterday afternoon."

"What happened?"

"Did he file a charge against me? Is this what this is about?"

"Mrs. Jones, please just answer the question."

"Fine. We went to my house to get my things because I was leaving my husband. He's not the man everyone thinks he is and I no longer wanted to be married to him. While we were there, he showed up and said some nasty things to me—"

"What'd he say?"

I sighed and looked up at the ceiling, taking a deep breath. "He said that he'd never loved me and only married me because I looked good on his arm."

"And that pissed you off?"

"Well, of course it did, detective." I hissed.

"Enough to kill him?"

I sucked in a breath again and stared at his face, not saying anything for a few seconds. "What?"

"Were you angry enough to kill your husband?"

"I ... You're ..." I paused again, trying to form the words in my head. "Are you saying Rich is dead?"

"You didn't know?"

"How was I supposed to know? I left him and haven't seen him in twenty-four hours." I looked down at my lap, feeling a lump form in my throat. I wanted to fight off my tears. Rich wasn't worth them, but my heart didn't know that. Detective King didn't say anything while I ran my hand over my forehead, still looking down at my lap as if I had a headache, thinking of how this was possible. "How?" I asked, not lifting my head.

"We're not sure yet."

I raised my head to meet his gaze again. "You don't know how?" A single tear spilled over my bottom eyelid and I wiped it away.

He shook his head. "No, we're still running tests."

"So he wasn't shot or something obvious?"

"No, we're still reviewing the footage from the video cameras in your house."

I scrunched my eyebrows. "Where? I don't even know where

that's kept."

"Your husband had an app on his phone that can play back live footage and anything within twenty-four hours."

"I always suspected he had the feed in his office at his work."

"We haven't checked there yet. If you could give me the address that would speed up this process."

I gave the detective Rich's work address. "Who found him?" I asked.

"His campaign manager Trista."

"When?"

"This morning. When he didn't show for their meeting, she drove to your house and found him."

"What about Remo?"

"Mr. Romero was found with him."

"Dead?" I whispered.

I didn't know if I should feel relieved Rich was dead or sad. Even though I hated him for what he did and said to me over the years, I'd never wish for someone to die.

I walked out of the tiny room and into the hall after the detective asked me every question under the sun. I didn't think I was a suspect, but he told me not to leave town. If they didn't find anything on the footage they retrieved from the saved feed, then I was sure they'd have more questions for me since I had motive.

"You okay, angel?" Gabe asked as soon as he saw me round the corner.

I gave a weak smile and nodded. "Yeah. I just want to go home …

Your home," I clarified. "They said they'd let me know when I could go back inside my house."

'Of course."

"So they told you?" I asked as soon as we shut the doors to his Yukon.

"About Rich?"

"Yeah." I nodded.

He sighed. "They did."

"Paul didn't have anything to do with it, right?"

He scrunched his eyebrows. "Um ... no."

"I know we didn't have anything to do with it since we were together," I motioned between us, "but Paul left and you said he was on a date."

"He was."

I stared into his green eyes before he turned to look back at the road as he drove. "Sorry." I sighed. "Everything's running through my head."

"I get it, but I know for sure that Paul had nothing to do with it."

"What if he did and you just don't know?"

"Because we're soldiers. If he killed Major Dick, it would have been by a gunshot."

I let out a long breath and stared out the passenger side window. "Right."

"You sure you're doing okay?" Gabe reached over and grabbed my hand, lacing our fingers and then brought it to his mouth to kiss the back of my hand.

I answered, not able to look at him. "As good as I can be knowing my husband's dead."

"Okay. If you need to let it out, you know I won't care right?"

I turned my gaze to his. "Don't think it's hit me yet. I'm still trying to process how this happened."

"Let the cops do their job, it's not for you to worry about, angel."

Gabe was right, but my brain wouldn't shut up. We drove not speaking again with Ed Sheeran serenading us. By Gabe's last question, he probably thought I'd be a bubbling mess. After everything that had gone on, I was surprised I wasn't. Knowing I'd never see Rich again was almost bittersweet. He could never hurt me again. I didn't have to hide anymore. I was free. Unless ...

"What if he's not really dead?"

Gabe grunted. "What?"

"What if he paid those cops to say he was dead so we put our guards down and then he attacks?"

"I know last night we were watching a rerun of Law and Order, but that's just TV."

"But we didn't see his body."

"They said they're running a tox screen. They'll contact you when it's time to bury him."

I groaned. "I know. It's surreal, you know?"

Gabe gave a tight smile. "Actually, I do. Why don't you call your parents and tell them they can go home and we'll meet them there and tell them everything?" Gabe quickly changed the subject and I didn't think anything of it.

"Can we go by my house first? If it is a crime scene, it should look like one, right?"

"Yeah, angel. We can do whatever you want."

I called my parents on the way to my house. Of course, my dad questioned everything, but I'd convinced him I would fill him in once we met them there. I also needed to reassure myself Rich was really dead.

When we rounded the corner onto my street, I immediately saw the yellow tape. A lump started to form in my throat again and my eyes started to sting. My breathing increased as I tried to keep my tears at bay.

"Angel—"

"Stop the car."

Gabe drove slowly in front of my house and stopped. I got out and walked to the sidewalk toward the yellow tape that blocked anyone from stepping onto my property. There were no police cars, no medical examiners—nothing. I didn't know how long it would take the police to collect all the evidence they needed, but it was getting late so they'd probably gone home for the day.

I ducked under the caution tape and took a few steps on the grass toward the front door. I didn't make it past the middle of the yard before I collapsed, the weight of everything beating down on me. The tears I was trying so hard to fight started to run down my cheeks. My body shook as I closed my eyes and let the tears try to do their job.

I felt Gabe sit down next to me and wrap me in his arms. "It's okay. Let it out."

"I don't know why I'm crying," I admitted.

"Because you loved him. Even though he treated you like you didn't matter, he mattered to you."

"But I didn't cry when I left him. Why am I crying now?"

"Crying doesn't always show weakness, angel. You were strong for so long maybe you feel relief that it's over?"

I nodded against his chest. "It is over, isn't it?"

"The living in fear part is over. Once they determine how he died, you'll need to deal with everything else, but I'll be here with you."

I nodded again as I wiped the tears from my eyes. Rich put me through hell and I despised him, but in the end, he'd made me stronger. I always thought I'd resent him, but the more he pushed, the stronger I got. He made me learn. He made my skin thicker. He made me—me. I was a fighter. And now that he was gone ...

I would no longer be the victim.

TWENTY-SIX
Gabe

I GROANED AS I CHECKED MY BACK OFFICE. FUCK, I HAD A DATE tonight. For the last few days, all my thoughts were of Autumn and what she was going through. I had no idea how I was going to slip away and go on this date.

"Is it okay if I go to coffee and dinner with Brandi?" Autumn asked as we cuddled on the couch.

"You don't need to ask permission." I laughed, but then stopped when I saw the expression on her face.

"Sorry. Habit." She shrugged.

I kissed the top of her head. "Go have fun. I have stuff I need to take care of."

She sat up and smiled. "Work stuff?"

I stared into her hazel eyes, contemplating if I should tell her the truth. I knew I should, but I didn't want to drop the bomb on her when she was finally in a good mood and not crying. Before I met with my client, I would tell my boss it would be my last date. After that, I'd finally explain to Autumn why I was an escort.

"Actually, yeah. I need to do some work."

"And what is it that you do?"

"We don't have time to get into all of that. I'll tell you tonight. Go enjoy your time with Brandi." I kissed her lips before she stood, then texted my boss and told him I wanted to meet with him before my date.

I arrived at S&R an hour before I had to pick up my date. I was to meet Liz for an early dinner next door to her ex-boyfriend's workplace. We never questioned why a client wanted to have a date a certain way. Usually with jealousy dates, the ex-boyfriends got one look at us and didn't do anything because most of the time we were bigger than them and much stronger.

After the date, the ex-boyfriends typically came crawling back because they realized what they had with the woman was something another man would want—and they didn't do well with having it flaunted in their faces.

"Gabe, what can I do for you?" Mark asked as I entered his office.

I sat in the oversized, plush black chair in front of his desk, crossing my leg over my other knee. "I know you transferred me because you needed more guys at this location—"

"Right." He nodded.

"I hate to do this man, but today's my last day."

He cocked an eyebrow and tilted his head. "Why?"

"I met this girl—"

"Ah, it's always about a girl. They don't like to share." He smiled.

I instantly relaxed and chuckled. "I haven't actually told her what I do, but yeah ... She probably doesn't like to share."

"All right." He nodded. "I'll keep you on the books just in case, but I'll make you inactive on the website. If you ever change your mind, or if it doesn't work out with your girl, you're always welcome back."

"Thank you." I stood and shook his hand. "I'll come by tomorrow to get my cut for this evening's date."

"Perfect."

"Oh, about the house. Is it okay if I stay? I'll still pay rent, of course."

"Sure no problem." He waved off my question as if it were ridiculous. "The house was rented so you two had a place to stay when you relocated. Since Paul's still living there, I don't see why you can't as well."

"Okay, thank you."

"Plus, I'm hopeful you'll change your mind and come back."

I chuckled. "Honestly, I hope I don't. I really like this girl."

And just like that, I was one step closer to starting a real relationship in—forever.

I met Liz at a small café next door to a coffee shop. After Liz and I had made introductions, we sat on the patio near the front doors.

"Every day after work, my ex buys a coffee from there." She pointed toward the shop and I turned around to get a good look because my back was facing the door.

"Why'd you break up if you don't mind me asking?" I asked when I turned back around.

"Josh would rather spend time with his friends than me." She shrugged.

"And you still want him back?" I took a sip of my ice water as I waited for her reply.

"We were together for two years. I still love him, and if he thinks I moved on then maybe he'll realize what a hot commodity I am." She smiled.

Women and their games. Sure this plan of hers might work, but if this dude let her go so easily, he didn't want her. Men fight for what they want or who for that matter.

"What do you want me to do when we see him?"

She shrugged. "I don't know? Flirt with me."

I smiled. "I can do that."

She looked down at her phone. "He should be getting off now."

We waited a few minutes and the moment her eyes became huge, I knew Josh was walking behind me. I grabbed her hand, holding it with mine and ran my thumb across her knuckles. She smiled, blushing as she looked down at the contact. I didn't know if she was playing her part or was really embarrassed in front of this guy.

My thumb continued to brush against Liz's skin and all I could think about was Autumn. Everything felt wrong as I sat holding Liz's hand. I wasn't looking into Autumn's familiar hazel eyes. I wasn't smelling the warm vanilla sugar I loved.

I let go of Liz's hand and her eyes dropped down at the loss of contact. My head wasn't in the game, but I needed to be on point and get it over with. I could see the end of the tunnel and it felt as if each minute was the equivalent to five.

"I think it worked. You should've seen his face when he saw us sitting here." Liz looked back up at the coffee shop's door and smiled.

"Not my first time." I stood and moved my chair next to hers. We waited, both of us not speaking until I saw Josh exiting. I leaned into Liz and whispered into her ear, "Is he looking?"

She smiled. "Yes."

I looked up, and through the veil of Liz's strawberry blonde hair, my gaze fell on the multicolored eyes I wanted to look into forever.

"Fuck," I murmured.

"What?" Liz asked through clenched teeth as she continued to smile.

I didn't respond. My stare didn't leave Autumn's as she stood, Brandi's passenger side door's handle in her hand. I didn't know why she and Brandi were here, but it wasn't going to turn out good for me. The look on her face broke my heart into a thousand pieces.

I should have told her sooner, but everything had happened too fast. I needed to explain myself, but I didn't have the time at the moment because my *date* was questioning what was happening.

"What is it Gabe?" Liz asked, her stare still on the coffee shop.

I broke my gaze from Autumn's briefly and leaned away from Liz. "Nothing, I'll be right back." I went to stand, but Autumn slid into the opened door of Brandi's car. "Fuck!"

"What's going on?" Liz questioned.

I didn't know what to do—I felt as if I were trapped in a Plexiglas box with no way out. "Sorry. Is he still here?" I asked, looking toward the coffee shop door. Josh was staring at us, so I sat back in my chair and whispered in her ear, "The girl I want to start a relationship with just saw us. She doesn't know what I do for a living and I need to cut this date short and run after her. I need you to start laughing like I'm telling you funny shit then lean your head down like you're blushing. You help me out and I'll refund you your money."

She lifted her head and our gazes met. "Are you serious?"

I looked over at Josh and then quickly back to Liz. "Yes, he's still standing there so just pretend I'm whispering sweet nothings into your ear until he leaves. I bet he'll call you tonight."

"You think so?" she whispered.

"Well, he's still standing there." I reached into the pocket of my leather jacket and grabbed my cell phone. I wanted to go after Autumn, but a text would have to do for the five minutes I needed to finish this *date* with Liz.

"And he's staring at us," she murmured and looked down at my hand that held my phone. "You need to call her?"

"I'd like to, but I can't. I can't imagine what she's thinking right now."

"Well, it looks like Josh is leaving. Go ahead and call her."

I lifted my head and sure enough Josh was leaving. "If he doesn't call by tomorrow, I'll set you up on a free date with my friend Paul. He's a great guy and *very* single. I'm sorry this turned out this way."

"It's okay."

"Let me walk you to your car just in case Josh is still here."

"Okay." She smiled and stood. "You're a great guy, Gabe. I hope it works out for you."

"Thank you."

Me: *Angel, it's not what you think. Please meet me at home. I'm on my way.*

I grabbed Liz's hand and laced our fingers. Autumn was long gone and Liz needed this if Josh was spying on us. "I'll handle your payment with Saddles & Rack, but call me if it doesn't work out with Josh and I'll get my buddy to do a better job." She handed me her phone and I entered my number for her.

I jogged to my Yukon in hopes Autumn would be waiting for me at home.

TWENTY-SEVEN
Autumn

I SHOULD HAVE KNOWN GOING TO A NEW COFFEE SHOP wouldn't be a good thing. Brandi wanted to grab coffee and dinner near the movie theater where we decided we wanted to see a new movie at. I still hadn't told Gabe we were going to a movie, but I knew he wouldn't care. He wasn't like Rich.

Or so I thought.

The moment my gaze fell on Gabe's and the woman with the strawberry blonde hair, I knew I was right about one thing—Gabe wouldn't give a shit where I was. I just didn't know it was because he was out with another woman. I couldn't believe my eyes. We were just starting our relationship and since we had been together, we were inseparable. I'd had no idea he was seeing someone else.

"Who was that?" Brandi asked, pulling out of the parking lot.

"His ... Gabe's ..." I couldn't finish the sentence.

"His girlfriend?"

"What did it look like to you?" I asked, staring out the windshield.

"It looked like he was cozy as fuck with her."

"I know," I sighed.

We'd sat in silence for a few seconds before Brandi asked, "Do you still want to go to the movies or should I take you home?"

"Home ..."

Where was home? The house Rich died in? Gabe and Paul's house? Did I even have a house to call home?

"No. You know what, B, let's go out drinking. Fuck this shit, I'm single. I can do whatever I want to."

"Are you sure about this?"

"Should I just go back to Gabe's and wait for him to tell me another lie?"

"No, you're right. Fuck the movie. Let's go have shots!"

By the time we arrived at Blue Martini, it felt as if my life was spiraling out of control. I didn't know when my life had changed. Maybe it was the moment I'd decided to leave Rich, or maybe it was the moment I bumped into Gabe.

The man I was married to was dead.

The man I wanted as a possible boyfriend was out with another woman.

I grabbed my phone, my ID, and some money to stick into my pocket because I didn't want to carry my purse into the bar. I noticed I had a missed text message:

Gabe: *Angel, it's not what you think. Please meet me at home. I'm on my way.*

I groaned. It's not what I think? What was I supposed to think? He was up close and personal with some chick and it's not what I think?

Whatever.

I didn't respond, and I sure as hell wasn't about to run *home.* I stuffed my cell phone in the back pocket of my jeans and rounded the hood of the car to wait for Brandi to be ready.

"I'll buy you your first shot." Brandi smiled as we walked toward the entrance of the bar.

I smiled back. "Thanks."

We made a beeline for the heavy oak bar.

"What do you want?" Brandi asked as we waited in line.

"Fireball, of course."

Brandi laughed. "It's a cinnamon whiskey kinda night?"

"Damn straight. I'm tired of men fucking with my life."

"That'a girl, let's get you drunk." She laughed.

As Brandi ordered our shots, I scanned the floor. I wasn't looking for a new guy to be with long term, but I was definitely looking for someone who would take my mind off Gabe and whatever he was doing with that redhead.

I felt my cell phone vibrating in my pocket. I knew who it was, but I still didn't want to deal with Gabe. I needed to be at least tipsy while Gabe told me what he was doing so I didn't yell in his face.

"Here you go." Brandi handed me the shot glass filled with amber liquor.

I turned and took the glass from her hand. "Here's to it and to it again. If you ever get to it and can't do it, I'll strap you to it until you learn how to do it." We clinked glasses and downed the fiery goodness.

She laughed. "What the hell was that?"

I giggled. "I don't know, but it's something my dad always says."

We sat our empty shot glasses on the bar and then moved to a table that had opened up nearby. I watched as people danced, enjoying the live band, and having a good time. That's what I should've been doing—having a good time and not thinking about Mr. Green Eyes. But I needed more liquid courage before I could dance with strangers.

"How are your parents taking everything?" Brandi asked.

I shrugged. "As good as they could be. I know this is bad to say, but I think my parents are relieved that Rich is dead. I know they liked him a lot, but after finding out what he did to me over the years, it's a relief."

"It's totally a relief. We all liked Rich, but we all didn't know the real Rich. Not even you."

"I know," I sighed. "Let's not talk about the past." I groaned. "I was really starting to like Gabe. I can't believe he's out with another woman."

A waitress came over and we each ordered a shot of Fireball and a Jack and Coke.

"He hasn't called you or anything?"

"He texted me saying some bullshit that it wasn't what I think and to meet him at home."

There was that word again. *Home.* In the short time I was living with Gabe, it had really started to feel like home. But now the word felt foreign on my tongue.

It had almost been a week since Rich died. I was still waiting to hear how. I was told he was poisoned, and we weren't allowed to leave town because they had yet to determine how and by what. My house was no longer an active crime scene, but I still couldn't bear being there at night by myself. Gabe had offered to stay with me—to make me feel safe, but even though it was my house, I still felt as if Gabe didn't belong. I needed to sell the house and buy one of my own. It needed to be something new in my life—like a new beginning and I thought all along Gabe would be my new beginning.

"Maybe he has a good reason for being out with some chick?"

"Come on, B. What *good* reason could he possibly have? He told me he had some *business* to take care of. That didn't look like business to me."

The waitress returned with our drinks.

"All I'm saying is that Gabe has been nothing but a good guy toward you. He hasn't shown you once that he has anything to hide, right?"

I stop swirling my straw in my drink. "Except his job. Every time I ask him about his job, he changes the subject or we get interrupted. He hasn't told me what he or Paul do for a living. Do you know what Paul does for a living ... What are you doing here?" I asked, looking over as both Gabe and Paul walked to our table and stopped in front of us.

"I need to explain," Gabe professed. "But not here. Please come back *home* and I'll tell you everything. I promise."

"Don't you see I'm out with my friend? Why don't you return back to *your* friend? You two looked very co—"

"Stop. Please, angel," he pleaded.

246

"Let's all four go back to our place. Brandi needs to hear this too," Paul interjected.

"I do?" Brandi asked.

"Yes," Paul said.

"I agree. You both need to hear this," Gabe said.

"What? Are you two like secret agents or something?" Brandi laughed.

Paul laughed. "Sometimes."

Gabe nudged Paul and then Brandi spoke as if she didn't hear Paul's response. "Let's just go and see what they have to say, Autumn. If you still don't like it, you can stay with me until we figure out your house situation." "Fine, let's go." I downed the rest of my drink *still* needing the liquid courage.

The alcohol was starting to heat up my veins by the time we arrived back at the house. He was ready to talk and so was I.

"You might want to sit down." Gabe gestured toward the couch.

"Or have some more to drink." Paul laughed.

I gave Brandi a wary look as we both sat on the couch. "I'll take a shot of Fireball."

Paul walked toward the kitchen while Gabe sat in a chair in front of me. My gaze met his and I could see the worry in his emerald eyes. Whatever he had to tell me was scaring him.

"Promise that you'll let me tell you everything before you storm off?" Gabe pleaded.

I nodded and reached for the shot of whiskey from Paul.

"Do you want me to leave the room?" Brandi asked.

"No." Gabe shook his head. "Autumn will tell you eventually, and it's better if you hear it directly from us."

"Us?" I asked as I set the glass down.

"Should I have a shot too?" Brandi asked with a chuckle and looked up at Paul.

"You might need one, firecracker."

Brandi and I looked at each other while Paul poured her a shot and refilled mine. I eyed the shot glass then looked back up to Gabe. He nodded for me to take the shot. I didn't question him. Whatever he was going to tell me was probably better not one-hundred percent lucid.

After taking a deep breath, Gabe glanced at Paul and then back at me. "We're male escorts."

It felt as if the room spun. Like a dizzy spell came over me. Part of me had expected him to tell me he was in the Secret Service or working for the FBI, but I never expected him to tell me that people paid him for sex.

"Come again?" Brandi uttered.

"It's not as bad as you think," Paul said.

"We're paid to go on dates," Gabe said.

I still couldn't speak. I wasn't sure if I should be mad or find it funny. I never in a million years thought they'd be escorts. Last I knew, it was illegal to pay for sex. Apparently, I was attracted to criminals.

"I should clarify that today was my *last* date."

I felt three sets of eyes on me, waiting for a response. "I need some air." I stood and made my way toward the backyard. Gabe had asked me not to storm off, but it was too much. I'd only been with four guys in my twenty-nine years and Gabe apparently had been with ... well, *a lot* of women.

"Angel, I quit because of you."

My hand stayed glued to the door handle. I looked over my shoulder at him. "You did?"

"Tonight was the first date I'd been on since we've been together. I hadn't had a chance to quit before today."

Turning around to face him, I asked, "Why didn't you just tell me when I asked you what you did for a living?"

I could hear Brandi and Paul laughing in the living room. Seemed she was okay with her friends being male escorts. If Gabe and I were just friends, I'd probably find the situation funny, too.

"I didn't want to lose you before I could save you."

I crossed my arms over my chest. "You've had two weeks to tell me."

He leaned back against the kitchen counter. "I need to tell you why I became an escort and maybe you'll understand my hesitation to tell you."

"Okay, tell me."

He took a deep breath and closed his eyes. "I've been in love once before, and she died in my arms."

My eyes widened. "How?" I whispered.

"She was a medic in my platoon. Just like most days, we got a call to pick up a wounded soldier, but when we arrived we were ambushed and she took a bullet in the chest. As she lay in my arms dying, something changed. I didn't think my heart could ever love again—I never wanted to love again. But you've stolen my way to breathe, angel." He took the few steps to where I stood and reached his hand up to cup my cheek. I wanted to lean into it because his touch always made me feel safe, but instead, I stood there, peering into his green eyes and trying not to be inconsiderate. "I've gone on dates and I only see you. I don't need to fill a void with other women or a bottle of whiskey anymore. I just want you. Nothing compares to you."

"Why become an escort? Why not do something with your skills from the army or become a personal trainer?"

"Money. Paul. Not wanting to open up to anyone. I still had needs and it was the easiest way to satisfy them. And I got paid for it."

"I was lied to for four years, Gabe. How can I trust you?"

"I'm not him. I'll never be him."

"But how can I be certain?"

"When you've been to war, you tend to not take things for granted."

His words hit me like a ton of bricks. I'd heard those words before.

"What?" Gabe asked.

"Rich told me the same thing once. I have to go, Gabe. I need time to think. This is all too much."

"Autumn, wait!"

I didn't wait.

I needed air and I needed to be alone—away from everyone.

Without saying a word, I grabbed my purse, ran out the front door to my car and quickly drove away as Gabe stood on the curb begging me to stay.

The moment I pulled away, it felt as if I'd left my heart on the sidewalk with Gabe. Tears started to roll down my cheeks and I realized I'd had too many shots and shouldn't be driving. Instead of going left to leave to the main road, I went right and parked on the street. Cutting the engine, I leaned back against the headrest, closed my eyes and sobbed.

What was wrong with me? Why did I attract liars? Gabe's lie was only about his job. Was him getting paid to date a big deal? It was a known fact that escorts had sex with their clients, and the thought of how many women Gabe had been with had me feeling as if sex wasn't special to him. I'd spent too many years being forced to have sex with Rich. I wanted sex to be special.

My phone buzzed in my purse.

Brandi: *Are you okay? Where'd you go?*

Me: *I'm fine. Just give me a few minutes.*

His words rang in my head. *"Angel, I quit because of you."* He'd quit to be with me. We'd only known each other a couple of months, yet he'd quit his job to be with me. My heart swelled and ached at the realization. He wanted to be with me and knew that escorting wouldn't allow that to happen.

"I've been in love once before, and she died in my arms."

As I thought of everything he said, it dawned on me that he said he was in love *before*. What did he mean by before? Before me?

"... I don't need to fill a void with other women or a bottle of whiskey anymore. I just want you."

After replaying his words over and over in my head, I wiped my tears and drove back *home* realizing that I'd only left because I *could* leave. Rich would never have let me drive off without coming after me and punishing me. Gabe, on the other hand, had let me leave.

I parked in my usual spot in front of the house, then checked to make sure no mascara was running down my face in the mirror before I got out of the car and walked into the house. I spotted Brandi and Paul sitting on the couch, watching TV on opposite sides. When they noticed me, they both looked up and gave me a tight smile. At Blue Martini I thought something was going on with the two of them, but seeing them now, changed my mind. Brandi was telling the truth; she and Paul were just friends. In my gut I knew she'd never cheat on Todd and I shouldn't have doubted her. Paul was a great guy and friend.

"It's not good, Auttie," Paul sighed.

"What do you mean?" I asked, looking around for Gabe.

"When Cochran died in his arms, he turned to whiskey to sleep to try to forget her because he had nightmares. When he decided to get close to you, the nightmares stopped and so did the drinking—

251

until tonight. After you'd left, he grabbed the bottle of Jack from the liquor cabinet and went to his room."

I nodded and walked toward Gabe's bedroom—the room that we'd been sharing each night. I knocked softly on the door, but there was no answer. I took a deep breath and tried turning the door knob. It opened and I stepped into the dark room. I could smell the stench of the whiskey and I wanted to cry again. It was all my fault. I shouldn't have left Gabe begging on the sidewalk. I should have been a grown woman and talked it out with him. Instead, I'd let the past control my future.

"Gabe?" I whispered, but there was no response.

I stepped closer to the bed. The moment my hand touched his warm skin, I realized how much I'd miss him if I let his past ruin our future. He saved me and I needed to save him.

After stripping my clothes, I crawled into the bed, moving as close as I could to Gabe without being on top of him.

He groaned. "Angel?"

"Yeah, it's me."

"You left me," he slurred.

"I know. I'm sorry."

"You can't leave me again."

"I won't."

"I love you, angel."

My eyes widened at his words. I didn't know if he said he loved me because he was drunk or because he actually did love me, but one thing was certain ...

I was in love with him too.

TWENTY-EIGHT
Gabe

I woke and rolled into a warm, soft body. At first I thought maybe it was a chick I had brought home during my drunken stupor, but then I remembered that Autumn came home ...

And that I'd told her I loved her.

I do love her. I love her as much as I loved Alyssa—if not more. My relationship with Alyssa was hard because we had to sneak around. I wanted to marry her, but as I have gotten to know Autumn, I realized I didn't know Alyssa like I knew Autumn. The ability to *be* with Autumn was allowing me to be myself and not a sneaky person.

I slowly got out of the bed, trying not to wake her. She didn't wake and I went into the connecting bathroom and brushed the whiskey from my breath. I needed a glass of water, but instead I climbed back into bed with Autumn. Brushing her hair out of her face, I leaned down and kissed her lips. I was worried I'd never be able to taste her again. She moaned the moment my lips touched hers and then her eyes opened and a smiled spread across her face.

"I'm happy you came home."

"You remember?"

I groaned as I felt a sting in my heart. Rolling onto my back, I stared up at the ceiling. "After you'd left, I drank a lot, but I remember. I always remember. It was just hard to stay awake with all the alcohol—that's why I drink. I need it to sleep when shit gets real."

"I don't understand how you drank so much. I wasn't even gone an hour."

"What can I say, angel? Whiskey and I know how to get shit done."

She rolled over and placed her chin on my bare chest. "Are you feeling okay? Hungover or anything?"

"Nah. I've built up a tolerance over the years."

I didn't want Autumn to know my dark past, but she was grilling me about the drinking and I knew I couldn't lie to her ... again. I knew that trust was a big issue for her. If I let her know all of my dark demons and she didn't want to be with me, then I was only meant to meet her so she could get her away from Rich. But I love her ...

"Do you remember what you said last night when I came back?"

I leaned up and rolled her over so that she was on her back and I was hovering over her. "When Alyssa died, I never wanted to feel that pain again. I never wanted any woman to get close to me—until you. Part of me felt as if Alyssa sent you to me ... Like she wanted me to be happy and you would be that person."

I kissed her briefly. "So yes, angel, I love you. The moment you drove away last night, it felt as if you drove off with my heart. I wanted to go after you, but Paul told me to give you time. I was out of my mind and I didn't think you'd come back—"

She placed a finger on my lips. "I love you too."

"Yeah?" I asked, a huge smile spreading across my face.

She nodded. "From the moment I first saw you, I couldn't get you out of my head, and when I saw you with Trista ... I was jealous—so jealous."

"I was only her date."

"I know, but seeing you with another woman—"

"Isn't as bad as it was for me to see you with Rich."

She groaned. "Sometimes I think that this is all a dream. That Rich is alive and—"

"It's not a dream, angel." I lowered my head and kissed her softly. "No one is ever going to hurt you again."

She nodded her head, her eyes glassy. "I'm much stronger now. Thanks to you."

"You were strong the moment you decided to leave him. And thankfully, I ran into you that day—literally." I chuckled. "And you know what?"

"What?" she asked, lowering her gaze to my lips as if she wanted me to kiss her again.

So I did.

"I'm going to love the shit out of you. We may fight, bicker, slam doors, even want to strangle each other sometimes, but I will never lay a hand on you to hurt you."

"But you'll still *touch* me right?" She raised her eyebrows as if to entice me.

"Angel, I'll *touch* you every day and every way I know how until the day I die ... starting with right now."

I'm not going to lie. Waking up to a naked woman next to me is great, but waking up next to a naked woman I love is the best feeling in the entire world. It was new to me—everything I was feeling with Autumn was new. My heart felt different ... My love for Alyssa had never felt like this. I knew I'd never forget her. I couldn't; she was my first love. But Autumn was the one I was going to make happy forever.

I slid down her body, the sheets coming with me to expose her beautiful frame. I sucked on each nipple, making them harden before licking my way down her flat stomach. My dick started to stiffen, waking up and ready for action. The taste of her skin was like nothing I'd ever tasted before. She was perfect—perfect for me.

Her back arched as I made my way down to taste her. She spread her legs, opening herself for me. I could smell her desire and my mouth watered, wanting a taste. She moaned the moment my tongue took the first lick.

As I continued to lick, suck and pump my fingers into her, everything dawned on me. I had no more secrets to share with her. She knew about Alyssa. She saw firsthand my relationship with whiskey and she knew what I *did* for a living. I had nothing left to hide.

If I knew my angel up in heaven like I thought I did, Alyssa had sent me to Vegas to save Autumn from Rich. I wasn't truly happy until I met Autumn, and I didn't meet her until she decided to leave him. The timeline lined up perfectly, and everything worked out as it was supposed to.

"Fuck, angel. You taste like heaven."

"Do you call me angel because of *her*?"

I stopped licking and raised my head enough to see her face. "Who? Alyssa?"

She looked down at me. "Yeah."

I sat back on my heels and we stared at each other for a few beats. "Do you want to talk about this now or do you want to come?"

She laughed slightly. "I want to come, but I was wondering if clients ever pleasured you?"

"With a blow job?"

She nodded her head.

"A few times, but it was mostly about their pleasure."

"I want to do that for you."

A smile spread across my face. "I won't object to that."

I returned to her sweet pussy, tasting her until she moaned and squeezed her thighs against my head. Afterward, I kissed her, letting her taste herself before we switched places. My dick was hard as steel, and just the thought of Autumn's mouth wrapped around my cock had me aching with need.

"I might not be as good as other women who have done this."

"Angel, just the fact that it's you is already better than anything I've done in the past."

She chuckled under her breath, a blush spreading across her cheeks. Her soft hand wrapped around my dick and I instantly groaned. Having Autumn wrap her hand around my shaft felt perfect.

I watched her under hooded eyes as she kneeled between my parted legs and lowered her head. The moment her hot mouth engulfed the head of my dick, I thought I was going to come right then and there. Her tongue ran across the tip, tasting the bead of pre-cum that was oozing out, then ran along the sides before she took as much of me as she could into her mouth.

Her mouth was just the right size as it sucked, sending chills down my body that quickly heated up as I got closer and closer to coming. Autumn used her hand to pump while her mouth and tongue worked together until I was on the cusp. She then used her free hand and cupped my balls, making me groan as cum shot down her throat.

"Was it—"

"Yeah, angel, it was perfect. Now, how many more times do you want to come?"

TWENTY-NINE
Autumn

ALMOST THREE WEEKS AFTER RICH DIED, DETECTIVE EVANS and Detective King knocked on our front door.

"Is Mrs. Jones here?"

"Yes," I heard Gabe respond.

I didn't know how they knew that I'd be at Gabe and Paul's house. Maybe they stopped by the house I shared with Rich—I no longer called that house my home. Or maybe they took a chance and drove by Gabe's and saw my car. Whatever the reason, I was still nervous when I heard Detective Evans ask if I were available.

"Mrs. Jones." Detective Evans nodded in greeting as I sat on the couch in the living room.

I stood and shook their hands. "What can I do for you detectives?"

"We have news regarding your husband," Detective King said. They sat opposite me as Gabe leaned against the wall near me. "The tox screen came back. Mr. Jones and Mr. Romero were poisoned."

"Poisoned?" I asked, looking briefly at Gabe.

"With what? Do you know by who?" Gabe asked before I could.

"We were lucky enough to find the footage from the video cameras in the house," Detective Evans replied. "Do you know the guy who Mr. Jones got into an altercation with at the party a few weeks ago?"

"No, I don't. That was the first time I'd seen him and I didn't get a good look."

"You're husband had loaned him money, and we think Mr. White didn't want to pay it back."

"Think?" Gabe asked.

"Mr. White isn't exactly cooperating," Detective King replied.

"But you know he poisoned them?" I asked.

"The footage we recovered showed Mr. White going to the bar area and using a syringe to inject a liquid into several bottles. We tested those bottles and found Rohypnol."

"Wait," Gabe interjected. "Like the date rape drug?"

"Exactly," Detective Evans stated. "The medical examiner determined that both Mr. Jones and Mr. Romero consumed approximately eight to ten milligrams of the Rohypnol from the Grey Goose bottle. The other bottles we tested had anywhere from twenty to thirty milligrams of the drug in them."

"Wouldn't that just make them pass out?" I asked.

"In rape cases, the tox screen only shows one to one and a half milligrams of the drug in their system. Mr. Jones and Mr. Romero consumed almost ten times that amount. With that amount of Rohypnol, the medical examiner determined that their blood pressure dropped and then their respiratory system started to shut down until they could no longer breathe," Detective King stated.

Gabe sat down on the couch next to me and grabbed my hands. I needed the contact. I needed to feel that I wasn't alone in this, and having the comfort he provided was all I needed. If I hadn't left Rich that night, there was a chance I could have been killed. I took a few seconds to process everything while the room was silent.

"Now what?" I finally asked.

"Mr. White is being held in custody until his trial. He's pleaded not guilty in the bail hearing, but like I said, we have him on camera." Detective Evans answered.

I chuckled sarcastically under my breath; if he only knew why Rich had those cameras.

"Is Autumn in danger?" Gabe asked.

"We don't think so," Detective King answered.

"When is his trial?" I asked.

"In about seven months."

"Seven months? Will I have to go to the trial?" I asked.

The detectives looked at each other and then back to me. "We know you were leaving Mr. Jones, but the public doesn't. It would probably be in your best interest to play the grieving widow. From what we've learned and heard, Mr. Jones has a lot of enemies," Detective Evans confirmed.

"He never included me in anything to do with his business. I'm not even sure I know what he did."

"That's probably a good thing," Detective King said. "The less his enemies know, the better."

I nodded. "But they'll know about me if they go to his funeral."

"I got you, angel," Gabe said, kissing the top of my head.

I knew he did. Gabe had a way about himself that made me think we were bulletproof when we were together.

We received the information we needed to claim Rich's body. After Gabe had walked the detectives out, we sat in silence. I looked up at him.

"So ... I need to plan his funeral."

"I know you don't want to, angel. But I agree with the detectives and think you should keep up appearances."

"I guess." I sighed.

"Angel, you won. You beat him. You *survived* him."

It doesn't rain that often in Las Vegas, but it rained the day we held Rich's funeral. It felt as if it were one more jab toward me—like

Rich was looking down on us and wanted me to stand in a black dress while the cold rain surrounded me.

I hated that I needed to keep up appearances, but as Trista, Trina, and friends of Rich's arrived, I did the "wife" thing and hugged when I was supposed to, gave a tight smile when someone told me they were sorry and nodded when they said they couldn't believe he was murdered.

Gabe briefly said hello to Trista and I smiled. I couldn't imagine walking in and finding someone dead—let alone two people.

I was going to say hello to Trina, but she steered clear of me and I was okay with that. If she wanted to be the grieving mistress, then whatever.

As the service started, Gabe stood on one side of me while my dad stood on the other, the rain beating down on us. Paul, Brandi, her husband and my mom stood around us as I stared down at the mud, pretending to listen to how Rich was a great man. I wanted to stop the service, tell everyone that what the priest was saying were lies, but instead, I waited until it was my turn to throw dirt on Rich's grave. I didn't want to give a speech, and I didn't shed a tear until I felt the dirt in my hand. I felt a rush of relief wash over me as I tossed it onto the lowered casket.

The tears streamed down my face as I finally realized that he'd never hurt me or anyone again.

THIRTY
Gabe

In the two months since Rich's funeral, Autumn, Jackson and I attended a weekend course in Texas and had become certified as self-defense instructors. When I pitched the idea to Autumn, she cried. At first I didn't understand her tears until she explained that it was a perfect idea because she wanted to save other women like I'd saved her. She didn't want to go back to working at a bank and while Rich had left plenty of money behind, we both knew it would run out eventually if we weren't working.

What stunned us both was the amount of money Rich had loaned to people. Instead of dealing with Rich's clients, Autumn closed the doors on Jones Investments. I didn't blame her. Rich was involved in shady shit and since it had got him killed, we all knew the best thing was to forgive each loan. It would also increase Autumn's safety to anyone who Rich may have pissed off over the years. Autumn, Jackson and I had also become certified firearm instructors. It made Autumn feel safer even if we believed she wasn't in danger any longer.

"You know how you think I'm the smartest person in the entire world?" I joked.

"Yeah." She laughed and shook her head.

"I might know where we can teach our class until we can buy a warehouse."

She perked up. "Oh? Where?"

"Club 24."

"Really?"

"I need to talk to Blake first, but I think it would work out. Even if it were once a week."

Since we went to Club 24 almost every day, I'd become friends with the new manager, Blake Montgomery. His brother owned the gym, and Blake had relocated to manage the compound as Jackson would say. I knew I could talk Blake into letting us teach in a one-hour time slot.

"I think that sounds perfect." Autumn came and sat next to me on the couch. "We go there all the time anyway. Why not make money doing it." She chuckled.

I grinned and kissed the top of her head. "That's what he said."

She sat up and gave me a confused look.

"Why not make money *doing it*," I repeated.

She shook her head again as she smiled. "You're lucky that's not a sore subject for me anymore."

"I wouldn't joke if it were."

She rolled her eyes. "Men."

"Speaking of doing it ..." I raised my eyebrows with a huge grin.

She stood. "Last one in our room does all of the pleasing." She took off running down the hall before I was able to stand from the couch.

What my angel didn't realize was that I'd always let her win because nothing satisfied me more than making her come.

Multiple times.

Autumn fell asleep in my arms, and while sleeping next to her was one of my favorite activities, there was something I needed to do without her knowing.

I slowly got out of bed, making sure not to wake her and slipped on my basketball shorts. I never thought that I would be doing this again. If you had asked me eight months ago where I saw myself in five years, I would have told you dead.

While my laptop booted up, I jumped into the shower in the spare bathroom to wash the sweat from my body. Rolling around with Autumn was always a workout. I made sure I gave her the best of me each time. Sometimes my arms would burn as I pumped my fingers hard and fast to bring her to shattering, and sometimes my thighs burned as I took her from the back and made her come multiple times before I would. But each time we made love, I did whatever it took to make up for what she'd missed out on before we met. I knew I couldn't fuck the memory of Rich from her mind, but I was determined to make her forget his *touch*.

After turning off the shower, I grabbed my towel and began to dry my body until I saw the note on the steamy mirror.

She'll be good for you, C.H.

At first I thought that it was Jackson playing a trick on me until I realized it wasn't his handwriting. It wasn't Autumn's either. I didn't believe in ghosts ... but angels ... I believed in angels and I knew Alyssa was always looking down on me. I sat on the lid of the toilet, tears running down my cheeks. Alyssa's nickname for me was C.H. I didn't know how it was possible, but the note was from her.

"I miss you," I whispered. I "I didn't get to tell you that day and I hope you knew that I loved you. I know in my heart you had something to do with bringing Autumn and me together, so thank you. I'm not sure how the other side works, but please make sure I don't fuck this up. You're right—she is good for me." I wiped the tears from my face. "I'll always love you, babe."

When I stood and looked at the foggy mirror, the note was gone.

The last time I designed a ring, my world was turned upside down.

When I logged into my account, the ring I designed for Alyssa was still on file. As I stared at the princess cut diamond, I knew I could easily order that ring for Autumn and crawl back into bed with her. But there were three things wrong with that option: one, when I looked at the design, I saw Alyssa, not Autumn. Two, Rich called Autumn his princess and three, her engagement ring from Rich was a princess cut diamond.

So instead, I clicked the new design button as Jackson walked in the front door. He walked into the dining room, looked at the computer and said, "You gotta girl back home we don't know about, Cap?"

I turned to him, remembering he said that when he *caught* me designing a ring before. "Something like that."

EPILOGUE
Autumn

March 9th

THE FINAL CONNECTION WITH RICH WAS OVER.

I didn't want to go to the trial for the guy that killed Rich, but I decided to go on the day the verdict was being read for the double murder of Rich and Remo. I wanted to see his face as they read the guilty verdicts. I wanted to silently thank him for causing the commotion at Rich's party almost a year ago. Mr. White was a murderer, but he also *made* me put my plan into motion. He'll never know that he helped me, but I will. I'll always remember that night—it was the beginning of me being happy again.

Finally, the judge entered the courtroom and when asked, the foreman read the verdict.

Guilty ... On all counts.

Gabe wrapped me in his arms, hugging me tight and I cried. I didn't know why I was crying. It was as if I couldn't control my emotions. Finally everything to do with Rich was done and it felt like a weight was lifted off my shoulders.

While we drove home, I texted Brandi the guilty verdict and told her I felt sick to my stomach. She replied back:

Brandi: *Maybe you're pregnant.*

I read her text and chuckled under my breath then stopped. *Holy shit.*

The next day, I got a home pregnancy test and sure enough, Brandi was right: I was pregnant.

"Did you tell him yet?" Brandi asked as we watched our guys plus Paul, Nick, Vinny and Brad load our stuff in the moving truck. Gabe and I were moving into our own house today.

"Not yet."

"When?"

I shrugged. "I don't know ... Soon though."

"You just bought a house together. I doubt he's going to leave you high and dry."

"I know. I just haven't had a chance yet. We've been busy getting our business up and going. It just hasn't been the right time."

While I was with Rich, I thought the pill would prevent me from getting pregnant. I'm thankful that it did. When I saw the blue lines appear on the home pregnancy test, my heart stopped. I always hoped that God wouldn't have me bring a child into this world with a man like Rich. As I stared at the test, I knew God knew what he was doing.

Gabe and I were meant to be together and me being pregnant was just another sign.

"Angel," Gabe called, walking toward us. He knelt beside me. "Are you two going to help or—"

"Leave us alone, Gabe," Brandi said. "We're watching hot guys sweat."

"What she said." I laughed.

Gabe shook his head and stood. "Women." He chuckled and walked away.

"You're not supposed to lift heavy stuff." She nudged her shoulder into mine.

"Thank you." I smiled.

I knew I had to tell Gabe I was pregnant. I just didn't know if it should be on the anniversary of Alyssa's death. While he drank his coffee before everyone got to the house, he was quiet, but when I realized what day it was, I didn't question it.

"Holy crap, I'm exhausted," I said, falling onto the couch on my back. Everyone had just left and Gabe and I were officially moved into our own home.

Gabe walked over and leaned over me with his arms on either side of my shoulders. "How are you exhausted, angel? You and Brandi watched all day."

I laughed. "It's hard work watching my man all day."

He kissed my nose. "We just have to do one more thing before we shower and call it a night."

I furrowed my eyebrows. "What do we *have* to do?"

"Come on, you'll see." He stood, reaching out his hand to help me stand. "We haven't seen the backyard at night yet."

I grabbed his hand to stand. "We have forever to see the backyard at night."

"That's true, but I want to see it on the night we moved in."

"Whatever you say, Mr. Green Eyes."

I laughed slightly as he guided me toward the French doors that led to our backyard. When we got outside and I turned my head, I gasped. "How?"

"We have the best friends."

"But—"

The pool was lit by a pool light and what appeared to be fifty candles flickering as they floated in the water.

He led me closer. "I wanted this night to be special, so I asked our friends to help me out. Brandi distracted you while the guys and I lit all the candles."

He dropped to one knee and my hands covered my mouth as I was left speechless.

"For the past six years, March ninth has been a terrible day for me. It reminded me of what I lost, but when I woke up this morning, I knew what I wanted to gain." He reached into his pocket and pulled out a black velvet box. "I've had this ring for weeks now. There have been so many days that I've wanted to ask you, but none felt right. Until now. March ninth may be the day I lost my first love, but I also want it to be the day my last love told me yes. Angel, will you marry me?"

"Yes! Of course I will." I stuck out my hand and he slipped the round, solitaire diamond onto my left hand.

He stood and pressed his lips to mine. His tongue slid across my bottom lip and my mouth parted, wanting to taste him. After a few moments, we broke apart.

"I love you, angel."

"I love you too, Mr. Green Eyes." I wrapped my arms around his waist and rested my head on his chest. "I have something to tell you though."

"Oh yeah?"

I pulled my head back, my arms still wrapped around him. Peering into his eyes, I told him, "I'm pregnant."

He blinked and then his eyes got big. "You're ... We're having a baby?"

I nodded.

"I'm ... Damn, I'm speechless. You have no idea how happy I am."

"Good." I smiled. "I was surprised since I was still on the pill, but things happen for a reason right?"

"They sure do, angel." He pulled my head to him so it was resting on his chest again. "They sure do."

The End.
Keep reading for a bonus chapters about Gabe's bachelor party. Also, Paul's story continues in Tequila & Lace. Check out a sneak-peek after the about me page.

BONUS CHAPTER

Paul

My best friend is getting married.

And I get to plan an epic as shit bachelor party.

There are two requirements for a great bachelor party. The first one is getting shit-faced with your buddies while surrounded by naked chicks. The other is humiliating the guy. Women do the same thing where they make the bride wear penis attire and go on a stupid scavenger hunt where they make some pussy buy them a shot or have the bride kiss some ugly fucker. I've seen it happen far too many times.

Guys have a different way of embarrassing the groom, though. We're dudes, so we shit talk and roughhouse. We take things to the extreme, and we do it with force. We do it with bodily harm.

Gabe used to be a gigolo, and a damn good one at that before a woman changed everything and he quit the game. Normally, I would tell him that he's letting a woman drag him around by the balls, but the woman in question is Autumn, and I love her. She's like a sister to me, and he couldn't have found a better woman.

So how do you plan a bachelor party for an ex-gigolo who has seen more titties than he can count and already lives in Vegas, the city where most guys come to enjoy their last night of freedom?

This needs to be a night Gabe won't forget.

I called our buddies from Saddles & Racks and asked them to meet me for a few drinks so we can come up with a plan. We're at a place I found on one of my dates called Gold Spike. It has a full bar and has games like beer pong, pool, cornhole, and life-size Jenga.

After we get our drinks from the bar, we grab a high-top table, but I see the guys eyeing the pool table. We can't have that. We won't get anything done. One thing would lead to another, and we'll be betting money and not coming up with a plan for Gabe. *After* we've discussed the bachelor party, we can play games and I can take these fuckers' money in a few games of beer pong.

"I can't believe Gabe's getting married," Nick says, sliding onto a bar stool.

"We know the thought of one woman's pussy for the rest of your life makes your dick want to run and hide." Vinny shakes his head, grabbing a seat, too. If anyone in our group is next to get out of the game, it's Vinny. He stopped seeing a chick from out of town who couldn't handle what we do. He didn't want to leave S&R for *her*. He wasn't like Gabe.

"Fuck," Nick groans. "Just the thought of that scares me." He shivers and then takes a long sip of his grapefruit juice and *vodka* with a salted rim—which is also known as a salty dog—appropriate for him in my opinion. Out of all the guys, Nick is my go to friend when it comes to shit, but he's a real I'm-never-getting-married-dude. Hell, I'm never getting married either, but if this motherfucker fucks up Gabe's happiness by putting any kind of doubt in his head, I will personally beat his ass. After what Gabe went through with Cochran, he deserves to be happy, and if Auttie is that person, then I'm not going to try and change his mind. Like I said, I love Autumn like a sister.

"You better not fuck this up," I warn, pointing my finger at his face and narrowing my eyes.

Nick rolls his eyes. "I'm only going to get Gabe shit-faced."

"I don't want to only get him hammered. I want this to be something cool as shit."

He laughs. "It will be. He just won't remember it."

"And how do you know what will happen?" I ask.

He shrugs and looks to Vinny and Bradley. They look to me, waiting.

"That's why I asked you all here." I shake my head in frustration before taking a sip of my *tequila* and Coke. "*We* need to plan something fun. We can't just bring him to a strip club. We see tits and ass all day."

"Not Gabe. I bet he has to jack off twice a day now just to keep his sack from exploding." Nick chuckles.

I groan at his smart ass remark. "Trust me, I'm sure they're still fuckin'. They lived with me, remember? I'm pretty sure shit hasn't changed that much in only a few weeks."

"What do you have in mind?" Bradley asks, getting back to the task at hand.

"I'm not sure. He can go to a casino anytime, so that's lame."

Bradley takes a sip of his *gin* and tonic before he speaks again. "Have you seen that place where you can drive bulldozers?"

I shake my head. "No."

"I've never been, but a buddy of mine told me about it. You can drive a bulldozer or an excavator. You build huge mounds of dirt, push gigantic tires around, build trenches, and stack two thousand pound tires. You can even play bucket basketball—whatever the hell that is."

"Dude, that sounds cool," Vinny exclaims with a huge grin.

I watch Vinny take a sip of his *rum* and Coke while I consider the bulldozer idea. Playing with heavy machinery does sound fun, but it doesn't sound epic and I want something he'd never expect. I want something that we can't go do any given day. "I've never heard of that, and we definitely need to go do it one day, but I want something that's going to be the shit, not something that's just going to be fun."

They nod and then we sit in silence. We sit and think for what feels like forever. My drink is almost empty when, out of nowhere, Bradley slaps the table, causing us all to jump.

He turns to me, a big ass grin on his face, and asks, "How good are you at lying?"

273

I told Autumn that I was stealing Gabe for the weekend and to have his bag packed. She, of course, questioned me, but if I wasn't going to tell him what we were doing, I wasn't going to tell her. I did, however, promise her there would be no girls involved.

That was partially true.

Knowing that Gabe was at the range teaching, I stopped by his house to grab his bag from Autumn.

"Are you sure that's all the clothes he's going to need?"

I look at the small duffel bag and then back at her. "Yeah," I chuckle. "We're guys. We don't need a lot of clothes."

"I know, but all I packed was two pairs of boxers, two T-shirts, swim shorts, a sweatshirt and a pair of sweats."

"That sounds right."

"What if something gets dirty? You'll be gone for two nights and I didn't pack extra pants."

"Auttie, trust me. We can wear the same clothes two days in a row." Her eyes grew huge. Laughing, I add, "Guys don't care."

Shaking her head, she closes her eyes and then turns and walks to the kitchen as she mutters something I can't hear. I don't understand the big deal.

"I'm going to grab some stuff from the garage."

"Whatever," she calls back.

After grabbing what I need, I throw everything into my *Jeep* and then walk back to the kitchen. "Bye, Auttie. We'll pick him up at nine." I kiss her cheek and try to step away to leave, but she grabs my wrist before I can move and gets in my face, pointing her index finger at me.

"Just because I'm pregnant doesn't mean I can't kick your ass, PJ. If I find out there are women all over him this weekend ..." Her eyes narrow and I swallow hard.

"There won't be *women* all over him this weekend, I promise. Plus, this is Gabe we're talking about. You can trust him. You can trust *me*."

She stares at me for a few beats and I feel my heart rate kick up. I've never been scared of her. I knew she was a badass by the way she'd handled her ex-husband, but Jesus, I never expected to be on her bad side.

"Autumn," I say, using her given name because I need to let her know I'm serious and she can trust me. "I promise it's just a bunch of guys getting together. You packed him sweats for Christ's sake. You think chicks are going to be all over him in sweats?"

"Paul Jackson, I know how all you boys operate. It doesn't matter what you wear. Hell, you all work naked for a living, so don't give me that bullshit."

All right, she got me there.

I release her death grip from my wrist and bring her in for a hug. "Auttie, I promise it's not that type of party. We all fuck everyday—literally." I snicker.

"Not helping," she mumbles.

"We're going to go blow off some steam and do guy shit. Just drink and have a good time, I swear."

She pulls back and looks me square in the eyes. "Promise?"

"I cross my heart."

BONUS CHAPTER
Gabe

I'm DREADING TONIGHT.

It's my bachelor party and I don't know what's going on, but apparently, Autumn does. She's in on the shenanigans and I'm left in the dark. All I know is what Paul texted me this morning:

Paul: *Dress to impress tonight because it's about to go down!*

Usually, I'd be excited to hang with my friends, but Autumn and I are still *new*. She's having my baby and I want to spend every free second with her. Before she came along, I was drowning my sorrows in whiskey, hiding my pain from everyone. *Well, I thought I was hiding.* I didn't care if I woke up the next day, but now I have a reason to wake up. I don't want to get wasted at my bachelor party and not remember going to bed next to my angel. I want to remember *every* single night.

But Autumn has convinced me that I need this. Maybe we both need this. Sure I spend time with Jackson here and there, but it's been a while since I've hung out with the guys. A night out would be good. But I won't get plastered, even if it *is* my night to get hammered. Jackson can go fuck himself if he thinks that will happen.

As I head home from the range, I think about what I'm going to wear. I know, I'm a guy—*whatever*, but Jackson said I need to dress to impress and I have no idea what to wear or where the fuck we're going.

By the time I get home, I still have no idea what I'm wearing. I'm not good at this shit. Hell, Jackson helped me pick out my outfit my first night as a gigolo. Clothes just aren't my thing.

I grab my phone and send a text to Jackson as I get out of my *Yukon* and head inside:

Me: *Where are we going tonight?*

Paul: *Out.*

Fucker.

Me: *What are you wearing?*

I groan as I enter the house, shaking my head. I fucking sound like a chick.

Paul: *Is this Auttie because you sound like a girl.*

Me: *Just answer the question!*

Paul: *Clothes.*

I'm going to kill him.

"Angel," I call out. She doesn't answer so I call her again, moving toward the kitchen.

"By the pool," she finally responds.

The moment I walk through the French doors that lead to the backyard, I spot her in her bikini, lounging in the shade. I decide I'm not going out tonight no matter what Autumn and Jackson say. The sight of her with her small bump, *the bump that holds our future,* is enough reason to stay home and cuddle on the couch like we do every night. It's what I've grown to love.

She looks up from her e-reader. "Hey, how was the range?"

I sit in the lounge chair beside her and then lean over and kiss her. "The usual. Julie's getting better. Before long, she'll be as good as you." After everything that went down with Major Dick, we'd started our own self-defense classes at Club 24. In addition, we teach women how to properly shoot guns.

"That's awesome. I really like Julie. So are you ready for tonight?" Her smile is as big as I've ever seen it.

"You really want me to go?"

"Of course, I do. It's your bachelor party."

I lean back in the lounge chair and stare up at the blue sky. "But I want to stay home with you. No telling what they have planned. PJ told me I need to dress to impress and I have no—"

"Wait—what?" She sits up.

"This surprises you? I thought you know the plan?"

"One second."

She grabs her phone and I watch as she messes with the screen. "What are you doing?"

"I'm ..." She pauses longer than necessary, still on her phone, and I begin to wonder if she doesn't know what the plan really is.

"Ange—"

"I'm asking Paul what you need to wear."

"But you know where we're going, right?"

She gives a nervous giggle and I start to become even more suspicious. "Yes, but I didn't ask him what you need to wear."

"Why would you need to *ask* him?" This is definitely making me nervous.

"It's a special place."

I tilt my head. "Special?"

"Yes—*special.*"

"Like VIP special?" I grin.

She smiles with a shrug almost as if she is trying to hide something, then looks back down at her phone. "Well, it *is* your night."

He's probably taking me to a club on the strip with our own table and bottle service. Guys have to dress nicely to get into most Vegas clubs.

"Are you sure you're okay with all of this?"

She looks back up from her phone. "Yes, now let's go pick you out something to wear."

"I don't want to go."

"What do I have to do to convince you?"

I scrunch my eyebrows. "You want me to go *that* bad?"

She stands then straddles my hips. "I want you to go and have fun with the guys. You've been with me every night. Things are going to change once the baby gets here."

I grab her phone from her hands and then glance at the time. "We have time for a shower first."

"We?" She laughs, throwing her head back.

I nod, staring at her chest.

"I *am* covered in chlorine." She winks.

"Then we'd better wash you off."

I toss my wallet and keys on the table then start making my way to the bathroom. But when I turn the corner, I stop. She's leaning into our walk-in shower to adjust the temperature and all I can see is that perfectly round ass of hers.

After adjusting my dick that's now straining against the fly of my shorts, I lean against the doorjamb, fold my arms and simply watch her. A few short moments later, she looks over her shoulder and flashes me that seductive grin as if she knows I've been watching her the whole time.

Pushing myself off the wall, I strip a piece of clothing with every step I take until I'm toe-to-toe and nose-to-nose with her, I swept Autumn's hair back with both hands, bring her lips to mine and start moving us under the spray of the showerhead. We reach the other end of the shower and I pin her against the wall, grinding my hips to give her a little tease of what's about to happen. I pull my lips from hers and make my way to her neck, applying little nibbles to her jaw along the way. She reaches down and wraps her hand around my now rock hard dick. I let out a groan and bring my mouth to her ear.

"Turn around, angel. Hands on the wall."

Autumn turns around, puts both palms against the tile, and then rests the back of her head on my shoulder giving me open access to her neck. When I start alternating between nipping and sucking at it, she pushed her hips back, rubbing her perfect ass against me. One of my hands makes its way up to her tits, massaging between small plucks and causing her nipples to stiffen. The other hand moves between her legs.

At the first stroke of my fingers against her clit, Autumn lets out a moan. I push them deeper, gliding in and out effortlessly and I know it's not from the water that's beating down on us. *My girl is ready.* She's hot and slick and as my knees bend, lifting her slightly to slide my dick in, I think to myself that the guys can go fuck themselves. Who needs a bachelor party when you have this woman waiting at home for you? I don't give a shit what they have planned. Nothing beats her. *Nothing.*

My thrusts are slow because I don't want to hurt the baby. We'll both get there eventually. I reach my hand around to rub her clit. She turns her head and bites my earlobe. "I'm not going to break, Gabe."

She tells me every time we fuck that I won't hurt her or the baby. I know she's right, but I keep my rhythm slow and steady. *Just in case.*

"I want it harder," she moans.

I take a deep breath before I grab her hips with both hands and drive into her. "Anything you want, angel."

I'm feeling better about everything now that I've fucked Autumn.

I'm relaxed, I shave my face and head and then dress in dark jeans, a button-up dark blue shirt, and brown dress shoes.

"What are your plans for tonight?" I ask Autumn as we lounge on the couch waiting for Jackson.

"You're looking at it."

"Don't have too much fun," I joke.

"Someone needs to stay by the phone in case I need to bail your asses out of jail." I look down at her, fear starting to work itself back into my veins. "I'm kidding, Mr. Green Eyes. You're going to have a good time with your friends. I promise. Now stop worrying." She leans up and kisses me lightly.

Before I can say anything, Jackson walks in without knocking, *his usual style.* "Get your ass up and let's get this party started!"

Autumn stands and I immediately miss her warmth. PJ's shit-eating grin spread across his face tells me I'm going to regret this night. I'm not sure if it's because I made him do all kinds of shit in the Army and he's going to pay me back or what, but I don't like how excited he is.

"I love you. Have a good time and I'll see you when you get back." Autumn's warmth is back as she hugs my waist.

"You'll be awake?"

"Of course." She stands on her tiptoes and presses her lips to mine again.

Before she can pull away, I grab her face and deepen the kiss. PJ can wait a few seconds. I want my angel to know that I'll be thinking of her tonight and that she has nothing to worry about. No matter what the plan is, she can trust me. Even though we haven't talked about trust, we both know Major Dick cheated on her and bachelor parties are unusually infamous for cheating.

"I'll be missing the taste of your lips all night," I whisper and give her one final kiss.

"Ready, love bird?" PJ motions for the door.

"Fuck off, Jackson." I wink at Autumn as a goodbye. She laughs and follows us so she can lock the door once we leave.

"You need a drink," he mutters as we step out my front door.

I expect to see his *Jeep* parked in front of my house, maybe even a limo. What I don't expect to see is a medium sized black party bus. "What did you do?" I ask.

"Did you expect me not to drink tonight so I could drive your ass around?"

"I guess not." We round the bus with multiple tinted windows. I can't see inside. I can't hear anything coming from inside either. As we get closer to the door, I see the driver standing outside.

"Gabe, this is Alfred."

"What?" I half-laugh because I don't want to insult the guy, but come on—*Alfred?*

"I'm kidding," Jackson exclaims, slapping the dude on the back. "His name's Roberto, but *Alfred* is better for our little adventure."

My head whips to PJ. "Adventure?"

"Get on the bus, Gabe," Jackson groans.

PJ and *Alfred* step aside. I look up and meet Bradley's gaze.

"Party's up here, man."

I shake my head slightly, take a deep breath and decide that the sooner I get on the bus, the sooner I can return to Autumn. I mean, *what can go wrong?*

Jackson follows me up the stairs. The darkened bus is mainly lit by multicolored LED lights running along the baseboards and in the ceiling. There's a stripper pole in front of me that I assume is in every party bus—at least in Vegas. The moment the guys see me, the cheers are deafening. You'd think I won an award or something. Bro hugs are exchanged. Pats on the back go around and finally Nick shoves a *whiskey* and Coke in my hand once I'm steered to a place to sit.

The door of the bus closes and music starts to blare. Strobe lights flash and I feel as if I'm in a mini club—I guess I am. I'm not exactly sure what five dudes are supposed to do on a party bus but it makes sense to have a driver to take us around town when *they're* drunk off their asses.

"Where are we going?" I ask.

"Around," PJ answers. The guys laugh.

The bus is moving and I can barely see out the tinted windows except for passing lights. *Why won't they tell me anything?*

"Are you going to be in a shit mood the entire night?" Nick asks.

"I just want to know where we're going."

Paul nudges his head toward my drink. "It's a surprise. Now drink your drink, loosen the fuck up and have a good time. This is your night."

I crack my neck, nod, and take a long gulp of my drink. The whiskey burns as it goes down my throat. I should have known that the *Coke* color was only a splash.

Bradley, Nick, Vinny and Paul are all watching me with grins on their faces. I'm about to ask them why they're so quiet, why they're looking at me the way they are, but before I can, a shadow appears out of the corner of my eye.

A chick walks through a back door and stops, hand on her cocked hip. She's dressed in a red sparkling bikini with fishnet stockings and stilettos. Usually, a man's reaction would be "Hell, yeah!" but my first thought is, "Autumn's okay with this?" We're five minutes from my house and a chick is coming toward me half-naked and my future wife who's carrying my baby approved a stripper? Nope, not buying it.

"What did you do?" I ask Jackson for a second time in ten minutes.

"Me?" he asks, bringing a hand to his chest as if he's innocent. I see a smile start to spread across his face.

"Autumn knows about this?" I wave my free hand up and down the length of the chicks body as she stands before me.

"Well ..." he starts to say and the guys laugh.

"Just relax," the stripper says and kneels before me.

"Look, lady—"

She stands again and straddles me. "They told me you might be difficult," she whispers in my ear while grinding her hips. "It's your bachelor party and they hired me to strip, so let me do my thing. I won't fuck you, that's not my style. Do what your friend said and just relax. Have a good time. This is the last time you're going to see another chick's boobs in person."

She pulls her head back and her stare meets mine. If she only knew *who* the bus was carrying. Jackson should have known I couldn't care less about strippers. Does he expect me to pretend to be into this chick? Am I supposed to pretend this part of a bachelor party is what I want?

"What's your name, sweetheart?" The moment the pet name comes from my lips, I'm no longer *me*. I'm S&R me, the one who can tap into a woman, have a connection with her, know what she wants even if she doesn't know.

"Tessa."

"Well, Tessa ..." I pause and look over her shoulder at Jackson. "Do your thing."

The bastard smirks and I flip him off as Tessa goes to work. I expect her to start taking off her clothes, dance on the poll, do shit like that. Instead, she stays on my lap and one-by-one she unbuttons my shirt until she has it off my shoulders and down my back. I reach up to untie her bikini because she promised me tits. I know Autumn will kill me, but everyone keeps telling me that this is my night and well—fuck it. I'm not going to touch, I only want to see.

As I reach up, Tessa slaps my hand. "No touching."

"Are you serious?"

She stands, taking my shirt with her. "I am." She throws my shirt and Nick catches it.

"Sweetheart," I chuckle, "you promised me your tits."

"I vote for tits," Vinny chimes in.

My gaze turns to his and I nod. "See, we want to see your boobs."

"All in good time boys."

"Let the woman work," Bradley says.

Asshole.

"Now," Tessa begins, kneeling and grabbing my belt buckling, "You won't be needing this."

"Whoa!" I start to crawl away, but she acts fast and jumps on my lap.

"Someone needs to be handcuffed so he can't move."

I shake my head. "You're not handcuffing me."

"Yes, I am."

"You're stripping me of my clothes before we go to a club? That defeats the purpose."

"You don't know how to dress yourself?" she sneers.

"I ..." I turn my gaze to the guys, who are all laughing at my expense. I'm supposed to be S&R Gabe. How is this chick turning the tables on me? "You don't need to handcuff me."

Her steel-blue eyes stare straight into mine. Seconds tick before I finally agree. What harm can come of her handcuffing me? She said she wasn't going to fuck me and I trust Jackson with my life.

The handcuffs she uses to bind me have an extra-long chain. I'm tempted to break them, but I know this is for fun. It's probably also for comfort. It allows my hands and arms to not be as high up on the bar behind me and I'm almost in a resting position once she's finished cuffing me.

The guys refill their drinks as they continue to watch the show. The drive to the club is taking a long time, but maybe *Alfred* is driving around until Tessa is done with me. After I'm handcuffed, Tessa removes my belt and then stands. She's facing me, her legs spread for balance, and a wicked grin spreads across her face. *Pony* by Ginuwine blares through the speaks.

"That's my cue," she confesses. Her hips sway and roll, her hands roaming her upper body. I'm in a trance, mesmerized by what I'm seeing. I'm no longer fighting to resist these bachelor shenanigans. I'm going with them. I want to see whatever Tessa has up her sleeve—well, under her bikini.

She moves to the poll and my gaze slips to the guys. They're caught in the reverie, too. We're all watching her as if we've never seen a woman before. Tessa walks around the pole, giving each guy attention, but lingers on Vinny for a little longer and I wonder what's up with that. She rubs his bald head between her breasts and then moves on.

With her back to the pole, her hands glide up her breasts, her neck and then behind her nape. We watch as the strings fall. I expect her tits to pop out, but her hands keep her top on and I groan. I stare at her chest, waiting. I can't tell you what song's playing right now—hell, I can't tell you how long I stare.

Tessa bends and her gaze meets mine. She grins and her top falls down. They're nice breasts, but not my angel's perfect ones. Her hands go behind her back and she loosens the rest of her top, finally removing it completely. She flings it at Vinny. It's my day, but she gives *him* the red top? *Whatever.*

I expect her to do some shit on the pole. Instead, she kneels in front of me and begins to work on the button and zipper of my jeans.

"You're not going to do pole tricks?"

Her hands still and she looks up at me. With a chuckle, she says, "In a moving bus?"

I laugh. "Oh, right."

She continues on my jeans. "So you have a thing for Vinny?" I whisper.

Her head turns and she looks at him then back up at me. She tugs on my jeans causing me to raise my hips so they slide down my thighs. "What can I say, there's something about bald guys."

"He's single." *Was I having girl talk? I was definitely hanging out with Autumn too much.*

"Good to know." She slipped off my shoes and then my jeans, leaving me in my boxers.

"Finally!" Jackson blurts.

My gaze darts to his. "What do you mean *finally*?"

"Well, we're about to be at our destination any second. Tessa, put his shoes back on."

I look down at her and she gives me an apologetic grin as she slips them back on my feet.

"My shoes? You mean my clothes. Nick, give me my shirt, asshole."

"Sorry, man. No can do."

The bus pulls to a stop and the guys rise. Bradley comes over and releases the bar above my head so my arms fall but I'm still hand-cuffed. I go to stand, ready to strangle Jackson, but the door of the bus opens and he's out before I can make a move. Nick blocks me before I can pass. I move around him, thinking I have the upper hand because when it comes to Jackson, I usually do, but when I run down the two stairs toward him, I stop in my tracks.

"I wouldn't do that, Captain."

The barrel of a gun is pointed at my chest.

I look around. It's pitch dark, the only light coming from a flash-light being held by *Alfred* and the headlights of the bus. I shake my head as if to make sure what I'm seeing is correct. The bus has pulled over on the side of the road in the middle of nowhere and my best friend in the entire world is pointing a pistol at me.

"What—"

Alfred moves the flashlight a little and then I see it's *my* paintball gun from *my* garage. The manufacture's name catches the light and I relax because my best friend isn't going to kill me in the woods —naked.

I watch the rest of the guys come out, each carrying their own gun. PJ is the only one with a handgun. The others are holding typical paintball guns with long skinny barrels and feeders on the top.

"Are you going to shoot me?" I ask.

"This is how it's going to go. You're going to run and we're going to chase you—"

"You want me to run in the woods naked?" I laugh sarcastically.

Nick shoots a paintball near my right foot and my head jerks toward him. "Let him finish."

"Are you fuckers for real?" I spat. This party is no longer fun.

"Yep," Bradley states.

"Like I was saying," PJ hisses, "you run, we hunt. Think of it like hide and seek."

"Motherfucker, I'm gonna kick your ass." I move to strangle him with the long handcuffs but stop when all guns point at me.

"Boss, you need to hurry up before a car comes," *Alfred* interjects.

"*Alfred!*" Jackson shouts. "Jesus, I know. We're parked on the side of the road. I get it. Now if everyone will shut the fuck up, we'll be on our way in two minutes!" He pauses for a second. "Okay, you'll be running, yada-yada, and if we catch you, we shoot you with these." He gestures to the guns. "There's a campsite just behind me that you need to find."

"How am I supposed to find it?"

"Don't give me that shit, Captain Hastings."

"You're serious?"

He nods.

"And I don't get a gun?"

"Nope, but you get a flashlight." All the guys laugh.

"You know paybacks are a bitch right?"

He laughs under his breath. "Shit, I'm never getting married."

"No, but I know where you sleep."

"Touché. We'll give you a thirty-second head start."

They release my handcuffs with their guns drawn. Before I run off, I see Vinny go back into the bus. I make a mental note to ask him about it. Not because I want to talk girls with him, but because if he gets involved with a woman she might become a friend for Autumn. Major Dick robbed her of friends and the more she has, the more my heart feels complete.

As I jog away, I hear the bus drive off and the guys cackling about

how awesome their plan is. It's awesome for them because they aren't
being hunted in their underwear.

I'm out of breath, Nick on my tail. I've tackled him, taken his gun,
and now I'm running to what I hope is our campsite. I see a fire blaz-
ing, tents set-up and all I want is water.

Fuck!

Two figures are sitting in chairs next to the fire and in ten seconds
they're about to get a scare of their life because I'm coming out of the
woods in my boxers carrying a paintball gun, sweat dripping down
my body and I don't give a fuck.

My gaze meets one of theirs and I smile.

Fuck my life.

"You've got to be kidding me right now," I pant, trying to catch
my breath.

Blake tosses me a bottle of water. "Good news is you found us."

"I can't believe the Montgomery brothers were in on this."

"Someone had to tend the fire," Brandon says as he slaps
my back.

Brandon and Blake are the owners of Club 24 where we teach
our self-defense classes. We rent the room from them.

"Sit and let's get you a drink." Blake gestures to a seat by the fire.

I down half of the water and pour the other half over my head.
"Sorry about your side," I say to Nick as I walk toward a chair.

"How's your thigh?"

I look down at the welt where he shot me. *Fucker.* "Okay—maybe

I'm not sorry about your side." We laugh and I rub my thigh where I got hit then sit.

Brandon sits back down in his chair next to the fire. The other three guys are nowhere in sight. "Excited about the baby?"

"Extremely. Have any pointers?"

"We'll talk later."

Blake hands me a shot. "I thought you said a drink?"

"Blake has a thing for shots." Brandon laughs.

The other guys finally walk in, laughing. I take the shot, down it and then I charge Jackson. Snatching the pistol from his hand, I aim for his thigh and pull the trigger. Nothing happens.

"You really think we'd have ammo after what we just put you through?" They all laugh.

"I really hate you right now."

He laughs again. "Go sit down and have a drink. We're here for two days."

My eyes become huge. "Two days?"

"We're camping, Cap."

"What?"

He shakes his head as if he's frustrated. "The future Mrs. Hastings approved this. There, now will you go sit the fuck down and have a drink?"

My eyes narrow at him in frustration. Autumn doesn't control me, but it does make me feel better that I finally know which part she knows about. I look down at my almost naked body and then back up at Jackson. "Can I have my clothes back?"

He laughs. "Oh right, we wouldn't want to see your dick popping out of the slit. Auttie packed you a bag. It's in your tent over here." We start walking. "There's also showers that way."

I definitely sweaty from running from these fuckers. "Hey, Jackson?" He stops and turns toward me. "Thank you for planning all this, even though you tried to kill me." I smile.

He chuckles. "I didn't try to kill you, but you're welcome."

"And I *will* get you back when you get married."

"Dude, I'm not getting married."

"You say that now, but I bet that someday soon some woman will barge into your life and you won't know what to do without her."

Paul's story continues in Tequila & Lace. Continue reading for a sneak-peek!

NOTE FROM THE AUTHOR

Dear Reader,

I hope you've enjoyed *Angels & Whiskey*. Please take a moment to spread the word so everyone can discover Gabe and Autumn and the men and women of Saddles & Racks. Please also sign up for my newsletter so you can stay up to date on all the Knight news.

You can find the links on my website at *www.authorkimber-lyknight.com.*
    You can also follow me on Facebook at *www.facebook.com/AuthorKKnight.*

Thank you again, and I hope these two have captured a place in your heart! You can really help me out a lot by leaving a review where you bought the book as well as Goodreads and Bookbub. Your love and support means everything to me and I cherish you all!

XOXO,

Kimberly Knight

BOOKS BY KIMBERLY KNIGHT

Club 24 Series – Romantic Suspense

Perfect Together – The Club 24 Series Box Set

Halo Series – Contemporary Romance

Saddles & Racks Series – Romantic Suspense

By Invitation Only – Erotic Romance Standalone

Use Me – Romantic Suspense Standalone

Burn Falls – Paranormal Romance Standalone

And more ...

ACKNOWLEDGMENTS

First and foremost, I always need to thank my husband. When I wrote *Wanted* and *Anything Like Me*, we thought I was going through a lot with my health, but this time around, *it* was far worse. At first, I wanted to take my time writing *Angels & Whiskey* to be able to spend more time with you, but then we got the bad news and I had to get as much of it done as fast as I could before my surgeries. Thank you for understanding and for everything you do for me. I really couldn't have done it without you. I love you, you know?

To my editor, Jennifer Roberts-Hall. Do you like how I listened to you and in this book had babe lowercased? Even angel was lower-cased! One day you'll be like, "There's nothing to edit!" and I'll be like "Damn straight!" Thank you for saving my ass this time around and making sure this baby got the editing it deserved *on time*. And thank you for understanding that my draft of *the end* needed to be late because I was physically unable to write/type. I know how busy you are and I appreciate it. Super proud of you and your weight loss. Keep it up, sexy lady.

Kym *Alyssa Cochran.* Thank you from the bottom of my heart for answering all my questions regarding the Army. I know I was a pain in the ass, but thank you, thank you, thank you! Oh, and sorry for killing off Alyssa.

Lea Cabalar, *my* Boo and fellow member of the Cut it Off Crew. Thank you for all of our late night chats, all the memories we made in 2014, and for flying in when I was in the hospital. I love you so, so much for everything you do for me. I can't wait to make many more lifetime memories with you. I'm *sure* there are other towns with pregnant strippers.

Christine Stanley. If it weren't for you, we wouldn't have started the Cut it Off Crew. Well, if it wasn't for Dave, but you know what I mean. Thank you for all the hours you put into contacting bloggers for me, for doing all my release day blitz and everything else that makes you awesome. Oh, and also for listening to me bitch. I can't wait to make more lifetime memories with you and have more crazy chats about Slip N Slides. I love you, lady.

To my betas: Alexis Noelle, Brandi Flanagan, Cassie Kirkpatrick, Chauna Carlson, Elizabeth Broadway Lattanzi, Heidi Woodring, Jill the Book Fiend, Kylee Beck, Loralee Bergeson, Michele Hollenbeck, Michele Kubik Follis, Stacy Nickelson, Trina Marie, and Trista Cox Ward. Thank you so much for taking hours out of your day to help me get *Angels & Whiskey* on the right track. I really couldn't do it without y'all. If you ever need anything, please let me know.

To all the bloggers who participated in my cover reveal, release day blitz and review tour, thank you! Without bloggers, I have no idea where I would be. You've all taken a chance on me and my books time and time again, and I can't tell you how much I appreciate it. I never thought I would be an author, especially one with a fan base, and I owe a lot to y'all.

To Eric Battershell and Alfie Gordillo: Holy hotness, Batman! That's one smokin' image that's gracing this cover. Thank you, Eric, for capturing an image that will leave panties wet. Sorry for being crude, but it's true! Thank you, Alfie, for all the time you put into the gym and eating right to effin' have abs like you do. The first time I saw you (on your first cover!) I knew I wanted to write a book about you ... well, about your cute face and jaw dropping body. *fans self* Two years later and it finally happened.

Emmy Hamilton, you're the best proofreader. Thank you for being super-fast at it! I love your eyes and the way you delete words to make me sound more professional. Ha-ha! I'm glad Christine sent you my way and for hounding me to send you more because you love my work.

To Audrey Harte: Thank you for always being my BFFL. I love you, home slice.

And finally, thank your readers for believing in me and taking a chance on my books again and again. Thank you also for understanding about why I had to push the release date. I don't plan to get anymore tumors! I'll keep writing, if you keep reading.

Photogropher:
Eric Battershell
facebook.com/ericbattershellphotography
Male Cover Model:
Alfie Gordillo
facebook.com/AlfieGabrielGordillo

ABOUT THE AUTHOR

Kimberly Knight is a USA Today Bestselling Author that lives in the mountains near a lake with her loving husband and spoiled cat, Precious. In her spare time, she enjoys watching her favorite reality TV shows, watching the San Francisco Giants win World Series and the San Jose Sharks kick butt. She's also a two time desmoid tumor/cancer fighter that's made her stronger and an inspiration to her fans. Now that she lives near a lake, she plans on working on her tan and doing more outdoor stuff like watching hot guys waterski. However, the bulk of her time is dedicated to writing and reading romance and erotic fiction.

KIMBERLY KNIGHT

www.authorkimberlyknight.com

facebook.com/AuthorKKnight

twitter.com/Author_KKnight

instagram.com/KimBrulee10

pinterest.com/authorkknight

bookbub.com/authors/kimberly-knight

A Saddles & Racks Novel, #2

USA Today bestselling author

Kimberly Knight

ONE
Joselyn

I stared out of the tiny, grungy, living room window of our two-bedroom mobile home. Today was my birthday and for the past seventeen years, I couldn't remember a birthday when I'd woken up to presents and cake, or even my mother wishing me a happy birthday.

Today was no different.

"When are we gonna have cake?" my brother, Bryce, asked, tugging on the hem of my purple tank top.

I turned and looked down at him. I didn't know if we were going to have cake at all, so I did my best not to give him false hope. "I'm not sure, buddy. Maybe when Mommy wakes up."

"But I want cake now!" he whined, crossing his arms over his chest and sticking his bottom lip out.

I wanted to tell my eight year old brother that I wanted cake now too, but we didn't have money to go to the store. There was also no way I was waking up Mother in hopes she'd remembered my birthday—even if it was close to two in the afternoon.

"How about you draw me a cake and by the time you're done Mommy might be awake? You haven't given me my present yet." I reached out and ran my hand over the top of his hair, messing up the shaggy light brown length that was opposite of my dark brown. I knew I was only biding time, but once Mother was up and in one of her moods, he'd forget about the cake and watch cartoons instead to avoid her antics.

"Fine," he huffed, then turned on his heels. I watched as he ran down the hall toward the room that we shared. I silently prayed he didn't wake Mother. If he did, she'd yell and make him cry, then leave me to get him to stop. She was still asleep because she worked nights. I'd thought she worked as a waitress at an all-night diner or something, but when I was thirteen, I learned the truth. I'd woken up as she was coming home at four in the morning dressed in a red tube top, a short black skirt that barely covered her panties (*if* she were even wearing any), black fishnet stockings, and black high heels that I was certain I'd break an ankle in.

"What are you doing up?" she asked, narrowing her eyes and glaring at me as she closed and locked the small, metal trailer door behind her.

I swallowed. "I ... uh ... I'm getting some water."

"Hurry up and get back in bed, Joss." She brushed past me as she made her way down the narrow hall toward her bedroom. She smelled of cigarettes and sweat. All traces of her perfume I'd seen her squirt on her wrists before leaving were gone.

"Why are you dressed like that?" I asked. She had been wearing jeans and a T-shirt when she'd left the house, so I was curious, but I quickly regretted the question as she spun on her heels, anger flashing in her eyes. She backtracked toward me, pointing her index finger.

"I'm the adult. You don't get to question me."

I huffed. She'd left me alone every night for as long as I could remember. Luckily, I had Mrs. McKenna next door if anything were to ever happen to me and my brother. "You're dressed like—"

"Like what, Joss?" She put her hand on her hip and cocked it when she was a few feet from me.

My eyes widened. I should have known not to question her. Whenever I did something she disapproved of, she'd whip me with a flyswatter, a wooden spoon, a belt, a shoe—whatever was on hand, and I didn't feel like crying myself to sleep if she decided to ever use the end of her spiked heel.

"Like what, Joss?" she asked again. I wasn't sure, but it didn't

sound as if she were surprised by my question, or that she wanted to hide something.

I took a quick deep breath before I spoke. "A ... Uh, a hooker."

I'd expected her to reach down, slip off her heel and throw it at my head. Instead, she'd laughed while her eyes closed briefly. She shook her head, not necessarily telling me I was wrong. "I really didn't want to have this conversation at four in the morning, but you're bound to find out at some time." She motioned for me to sit at the light blue card table we used as a kitchen table. We sat and she lit a cigarette, the smell of smoke instantly clinging to my clothes as I watched it float in the air before she spoke again. "Yes, I'm a hooker."

Have you ever had one of those moments where your world felt as if it were spinning on its axis? Or as if your head was literally spinning on your body? Something was spinning inside my head because even though I'd said she looked like she was dressed as a hooker and she worked crazy night hours, I really hadn't suspected that my own mother was a prostitute.

"Are you going to say something?"

My eyes focused on her face as I realize I was staring at her, trying to wrap my head around what she'd professed. What were my friends at school going to think if they found out? "So you like ... stand on the corner?"

She blew a poof of smoke into the air above our heads. "Gotta make money to feed us and put a roof over our heads somehow."

"Why a hooker? Why not a waitress or something?" During the summer, Mrs. McKenna's grandson, Seth, would visit. We'd play house with my friend Catherine (or Cat as we called her) and choose professions like a doctor, lawyer, teacher, bank teller, waitress, housewife, but never a hooker. Seth was always a cop. He was four years older than us and wanted to protect us from all the bad guys.

She chuckled. "If your father hadn't left us before you were born, we wouldn't be living in a dump, Joss. I got pregnant when I was your age and your grandparents kicked me out for getting knocked up. I thought your father would take care of me. Instead, he left me at a gas station in the middle of nowhere between here and Fort Lauderdale.

"*I didn't know what to do or where to go. I thought your father loved me. I thought he wanted to be with me. I was young and stupid and so wrong. Luckily, I met Tony at a diner I'd walked to. After he'd bought me some food, he drove me here to Miami and gave me a room in his house. Long story short, after I had you and was able to have sex again, I started working for him.*"

I hadn't asked many questions after that. I didn't want to know what was going on when she left the house. I kept her *profession* a secret, even after Seth became a cop in D.C. Mother mentioned recently that her *duties* had changed a little—I still didn't ask questions. All I knew was she dressed more business like now. Her skirts were a little longer. Her shirts covered more. She seemed happier, but Bryce and I continued to be on the back burner.

Every night was the same. She left around four in the afternoon and I stayed home to feed us, make sure our homework was done and that Bryce went to bed at a decent hour. On school days, I took Bryce next door to Mrs. McKenna's before I took the bus to school. *She* was the one who took him to school and picked him up when it was over because Mother was sleeping at those hours. I wasn't sure if Mrs. McKenna knew what Mother did for a living, but I wasn't going to tell her. I felt terrible that she cared for a child who wasn't her own, but I saw the love in her eyes when it came to him, and I was only a kid myself. I had no other choice.

Now I only had one more year until I was an adult. I wasn't sure what was after high school for me. I didn't want to stay home and take care of Bryce. I loved him, but I wanted to get a job, save up money, and move out on my own. I wanted to be roommates with Cat, go to parties and live wild and free. But I knew college wasn't in my future, not even community college. I wasn't sure if I'd be able to afford my share of the rent, pay bills and obtain a degree. Hell, I didn't even know what I wanted to be when I *grew up*.

As I stared out the window, thinking about my future and the year to come, there was a slight knock against the screen of the front door. "Mrs. McKenna," I greeted. I always used her formal name. I was introduced to her as that and it had stuck.

"Happy birthday, dear. You have a phone call." She smiled and reached her hand out to pass me her cordless house phone. "I'll watch Brycie. Go ahead and use my phone inside." She motioned with her head toward her trailer.

I took the two steps down while holding the screen door so it didn't slam and wake Mother. "Thank you." I beamed and switched spots with her. I walked a few feet before speaking into the phone to Seth. "Please tell me for my eightieth birthday you'll show up and not just call?" I grinned then gave a slight chuckle into the receiver while I stepped into the other trailer that was less than twenty feet away.

Seth's mature voice rang through as he spoke. Over the years, I'd heard it change into a deep *manly* voice and now it did things deep in the pit of my belly that made me grin like a complete fool whenever we spoke. "I'll show up as your knight in shining armor. Should it be on a white or black horse?"

I laughed again. "How about a white or black car?"

"I could do that if I picked you up at the airport here."

"Oh my God. I could just see the look on people's faces as I got in the back of a D.C. squad car."

"Want me to handcuff you too?"

"No way!" For a split second, images of being handcuff naked with Seth kissing his way down my body flashed in my head. Teen hormones were no joke, but I was waiting. I wasn't sure if I was waiting to be with Seth when I turned eighteen and legal—since he was a cop and twenty-one, or if I was waiting until I found someone *special*. All I knew was I didn't want to treat sex like my mother did.

"I'm only joking, Joss."

I smiled as I envisioned him smiling on the other end. I loved his smile. When he did, his mouth curved enough to cause his cheeks to meet his eyes, and when they squinted, you knew you had a genuine smile out of him. I knew at that moment—on the other end of the phone—he was giving me that smile. We were silent for a few beats as I looked around at the pictures of Seth from his childhood that were scattered throughout the small living room.

"It's actually white."

"What?" I asked, my eyebrows scrunched in confusion.

"The squad car. It's white with red decals and blue writing."

"Oh. Well, I've never been on a plane before. Not sure if I'd even make it up to see you."

"You've never been on a plane?"

I frowned. "Nope." I'd actually never left the trailer park for more than one night.

"All right. For graduation, I'm taking you somewhere on a plane."

I sighed and fell back onto the cream colored velvet couch with burnt orange roses. "Aw, man. I gotta wait over a year?" I was teasing, but getting away sounded like heaven, especially with Seth.

"Not my fault you're a baby. We gotta wait to get you an I.D. so you can go places since Cruella won't let you get one."

"I have my school I.D."

"Tempting, but you're still a baby."

I rolled my eyes. "And you're still an ass."

"Not my fault you don't have an older brother. I have to step up." I cringed at the word brother. "Anyway, birthday girl, I gotta go. Duty calls and all that shit—"

"Yeah, yeah, go catch those bad guys."

He chuckled. "Have Grandma cook you something good for dinner. You know she will."

"I know," I sighed. "I just want cake." *And candles ... And to make a wish as I blow out the candles.*

"She'll bake you one, Josie. She makes a mean 'better than sex' cake."

"Come again?" I covered my mouth with my hand as the words

spilled from it. *Sex. Cum. Talking to Seth about sex and cum. Fuck my life.*

"It's a chocolate cake, Joss. And it's fucking awesome."

"All right. Go catch those bad guys and I'll just be over here having an orgasm while I eat cake." I hung up the phone before he could respond. I wanted the last word and I wanted him to think about me having an orgasm ... even if I was a *baby* in his eyes.

Fucking teenage hormones.

After placing the phone back on its cradle, I returned to my trailer. Mother was still asleep and Bryce was just coming out of our room, running with a sheet of binder paper in his hand.

"Shh, B, you're gonna wake Mom." I gave Mrs. McKenna a tight smile after I lifted my finger to my mouth.

"I drew you a birthday cake," he whisper-shouted.

"I love it," I whispered back and took the paper from the palm of the hand my mother had used as an ashtray.

I was thirteen and Bryce was only four. Mother had the night off from her job, which was rare, and we were watching 101 Dalmatians. We didn't have cable and the only VHS cassette we owned was the cartoon from 1961, so we knew this movie by heart. I hated when she was home because she was usually pissed off at us, and she'd end up passed out on the couch after drinking a bottle of gin. This night was no different. She was angry at Bryce for something that was "all his fault" and he was crying. Before I knew what was happening, she'd yanked his hand and used it as an ashtray. I rushed him over to Mrs.

McKenna's trailer, telling her he'd burned it on the stove. She bandaged his hand, and when we returned home, Mother was passed out on the couch. The next few months, Mrs. McKenna made sure to check on us nightly.

"Want me to bake you a cake?" Mrs. McKenna asked.

"That won't be necessary. She won't be home."

My eyes darted toward the hall as my mother came around the corner, tightening her belt on her baby blue robe around her waist. "I won't?" This was the first I heard about it.

She shook her head. "You have plans."

We never had plans; especially plans for my birthday. "*We* do?"

"Yes." Her tone was short, so I wasn't going to question her again.

"Well, then I will let you get to your plans," Mrs. McKenna remarked, reaching for the front door.

"Thank you again." I gave her a quick hug. She nodded to my mother then left.

"What was that all about?" Mother asked, a cigarette between her lips as she flicked her lighter. I watched as the flame burned the tip.

"Seth called to wish me a happy birthday."

She blew a puff of smoke from her mouth. "That's nice. Go shower, Joselyn. When you come out, there will be a dress on your bed for you to wear."

"Where are we going? What are we doing?" I asked, not taking a breath. I didn't care that she hadn't wished me a happy birthday. She had bought me a dress and was taking me out.

"Just go take a shower, dammit!" she spat, causing me to jump.

I paused, glaring at her for a beat, then turned my head to look at Bryce. He was watching cartoons without a care in the world. I tried hard—really hard not to roll my eyes as I brushed past her. I was used to her yelling, but for one day—just one—I wished she would take into account that it was my birthday and act sweet.

Before I went to the bathroom to shower, I folded Bryce's picture and put it in my purse to take with me. I didn't want Mother to do something with it. I didn't trust her. I never kept anything I didn't want her *not* to throw away. Granted I didn't have much to begin with. I didn't have jewelry. I didn't have nice clothes. I didn't have CDs. I didn't have books. I didn't have DVDs. I didn't have anything except a photo of me and Bryce, one of me, Cat, and Seth from three summers ago that we took during Seth's last summer visit, and a few pictures Bryce had drawn for me at school. I kept Bryce's pictures he colored for me under my mattress and my photos in my purse.

Tonight I was going out for my birthday, and I was dressed up—something I'd never done.

When I returned to my room, there was a dress lying on my twin bed. I held it up in front of me; it barely came to my mid-thigh. It was a simple, sleeveless black dress. I didn't have a strapless bra, but I could go one night without one—depending on what we did. I didn't care. I was happy for once. It was getting to be dinner time, so hopefully we'd have a nice meal because I could go for something other than soup or a grilled cheese sandwich.

Still smiling, I slipped the dress on. Before I could slide into the sky-high, black heels my mother had placed by my bed, she came into my room without knocking. "You need to do your hair and makeup, too."

"Are you going to tell me where we're going?"

"No." There was the short, snappy answer again.

Whatever.

I went back into the bathroom and found Mother's makeup. I didn't have money to buy my own and she'd never bought me any, so I had no idea what I was doing. I didn't wear makeup. Hell, I didn't even know what she meant by I needed *to do* my hair. I covered my entire face with foundation, brushed a light beige across my eyelids, and then put on a little mascara. After I quickly dried my hair, I returned to my room.

Mother was sitting on my bed, still dressed in her robe. "You need more makeup."

"I do?"

She huffed and then stood. "Let me show you." She grabbed my wrist and tugged me behind her toward the bathroom.

"Ow! You're hurting me," I whined.

"Oh shut up, Joselyn. Stop acting like a baby."

I could feel my blood start to boil. She was such a bitch. It was my birthday. The one day that was supposed to be *your* day; a day when *you* got whatever you wanted. Before Seth became an *adult*, I'd had him and Cat to watch movies with, make me lunch, cake—*whatever*. This year Cat was off on a family vacation in Hawaii. They'd wanted one last family trip before she graduated and left for college. I wanted a first one.

Again—*whatever*.

I leaned against the olive green pedestal sink while my mother painted my face. When I turned to face the mirror, I didn't recognize myself. The freckles that lightly dusted my upper cheeks and nose were covered up completely with foundation. My eyelids were caked with pink eye shadow and black eyeliner circled each eye completely.

"Wow," I whispered.

"You look beautiful, Joss."

My gaze flicked to hers. I'd never heard her compliment me before. "Now will you tell me where we're going?"

"We're not going anywhere. *You* are."

"Huh?" Thoughts of Seth and Cat surprising me for my birthday flashed in my head, but I knew they were both out of town.

"Get your shoes on and let's go."

I didn't want to argue with her—I knew the consequences. I went to my room, slipped on the heels, grabbed my black clutch purse that

313

had nothing in it but my pictures and lip gloss, and stumbled my way to the living room where she was waiting for me.

"There's a limo waiting for you outside," she affirmed, puffing on another cigarette. She really needed to stop that nasty shit. I was tired of smelling like stale smoke all the time.

"There's a limo waiting for me outside?" I motioned between my chest and the door.

"Yes. Now go." She urged me to take a step and I caught myself before I fell flat on my face. I wasn't used to wearing heels.

"Bye, B." I waved to Bryce as he continued to watch *101 Dalmatians*. He didn't look away or say goodbye as he recited every line.

As I stepped out of the trailer, excitement flowing through my veins. I had no idea what was going on, but finally my mother had remembered my birthday. This was going to be the best birthday ever! I turned to give her a hug. I wanted to show her how thankful I was that she'd finally remembered my birthday, but something flashed in her eyes. Instead, I stopped and only said, "Thank you." I thanked her for the dress, the limo, but most of all, I thanked her for finally remembering it was my birthday.

"No, *thank you*." She smirked.

"What?" The humid Florida air caused my long hair to cling to my neck and chin as I whipped around to see what she meant.

"Just go, Joselyn."

When I turned toward the dirt road, there was a black limo with a man in a suit waiting outside the open door. *Fancy*. A smile spread across my face as I walked to the car. "Hi," I greeted the mystery man as he gestured to the open door. I slid into the car, the cool, black leather kissing my bare legs. A moment later, the door closed and I looked straight ahead at an unfamiliar face.

"You look just like your mother did when she was your age," he mused.

My heart stopped and my palms became clammy. "Um ... okay?"

"We've met, you know." His Latino accent laced his words.

"Um, okay?"

"You were just a baby."

"Um, okay?" I had no other words. I was in a moving car with an unfamiliar man who apparently knew me—a man who my mother had sent me to.

"I'm Tony, sweetheart."

Continue reading Tequila & Lace, purchase your copy today!

16086801R00197

Made in the USA
San Bernardino, CA
18 December 2018